HEATSEEKER

Also by James Classi

Nine Lives

Heatseeker

Tommy Boy,

"IT ISN'T about how hard you hit, it's about how hard you can get hit and keep moving Forward."

GeT Ready To Rock!!

JAMES CLASSI

authorHOUSE®

AuthorHouse™
1663 Liberty Drive
Bloomington, IN 47403
www.authorhouse.com
Phone: 1-800-839-8640

Published by AuthorHouse   08/29/2012

ISBN: 978-1-4772-6457-7 (sc)
ISBN: 978-1-4772-6453-9 (hc)
ISBN: 978-1-4772-6454-6 (e)

Library of Congress Control Number: 2012915840

For Thomas A. Fierro
The toughest son of a bitch I have ever known.

CONTENTS

Life doesn't run away from nobody, life runs at people.

Joe Frazier

A champion is someone who gets up when he can't.

Jack Dempsey

Fight one more round. When your feet are so tired that you have to shuffle back to the center of the ring, fight one more round. When your arms are so tired that you can hardly lift your hands to come on guard, fight one more round. When your nose is bleeding and your eyes are black and you are so tired and you wish that your opponent would crack you one on the jaw and put you to sleep, fight one more round-remembering that the man who fights one more round is never whipped.

'Gentleman' Jim Corbett

PROLOGUE

He didn't know it at the time, but he would never see the animal alive again.

The boy felt about a mile high sitting on top of the mare whose coat was as black as a starless evening sky.

He looked out over the barren, sandy landscape and inhaled the strong smell of salt. The sun boiled up off to his right, just starting to peek above the ocean's surface. It was late August and the day would be a hot one.

The night before, his father had arrived to take him back home to North Reading, another Long Island summer was at its end. In less than a week he would be starting the tenth grade at Wilmington High; circumstances had seen to that.

The boy wanted one more ride, one more chance to "save the world." He smiled to himself.

With his feet secure in the adjusted stirrups and his hands loosely grasping the reins, he ran the palm of his right hand along the animal's warm neck and tapped her softly.

"That's a good girl, are we gonna do it this time? It's our last chance, we got one more shot."

The horse whinnied quietly.

It was a game the boy liked to play before his morning ride on the Arabian. He would think of something, some child's fantasy, and imagine he and the horse would have to run down the problem, race along the beach to save the day, before time was up.

The boy lost himself in the semi-quiet for a small time, the only sound, the gentle rolling of the ocean surf, was comforting. At this very moment he owned it. The whole open space was his. The view before him was empty and constant; a warm breeze rustled itself over the sand.

Everything within his view was either blue or white, save the thin red line that ran across the horizon where the Atlantic Ocean met the sky. It almost looked like a child's drawing.

"This is it, girl, until next summer, just you and me."

He gave the horse two hard pats on the right side of her neck, and squeezed his thighs into her sides.

Reaffirming his grip, he drew back on the reins in a continuous, hard pull. With tears in his eyes, the boy spoke the single sentence that would send him, send them, on their run, their final ride.

The Arabian lifted her body, rearing back onto her hind legs, defying gravity, her front hooves pedaling in the air before them.

The boy dropped the reins and held on tightly, his left hand now grabbing the saddle horn, his legs crunching together for purchase. He was John Wayne in *True Grit*; he was the man with no name.

"Yeah! That's it, girl Yeah! Let's go! Time to save the world!"

At once, the mare dropped down and took off. She ran close to the sliding waves as the salty mist sprayed the boy's torso, neck, and smiling face. The hoofbeats sounded like thunder along the packed sand, a drumming, stampeding tempest.

The boy held his right hand high in the air, reaching for the sky . . . the sun . . . whatever there was to grab and make his own. On this animal, there was nothing he couldn't do.

As they charged up the beach, a single living entity, the boy felt like he was flying, as if there was only the rushing wind between the ground and the mare.

He felt unstoppable.

ROUND ONE

The Heavyweight Championship
January 20, 2013
Madison Square Garden

Flashbulbs popped outside the boxing ring like the prelude to a violent thunderstorm; or, as Tommy Farrow dreaded, was the light show due instead to corneal starbursts behind his swollen eyelids? The handy-work of Johnson's right jab followed up by his trademark left hook.

Like his idol Smokin' Joe Frazier, what Joltin' Jeffrey Johnson was known and most feared for was his devastating southpaw attack. And tonight, more so than any other night, it was landing with increasing frequency and pinpoint accuracy.

The fact that Farrow could no longer reliably discern between the two visual sensations was an ominous sign that no good could possibly come of this. His strength was slowly ebbing like the sands in an upturned hourglass. Sheer will, the guts and determination which were a by-product of his natural constitution and physical conditioning, was the only thing preventing him from floating out to sea with the flotsam and jetsam. But Farrow was well aware even in his semi-conscious state that this was not an infinite resource. That, despite a second-round knockdown and building up an early lead on the judges' scorecards, his time was running out and his share of the heavyweight championship was doomed along with it, but that was alright.

Okay, I put on a good show; time to end this thing, he thought.

"A vicious left has Farrow's knees wobbling," said analyst Jim Lampley. "Backed into the corner, blood now streaking his right cheek. I don't know how he is still standing."

"Survival instinct," said Larry Merchant. "Nothing more, nothing less. Oh, a right jab and another left and . . . I don't believe what I'm seeing! Farrow has dropped his arms! Tommy Farrow is no longer defending himself! What on earth is he thinking?"

The volume produced by the thousands of fight fans surrounding the small, roped boxing stage went from a deafening chant of "Far-row! Far-row! Far-row!" to a thunderous roar.

"Tommy seems distracted," Lampley again. "He keeps looking into the stands."

Flashbulbs continued to flicker and sizzle around the ring that now seemed to spin violently through the roaring mob and the thick cigarette smoke.

"That's gotta hurt! Another Johnson combination and Farrow has still not raised his arms. What could possibly be going through his mind?" said Merchant.

"Farrow, now thirty-six years old, is not the same man who started this fight. Something must have snapped . . . Ow! A big left by Johnson!" said Lampley, the volume of his voice increasing with excitement. "A right jab . . . another left, and Farrow is still looking out ringside."

Due to the measure of noise in Madison Square Garden it seemed the roof would likely blow off and up into the vast expanse of night sky like a soda bottle top fueled by the violent, shaken fury of carbonated air.

"A hard right followed by a punishing left hook! The round steam-training to a close, just under twenty seconds to go!" Larry Merchant yelling into his microphone now, trying to edge his voice above the havoc in the arena.

"A quick right jab to the face, another left, an assault to the body!"

Merchant was talking without breathing, calling the attack as it played out before him. The sickening sound of Johnson's leather gloves pounding into Farrow's flesh was not unlike Keith Moon destroying his drum kit in a ferocious blurred rage.

"The left hook again perfectly executed and Farrow finally hits the deck! My God, what has happened here tonight?"

The commentator's voice, now very small, was lost somewhere in a sea of cheers and yells, a tidal wave of shrieks and frenzied screams. The referee sends Johnson to a neutral corner and begins a count that Tommy Farrow looks to have no chance of beating.

One . . . Two . . .

"Tickets! Tickets! Who needs two for the big fight tonight?"

The scalpers were working Seventh Avenue earlier in the evening, their breath misting before them on the cold January air as they sought suckers or out-of-towners to part with double or triple the face value on tonight's main event at the Garden. A unification bout between the two reigning divisional heavyweight champions whose menacing profiles and career records were on vivid display on the giant screen outside the arena.

TOMMY "HEATSEEKER" FARROW
37-0 (32 KO) WBO HEAVYWEIGHT CHAMPION

JOLTIN' JEFFREY JOHNSON
32-0 (29 KO) IBF HEAVYWEIGHT CHAMPION

THERE CAN ONLY BE ONE KING IN THIS TOWN . . .
AND KONG IS DEAD!

"Sold out, baby," said one of the scalpers to two guys from Long Island hoping to score a couple of cheap nosebleed seats just to be there. "I got your only way inside right here."

He waved a handful of tickets, the legitimacy of which was dubious at best.

Highlights of both Farrow and Johnson's previous fights played on the video monitor overlooking the pandemonium in front of Penn Station, where the excitable fight crowd was tame in comparison to the tourists and club-hoppers impatiently vying for cabs to whatever Saturday night destination they couldn't seem to get to soon enough. Shopping, drinking, dancing, fucking?

Only the Vegas odds-makers, promoters, and Pay-Per-View providers whose personal gains from this event were believed to rival that of the contestants themselves, outdid the level of anticipation for this long-awaited match-up among the boxing faithful. Much was to be gained, or lost, according to what side of the action you happened to be on this night and everyone wanted to be as close to it as humanly possible. To feel the electricity, see the blood, smell the sweat, hear the sadistic pounding of leather against flesh, perhaps touch the robed gladiators as they made their memorable entrances into the 20x20 foot slaughterhouse. Sensory overload.

No two people, however, experienced the gravity of the situation on a more visceral level than Tommy Farrow and Jeffrey Johnson: the pre-dawn roadwork, running the streets of Farrow's freezing Boston and Johnson's sweltering Atlanta respectively, which began while the nine-to-fivers were still snug in their beds, hitting the snooze alarm for the first of many times. The seemingly interminable weight training and sparring sessions in stinking, too-hot or too-cold gyms, black eyes, broken noses, bruised ribs, plus the pissing of blood and the dozens of amateur bouts, tournaments, and competitions. Both were Golden Gloves champions, Farrow in New England after having lost in the previous years' finals, Johnson a two-time titleholder in the mid-south region.

Never had the two squared off against one another, as amateurs or professionals, before tonight. As both rose steadily through the heavyweight rankings at roughly the same time, much intrigue and speculation did abound, but it was thought best by the powers that be to wait for the right time and, more importantly, a huge payday.

Nearly seventy wins between the two. Not a single loss or draw, each with shares of the World Heavyweight title. It was beyond obvious that the time was now.

Three . . .

Linda Farrow, formerly Canzoneri, was born and raised in Boston's Italian North End, her husband James an Irish Southie transplant from County Cork and reformed street-tough. Both tall and attractive, it came as little surprise to family and friends that their first-and only-born, Thomas, quickly grew into his eventual six-foot-two frame, supplemented by muscle, natural and hard-earned by way of dock work down at the harbor from the age of fourteen.

Struggling to retain some semblance of consciousness, Tommy even now knew that relinquishing his title tonight was a foregone conclusion and the grasp on his very life was becoming more tenuous with every passing precious second . . . *but that was okay.*

His thoughts turned toward his mother and father at home in North Reading some forty miles north of Boston. They did not disapprove of their little boy's profession, indeed they were proud of his accomplishments as any parent could possibly be. And James could hardly protest after the shenanigans that earned him multiple stretches in juvenile hall and a very long weekend at the Suffolk County Riverhead Jail in his twenties when he would spend summers with his family on Long Island. They, however, could not, and never did, attend one of Tommy's fights. Tonight's bout was an example of why.

He reflected on holidays together, opening what felt like a never-ending pile of presents amidst mugs of steaming hot chocolate and shredded, multi-colored wrapping paper. A family vacation to the Grand Canyon where his father's reluctance to stop and ask directions resulted in the Farrows becoming hopelessly lost, and James exclaiming: "We'll know when we get there now, won't we? It's a giant fucking hole in the ground. If nothing else, we'll drive straight into it."

The remark relieved the tension that had been building in the car all morning into the afternoon and the three of them burst out laughing, pulling over for lunch and gas and, yes, proper directions.

Tommy would have laughed now had he the motor skills and respiratory function necessary to do so.

The crazy shit you think of at times like this.

Four . . .

ROUND TWO

. . . Three. Two. One.

Farrow heard the sound of snapping fingers close to his ear. There was something wrong with the number sequence. Shouldn't the count be ascending, instead of descending?

The noise clicked off next to his head a second time.

What was that?

His mind was clearing quickly. He had to stand. He'd been knocked down. If he intended to win this bout or at least continue the show . . . he had to lift his body, but something was wrong. He worked his back around for better purchase, the canvas did not feel right.

There was a peaceful silence surrounding him.

Where were the cheers? Where was the smell of blood? Why was the damn count going the wrong way?

Three. Two. One. Snap.

Farrow opened his eyes and hurriedly closed them again. Bright sunlight assaulted his pupils. He was not lying on his back in the center of a boxing ring. Of this he was sure. He kept his eyelids closed awhile before opening them again. He did so this time squinting with the palm of his left hand shielding his vision, like the captain of a sea vessel looking out over a misty, wind-swept horizon.

Farrow pulled himself up onto his right elbow before advancing to a full sitting position. He cupped both hands over his eyes. Was he resting on sand? For a moment he thought he heard seagulls off in the distance, but maybe not. He lowered his hands and recovered from the squint, turning his head left to right, absorbing the surroundings. The punishing

6

sunlight seemed to simmer down a bit, returning his vision to somewhere around normal.

Everything, as far as he could distinguish, was a washed-out, blurred white. His body was undeniably sitting on sand, this he knew now with finality. *A beach somewhere?*

Farrow was shirtless and still wearing his boxing trunks and shoes. He thought he could hear what sounded like rolling ocean waves breaking on the surf. He imagined the white foam sizzling and dissolving over seaweed and discarded shells. The smell of sea air was strong in his nostrils. But subsequently the sounds, and the not unpleasant aromas, were gone, almost like these sensations had been hinted at, floating in and out, not holding onto reality. There was nothing tangible for him to grasp.

Farrow, blinking rapidly now, looked around some more. He made fists in the warm sand at his sides, trying to grasp something real. It felt comforting. As a matter of fact, he decided, everything felt all right. He remembered flashbulbs bursting, a right jab and a hard left to his jaw. The canvas. Cheers and more flashbulbs, Johnson standing over him. The referee counting . . . he brought a hand up to his mouth. No swelling, or any pain or bruising seemed evident. *Where are my gloves?* He held his hands in front of his face. Gloveless. Except for the white particles sticking to his palms, they were clean. Turning them around, he now saw his fingernails appeared to be manicured.

"What the fuck?" he said under his breath.

"Hello, Thomas," said a soft voice behind him.

"Thomas A. Farrow. It's an absolute honor!" said another.

He immediately recognized the voice as the one that had been counting backward a few moments earlier. He turned his head quickly, and without realizing it, was on his feet. The reflexes of a prizefighter. He towered over the two men he now faced.

"Okay, guys. What's the joke? Where am I?"

The two smaller men looked at each other. Their eyes were kind.

"I'm John," the taller and obviously older of the two said through a neatly cropped, gray beard, "and this is Keith."

The man known as Keith sported a bowl haircut, had thick black eyebrows, and a generous belly. He gave a polite nod in Farrow's direction. "It's a real honor to meet you, sir. I have been a fan since the early days. I still remember your demolition of John Michael Walker in the beginning of the fourth round at the Boston Garden, and then there was . . ."

"Excuse me," Farrow said suspiciously, "who exactly are you guys? And where am I?"

"Like I said, I'm John and this is Keith."

"Yeah, I got that much," Farrow said, staring at the ground. "I remember fighting Jeff Johnson and taking a beating." He looked up at the two men with an almost embarrassed expression.

"I was about to turn things around," he lied. "I hit the deck and remember all this bright flashing and popping . . . and spinning . . . then I woke up here. I'm not . . . I mean, was I hurt? Was I hospitalized? Is this some kind of recovery retreat?"

John and Keith looked at each other. Farrow could tell they were holding something back and not ready to give it up yet. The sound of the churning ocean spraying on rocks sounded again. He looked beyond the two odd men, but still saw nothing.

"Listen, Thomas, maybe you should sit down," said John.

"Sit down? I want you two to tell me what's going on right now!" he shouted, his patience draining as his voice elevated. "And where the hell would you like me to sit? I don't see any chairs. Fuck, I don't see anything."

The two men stared at him, but didn't speak. Farrow threw his hands into the air in a frustrated gesture and planted his ass back onto the warm sand. Seagulls far above sounded again, but he ignored their song and just stared the two men down until they joined him in the sand.

"There is a rare opportunity," John started, "a unique and rare opportunity presenting itself to you."

Both men, their legs folded beneath them, seemed to be blanketed by a peaceful, soothing aura.

"What opportunity? Come on, guys, enough is enough. Where am I?"

"Please," now it was Keith's turn to speak. "We need you to stay calm. We're trying to explain everything to you." He looked to John, and then trained his eyes back on Farrow. "Just bear with us, okay? Did you ever hear of Robert Scalia?" The question hung out there for a second before Farrow answered.

"Robert who? Scalia? No, never heard of him. What's this got to do with me? What's going on here?"

"Please, Thomas," John's voice now, calming. "We're trying to explain everything in a most delicate manner."

Waves crashed again, and Farrow's nostrils were filled with the scent of an old-fashioned Long Island summer.

John continued, "A man named Robert Scalia was in a terrible car accident. I'm sad to say he passed while the doctors were trying to revive him. He just slipped away from us."

"Okay, I'm sorry to hear that, but what the fuck does this have to do with me?" said Farrow.

He looked at John and Keith, really looked at them for the first time, taking them in, absorbing what he was seeing. Both men spoke with slight British accents. The one named John looked as strong as an ox. They wore loose-fitting, white robes, and both had kind blue eyes; but Keith, Farrow saw, had a certain mischief flickering behind his. It was a trait he knew well, identified with.

"Who did you guys say you are?"

"We told you. I'm John, and this is Keith."

"Yes, yes, I know that much, but *who* are you?" The two men looked at each other with sly smiles. "And why are you dressed like that?" Farrow added.

"Thomas, listen," Keith began. "I've been a fan of yours since the beginning. I've seen almost all your fights, and I was quite literally always in your corner. I mean 37-0, with 32 knockouts. You sure were something!"

"Wait a minute, what do you mean, I sure *was* something?"

"What?"

"You said, '*You sure were something*' like in the past tense, like I *was* something, but no longer am."

"Let me ask you a question, Thomas," John this time. "Who do you think won the fight between you and Johnson? No bull. Who do you think really won?"

"I . . ." Farrow started. "I can't remember. I know I was hit hard, and I went down probably even harder. I remember a bunch of bright flashing lights and Johnson standing over me, that son of a bitch's bald head gleaming . . ."

"Let me ask you this, do you think you could beat him? Extend your record to a perfect 38-0?" John asked.

"You bet your ass I can beat that dirty . . ." Farrow's voice was climbing again before remembering why he actually lost the fight. *I could have beaten him if I wanted to.* Farrow stood.

"There's no need for emotions to flare, I was just asking a simple question."

Farrow pinned John with his eyes.

"What would you say if we could put you back in your body . . ."

Looking down at himself, "Back in my body? What are you two lunatics talking about? I'm in my body." His voice had a noticeable quiver now.

"I'm sorry, Thomas. At almost 11:00 this evening, less than half a minute after Robert Scalia died . . ." Keith began.

There's that name again, thought Farrow.

"Jeff Johnson knocked you down near the end of the tenth round in front of thousands of people."

"He won the fight?" Farrow asked, his voice soft now, knowing the answer before John responded.

"I'd say he won. You see . . . last night in front of the whole world, after that left hook to your head, you suffered an intracranial hemorrhage . . . and it killed you."

Farrow was silent and, without realizing it, he curled his hands into fists, the blood leaving his knuckles. He closed his eyes and leaned his head on his chest. Nobody spoke. Farrow stood motionless like an ancient sculpture portraying a mythical god. His skin seemed to glisten, his breath slow and even. The sound of the seagulls returned, but was now complemented by the tumbling ocean waves and that great sea smell he had loved so much as a child. He appeared to be deep in thought. John and Keith looked at each other with a hint of trepidation, and both men almost took a step backward when Farrow opened his eyes in what seemed an instant of panic.

"Okay," he said. "I'm ready to listen." His voice was soft.

He felt composed, at peace. He slowly opened his hands and wiggled his fingers, shaking away the dangerous fists. A refreshing breeze sifted off an ocean that he couldn't see and worked its magic over his skin. He could almost feel the spraying of the salt-water mist baptizing his near-naked torso.

As Keith and John took turns speaking, things came slowly into focus. Behind the two smaller men Farrow could see a large body of water defining itself and the sea smells grew stronger with real staying power. Opening and closing his hands he could feel the stickiness of the salt. The crash of the waves slid along the beach that was, and always had been, just about twenty feet away. *How could I have missed it?* The seagulls, he now saw, were out in full force, white and gray, gliding above the Atlantic Ocean and dipping down to pluck breakfast, or maybe lunch, from the bubbling surf. *This is the Atlantic Ocean. How do I know that?* But with certainty, he somehow did. He had spent summers here as a youth. It was all familiar and comforting. The happiest days in his childhood took place on this very beach.

Now, just John was speaking. Farrow took it all in without interrupting. He didn't question anything. Displaying an amazing sense of attentiveness he just listened. Keith would interject from time to time, bringing forth a memory to Farrow of the old Abbott and Costello routine "Who's on first?"

Farrow noticed other people occupying the beach; at first the horizon was a blur, just a yellow smear, then there were people. Slim girls in bikinis, worshipping a quickly materializing sun that was low in the sky, blazing orange, like the burning end of a cigarette. A man was throwing a Frisbee to a small, excited dog, and a volleyball game was being played out about thirty yards away.

The people laughed and went on about their business, seeming not to even notice the prizefighter, or for that matter, his two new friends.

After listening to their elaborate plans, Farrow looked at them, something akin to amusement in his eyes. He began to pace.

"Now hold on a second," he said, "let me see if I have this right. Last night, I died in the boxing ring, and next thing I know . . . I wake up here. You two tell me if I walk down the beach a stretch I'll come to a cave that leads into hell, and you want me to sneak in with some stupid weapons. You're kidding, right?"

He stopped talking for a second, amazed at the nonsense he was rattling off.

"I have to rescue the soul of this guy Robert Scalia," he continued, "who by the way, also died last night . . . but his soul was kidnapped. He's supposed to write a book exposing some politician who turns out to be an asshole. That's a real surprise by the way, a politician who's an asshole, who would have thought? If Scalia does not write his book, this politician will eventually become president and cause a nuclear war. If this writer stays dead, he can't write this book and prevent that from happening."

Farrow stopped talking again, digesting the information.

"If I do this . . . if I'm able to get this guy out, you will then put his soul . . . and mine, back in our bodies?"

Openly smiling, Farrow continued, "Scalia will be resurrected and eventually write the book, and I'm back on the canvas. I'll be able to open my eyes and have a chance to beat Johnson."

Farrow stopped talking again, the playful grin no longer on his face. He stared at John and Keith. "Did I miss anything?"

Both men started to clap their hands happily.

The sun, a low burning coal on the horizon, seemed to sizzle as it was dragged beneath an ocean that had been thrown into twilight.

Keith broke the silence. "First of all, it's not a cave, although it may seem like just that when you first enter. It's called a Hellmouth. It provides a passageway into hell; to you, it's going to seem about a mile long . . ."

John interrupted. "You can probably run the thing in about six minutes. I mean, you used to be a professional fighter and all . . ."

"Used to be?" Farrow cut in, his tone bordering on violence.

"You know what I mean," John's voice shaking a bit. "You're in great shape, this shouldn't be hard for you at all . . . the run-a-mile in six minutes part I mean; but what I'm getting at is even though you could do it, run a six-minute mile . . . perhaps Scalia is not in shape for the chore. He is, after all, just a writer, probably sat on his butt all day eating Doritos."

"What he means," Keith added, "is you will have thirteen hours and thirteen minutes to get in and out of there. Don't cut it close, like down to the last six minutes; if Scalia can't run or is in bad shape and not up for such a long jog, you are going to want to give yourselves some extra time. Once the Hellmouth closes, that's it. There is nothing we can do to help you. You stay dead, Scalia stays dead, and you both stay in hell. Not to mention the world ends and millions of people are eventually going to die."

"That sure makes me feel better," Farrow said. "Ya know, you guys are laying a lot of shit on me. Why can't God, or whoever is running this loony bin, just take Scalia's soul back? I mean, isn't He all-powerful and everything? You know all that shit we learned when we were just dumb kids?"

"It doesn't work like that, Thomas. Trust us, we have been over every angle. This is the only way. The unfortunate timing of your death and

Robert Scalia's passing . . . well, his hijacking actually . . . has locked you two together," said John quietly.

"Listen, Farrow," Keith started, "I have been a fight fan most of my life, and all of my afterlife. You've been my hero for years. I have counted you out in so many fights . . . only to see you come back from almost certain losses, and I've seen you do this more than once. I have seen you resurrected from the dead . . . Oh, sorry, I didn't mean anything by that. Anyway, I've seen you come back and win fights nobody could have won. You have something inside you, this fighting spirit to win . . . and, yes, to live. I know you can do this, Thomas. All I'm asking you, all *we're* asking you to do is beat Johnson, raise your arms back up and beat him. Finish the fight, the guy's a jerk. I know you can do it. Be a hero one more time."

Farrow knew Keith was talking about more, much more than just winning a fight.

"Yeah, all I have to do is go to hell and back first," he said. "And another thing, I'm no hero, that's for sure."

"I believe everyone has the ability to be a hero," John said, "providing that you catch them at the right time."

"And now's that time, right?" Farrow asked.

Neither man answered.

The night air was cool and Farrow could see a group of people sitting semi-circle around a small fire about fifty yards away, probably drinking beer and eager to get laid. Looking this way and that, he noticed there weren't many bodies left on the beach. What seemed like just a few minutes ago, the sand was teeming with people laughing and bathing. The fast, almost too-fast, sunset seemed to erase them with the daylight.

"Let's not complicate things, Thomas." It was Keith who spoke first. "You were always my hero; now the *world* needs a hero."

Farrow was silent for a moment and then exploded with almost comedic enthusiasm.

"Okay, you want a hero? Is that what you want, for me to be a hero? Let's do this thing. I think both of you guys are nuts, but let's do this."

Farrow looked into Keith's eyes. "I'm going to wake up on that canvas in less than thirteen hours. I'll get off my ass and beat Johnson. I'll do it for you."

Pointing now at John. "I'll do it for both of you."

Farrow wore a sly smile on his face not really sure about anything that was going on or anything he was saying, just playing along.

"But before I do that, I'll get our writer friend and save the day. How does that sound?" Looking at the two smaller men, he said, "You got me, I'll play the hero, put on a real showstopper! Shit, I got nothing else to do, so until I wake up from this insane dream, I'll go along with it." Farrow's voice was echoing down the beach while no one who remained along its sandy terrain seemed to notice.

"Tell me about these so-called weapons," he said.

John stroked a quick contemplative hand through his closely-cropped beard, hesitated a second, and said, "Okay, here goes."

He bent down and opened what seemed to be a small wooden chest that sat in the sand next to his feet. The box was stained a deep brown and the wood from which it was made seemed very old, ancient in fact. Its top was covered with a piece of worn, black leather. The box was about a foot and a half long, a foot deep, and a foot tall.

"Now wait a minute," Farrow said with astonishment and more than a bit of uncertainty in his voice. "Where did that come from?"

"This chest has been here all along. It's been right next to us this whole time," said John.

"Been next to us this whole time? Bullshit! We've been here for almost an hour and . . ."

"Thomas, trust me . . . trust us," Keith said, motioning his hands to include John. "The chest has always been next to us. You just have to know how to see it."

Farrow started to talk, but was quickly cut off.

"You couldn't see the Atlantic Ocean or the seagulls at first, am I right? But it's right there."

Keith pointed toward the large body of water. A gust of wind blew the smell of sea salt under his nostrils. He looked out and the horizon seemed to be glowing.

"And the birds have always been right above us . . . well, as soon as the sun comes up again, any minute now, actually, they will be."

Farrow's eyes raced up and down the beach. It was now barren. No people. No campfire or children, nobody drinking beer or playing grab ass.

"Wait a minute," he said. "Where is everybody, and what do you mean when the sun comes up any minute? The sun just set."

"The people are long gone, Thomas, and it *is* almost sunrise," Keith said pointing at the spectral glow simmering just above the ocean that seemed more purplish than blue at this hour, whatever this hour was.

"Sunrise? The sun just set a little while ago, that can't be right."

"Oh, it can be, and *is* right. Thomas, everything is not as it seems here, especially time. What if I were to tell you that we have only been standing here talking for a minute or so?" asked John.

"A minute or so? It's been at least an hour, but I'd put my money on longer."

"Let me explain," John said. "When your soul left your body . . . it . . . you woke up here. Are you with me so far?"

Farrow nodded.

"Time as you know it virtually stopped. Your physical body is still in the real, well, as you would call it, real world, and I'm not talking MTV." John smiled before continuing.

"If time continued at the pace you're accustomed to, it would be found out that you had died in the ring. The referee would have finished the count and your corner would rush to your aid and see how badly you had been hurt . . . they would find you not breathing."

John let that sink in before he continued. "If that happened, we wouldn't be able to put you back when, and if, the time came. Right now, in Madison Square Garden, everything is frozen like a snapshot, a photograph." He ended this last sentence in almost a whisper.

Farrow spoke slowly, his voice carrying a bit of a tremor. Things were settling in his head, winding around his brain and squeezing.

"How come a little while ago the people on the beach seemed to be moving just fine?"

"This plane of existence is somewhere between your reality and ours. It's something to make you more comfortable, a place that you are, or at least were, familiar with, a place you loved as a child. As you can see, time is very strange here," Keith said.

"Do you understand things a bit better, Thomas?" John asked.

Farrow nodded.

"Let's stay on the subject of time for a bit longer," Keith stated. "As I mentioned earlier, when you cross through the Hellmouth," now looking directly at Farrow, "a timer will start. Look at your left wrist."

He did. It seemed he was now wearing a black watchband that was about an inch and a half wide.

"Has that always been there, too?"

Keith just smiled at him.

Still looking at the band, Farrow could see four digital numbers running across its length horizontally in what seemed to be a phosphorescent, tranquil blue. 13:13. Thirteen hours, thirteen minutes.

"Once you go through the Hellmouth, that read-out will start to count down. No matter what, do not let it finish. Do not let it reach all zeros before you get back out on the other side of that thing," Keith said.

"Why thirteen hours and thirteen minutes? Who came up with that number?" Farrow asked looking at Keith.

"Because . . . it's unlucky . . . doubly unlucky actually. Hell's rules, hell's game. Anything past that time, and you're stuck there. I guess it's just a way to show us they have a sense of humor."

"Yeah, and I can't stop laughing." Motioning toward his wrist, Farrow asked suspiciously, "Won't they find out I died once this thing starts to count down?"

"No," said John, "because we, well, I mean *HE*," he said pointing his eyes upwards, "can put your soul back into your body at the exact moment it left. Right after you landed on the canvas. You just won't suffer the intracranial hemorrhage."

"Nor will you have to worry about it again," Keith added. "But, Thomas, if you do this, if you make it out and back into your body," he paused before continuing, for effect more than anything else, "it's all going to be up to you. You have to get back up and face Johnson yourself. Stand before him in the ring and raise your arms." Keith then added with a slight smile, "Truly back from the dead this time."

Farrow stared Keith down, and the smile receded back into his face, but a happy mischief still danced behind his bright, bird-like eyes.

"This is a Hellstick," John said, holding between the fingers in his right hand what looked to Farrow like a roll of quarters that had been wrapped in black electrical tape. Apparently John had been rummaging around in the "magic" chest at their feet while Keith had been making "back from the dead" jokes.

"A Hellstick? That's what you call a Hellstick?" Farrow said nearly laughing out loud.

Smiling and taking a full step backward, John said, "Watch."

He squeezed the small item in his right fist and almost instantly it came out, growing from his hand, extending to a full three and a half feet. The end of the Hellstick, Farrow saw, was slightly thinner than the part John firmly gripped, its tip glowing a sinister spread of yellow and orange. Farrow and Keith backed away together as John swung the item like a baseball bat. The black rod made a sizzling noise as it hissed through the air before them. Wisps of smoke rose from its length.

After the swing, John brought the weapon back to his side and lowered it; a thin smile cut the lower half of his face. He gave the rod a second squeeze and it receded back to its normal size, that of a roll of quarters. A strong smell of sulfur infused the air for a few seconds, before the overpowering aroma of sea salt once again consumed it.

"The Hellstick," John started, almost as if he were presenting the item on a Sunday morning infomercial, "will cut through almost anything or anyone you come in contact with."

The damn thing reminded Farrow of a *Star Wars* light saber.

"It will stop anything in your path, slash through anything that gets in your way. It's a very deadly weapon, and if you find the need to use it, its value to you will be absolutely essential."

John stopped talking and held out the hand holding the now shrunken version of the item to Farrow. The prizefighter hesitated a second before scooping it up.

"Where do I keep it?" asked Farrow.

"You're right-handed," Keith said. "So put it in the right front pocket of your jeans. It'll be easy to access there."

Looking down at himself, Farrow now saw that he was wearing a faded pair of blue jeans, black work boots, and a black t-shirt.

He started to ask where the clothes had come from and what happened to his boxing garb, but looking at the two men who saw he had a question on his lips, just said, "Yeah, I know . . . I was always wearing this stuff, right?"

John responded with a smile and a quick thumbs-up motion.

Farrow concealed the Hellstick, as was recommended, in his right front pocket.

When he completed this small task, Keith said, "Is that a Hellstick in your pocket? Or are you just happy to see me?"

The joke amused neither Farrow nor John.

Speaking to John, but with his eyes narrowed and pinned on Keith, Farrow said, "What else you got?"

He saw that John was already holding up what looked like a small pill; the item was surely no bigger than an aspirin. It was fire engine red, almost as if it had just been spray painted, still glistening.

"And what do I do with that? Does it help if I suddenly get a migraine? Or maybe it will send me on a nice trip," Farrow joked.

"This is a Spitfire," John said. "And it does just what it sounds like it does. Thomas, please do not regard this diminutive item lightly. It's a very powerful weapon. How it works is simple. You put the Spitfire in your mouth. After it mixes with your saliva for a few seconds, you spit the thing into the direction of your enemies."

"Oh yeah? And then what?"

"And then get your butt out of there. This little thing . . ." John continued, still holding the seemingly harmless red pill up high, "will cause destruction and mayhem the likes of which you have never seen. Only use it if you get yourself in a really tight bind, I mean really jammed up, and only as a last resort."

"Trust us," Keith added, "you don't want to stick around to watch the fun."

John handed the red pill to Farrow who hesitated for a second and rolled his eyes before depositing it into the right front pocket of his newly acquired jeans. It rested safely next to the Hellstick. Two seemingly innocent items, the purpose of both to cause death and destruction.

The sky over the beach seemed ready to burst with light. Dawn rolled over the Atlantic like a stampede of buffalo. The ocean glowed and the sand looked white hot. Electrified. The air was still and cool around the three men.

Keith cut into the conversation. "You can put these on now."

He was holding out to Farrow what seemed to be hand wraps. The same kind he used during his whole pugilistic career.

"These are a special item made specifically for you, Thomas."

"Hand wraps? Why am I starting to feel like James Bond being sent out on an impossible assignment? You know the way he always had to go see that guy with a letter for a name before each mission? Z? Or was it X? Some old guy played him in the early, well, most of the movies, then for some reason, John Cleese from *Monty Python* took over the role."

"Thomas, can we please stay on track? Stay focused?" John said.

"Q! His name was Q!" Farrow said with much excitement in his voice. "It's funny how James Bond always stayed young and debonair, but that gadget guy got older and older with each movie."

"Thomas, please," John begged.

"Okay, okay. Just trying to make sure that I'm not in a coma somewhere, or sleeping in my bed dreaming . . ." turning to look at John and Keith ". . . having a terrible nightmare.

"Alright," Farrow said smacking his hands and vigorously rubbing them together. "Hand wraps. What do they do?"

"You wrap them around your hands, of course, but the beauty of it is . . . well, put them on," Keith said, "and watch what happens."

Farrow took the wraps from Keith's outstretched arm and apprehensively, but quickly, wrapped them around his hands. Years of practice had the chore done in just under five minutes, a nice snug fit.

"Now what?" Farrow said, holding his large hands up, palms out for them to see, but the wraps were gone. Erased like they never existed at all. "Wait a minute, where did they go? Let me guess, they were never there, right?" he said sarcastically.

John said, "Oh no, Thomas, the wraps are there, you just can't see them." Then he added, "Nor can anyone else. If you come across someone, uh . . . something that wants to rock and roll, even though you were a professional prizefighter, you wouldn't stand a chance against anything that you may encounter on the other side of the Hellmouth. So the hand wraps that you can't see, but I assure you are definitely there, will even the score. Now when you hit something, if you have to hit something, you will hurt them . . . or it. Slow 'em down enough for you and the writer to get away."

"Okay," Farrow said, "if you say so."

He held his hands up, balling them into huge, meaty fists, and then reopening them trying to feel the wraps because he sure as hell couldn't see them. Farrow then proceeded to shadow box for a few seconds. He felt good. Dangerous.

"Just do me a favor, guys. Stop saying I *was* a professional prizefighter, like in the past tense. After I get this writer back out through that Hellmouth, or whatever it is you call it, I'm going to be a professional prizefighter again. Okay?" Then he smiled at them.

"Of course, Thomas," John said.

"Yes, of course," Keith chimed in. "I'm sorry. We're sorry."

"Okay, is that it? Is there anything else? Can James Bond leave for his mission now?" Farrow said, still smiling. "I have to get back. I still have a fight to win." He stopped shadow boxing.

"Another minute, Thomas. We have one more item for you. Well, it's not really a physical item," Keith said.

"What he means is you will have a certain ability to ask for stuff. Think of it kinda like making wishes, but you will only be granted the things that you really, really need," said John.

"Yeah," said Keith. "Don't get over there and start asking for a Coca Cola or a cheeseburger, 'cause it's not gonna happen."

"Can I wish for more wishes?" Farrow said grinning.

"Thomas, please! If there is absolutely no other way, and you are in dire need of something, you can ask, and we'll see what we can do," John said.

"Then why can't we just ask Him," motioning his eyes upward, "to get this writer of yours out?" Farrow said.

"We told you, it doesn't work like that. Nothing can be taken out without you actually going in to get it. Oh, and that reminds me, Thomas, only two souls will be allowed to leave hell, so don't get any ideas about taking anyone else out with you, it won't be permitted. If someone is there, they're there for a reason," John explained.

"Trust me," Farrow said. "I'm going in, getting the writer, and then the two of us are coming out as quick and as neat as you please."

"That's good, Thomas. Do things nice and clean. Quiet," John said.

"I'll do my best, but I do have another question. Just a small thing that's been niggling at the back of my mind."

"What's that?" Keith said.

"How the hell do I find him?"

"Ah, yes, Thomas. Excellent question. One we almost forgot to address," said Keith. "Since you died within seconds of each other, your souls are connected. You'll be able to sense him, almost feel him. It will be like a pull . . . a tugging in the core of your stomach. His soul will be like a beacon to yours."

"You said I only have thirteen hours and change to get in and out; how far away is he going to be? I mean, what if it takes me that long to find this guy?" Farrow questioned.

Keith said, "Scalia will be in the main holding area. Every soul is held for a twenty-four hour period in what will look like glass holding cells.

The structure is huge, and you should be drawn right to it, so he shouldn't be hard to find at all. That is why it's so important to get him out now, within this first twenty-four hours."

"It's about a three-hour journey on foot," John said. "Three hours there and three hours back. You should be out in six. Nice and easy."

"I really have to stress this next part, Thomas," Keith began. "As long as you don't involve yourself in anything or get into any trouble, you should remain virtually invisible to the, uh . . . well, I'll call them inhabitants. Once you cross through the Hellmouth that timer on your wrist will start, and that's something that can't be stopped. Don't talk to anyone, and don't even look at anyone. Believe me, the less you see the better. Keep your head down and stay focused. Get Scalia and get out."

"And if I meet that special someone?" Farrow joked.

"Thomas, please. Enough levity. This is serious business," said John.

"Okay, okay, I'm sorry. You guys are laying a lot of shit on me. I'm just a bit nervous. Hell, I'm real nervous. Scared to death actually."

"That's understandable, we'd be too, given the circumstances. Anything else you need to know? Anymore questions you might have that we can try to answer?" John asked.

"No, I guess not," Farrow said in a quiet voice, almost a whisper. "Just tell me one thing. Why is it I feel like I'm going off to my own execution?"

"Because," Keith said, "maybe you are."

The new morning sun brightened the sand as the first of its worshippers appeared on the beach. The three men started walking along the soft terrain in a palpable silence.

When they were close enough to the Hellmouth, just about six yards away, Farrow finally saw it, really saw it, and he was shocked into silence. He thought that it would be just a cave, or some sort of dark passageway; but he now knew with certainty that everything John and Keith had told him was true. He was not sleeping or the victim of a drug-induced coma, he was wide-awake.

Just a few feet away now, the Hellmouth floated before them a foot off the sandy beach ground. It was basically a rip in the air, as if something had torn a hole into existence through the atmosphere. There was a deep humming noise, an insect-like buzzing that sounded as if a thousand angry bees were coming from within the abomination. It was oval shaped, about six feet at its widest. Its edges seemed to be a burnt orange and black ash, red smoldering embers, an evil cigar burn.

Farrow could see the beach beyond and around this cruel puncture: laughing sunbathers featuring beach ball activity, and the midday sun in a cloudless eastern sky.

He looked from John and then to Keith, and said, "My God, what the fuck is that thing?"

With a comforting hand on his shoulder, John said, "That, Thomas, is the Hellmouth."

"I . . . have to go in there?" he said, motioning towards the buzzing rip. "Our writer is trapped somewhere in there? Make me understand how something like this could happen." Any trace of humor was now absent from his voice.

John gave Farrow's shoulder a comforting squeeze, and Keith began to speak. "When an incident occurs, where many people pass through, that's what we call it *passing through,* the souls all come through this area . . . this midpoint." He stopped talking so this information would settle in. Keith spoke slow and deliberately so Farrow would understand everything he was saying.

"Some people stay here for years. These are kind of 'borderline' people, it's almost like they have to do penance before we take them upstairs, while others go up instantly."

Now John cut in, rubbing a hand quickly through his beard, "While the rest go straight down there." He pointed into the endless black throat of the Hellmouth.

"So you see, Thomas, a place like a hospital, while hundreds of people don't die each day all at once, there is a pretty good turnover. A lot of souls pass each week. When Scalia came over, unfortunately, he was real close to the opening of this thing . . . and how do I say this . . . I guess he was hijacked, kidnapped from this limbo right under our noses. Something must have been waiting for him," Keith explained.

"Why was he on my beach?" Farrow asked.

"To Robert Scalia, it didn't look like a beach. It was the picnic area where he first made love to his wife. This place is different for everyone," John said.

"How could this have happened? How does somebody who doesn't belong in hell get kidnapped and held there?"

"Because of the particularly high volume of souls leaving the hospital. In the midst of the confusion, ol' Beelzebub pulled a fast one; he saw a chance to end the world. If Scalia does not write his book, a book that will keep an imbecile out of the White House and prevent a nuclear war . . . the world is going to end in about seven years," said Keith.

Farrow realized that this was it. He was a fighter, and to save the world he would have to fight for it. He would once again have to lift his arms. He took a single step toward the obscene opening of the Hellmouth.

"Thomas, no man can see the things that your are going to see over there and lead a normal life. I can assure you, that once you get Scalia out neither of you will remember anything that happened . . . nor anything you've seen. That's just a small consolation, 'cause you're gonna see some fucked-up shit."

"Keith! Language!" said John.

"Oh, I'm sorry. My Bad!" Keith said, smiling.

Farrow liked Keith. John, too. At a different time and place, he felt they could've been friends, good friends, maybe even start a band.

Farrow turned to the maddening buzz of the six-foot hole in the air, the Hellmouth. He could feel a chill draft filtering up through the dark passageway like a screen door left open on a frigid New England night. He took a step forward, stopped, and looked back at John and Keith one last time and nodded his head.

John returned the nod and Keith raised a single hand as if to wave goodbye.

In search of a writer whose soul was trapped in purgatory, a writer who would one day save the world, Thomas Farrow stepped into the Hellmouth.

ROUND THREE

The midday sun spilled in through the large, wall-sized windows on the east end of the cafeteria, bathing the students in warm light. Conversations buzzed around the room and the familiar stale smell of schoolhouse grub weighed down the stagnant air. Lunchtime monitors patrolled the area in their ugly attire with watchful eyes.

The cafeteria was more than just a facility to eat lunch in and catch up on homework. Important discussions took place, restricted meetings were conducted in secret, and, sometimes, something that started out completely innocent became something more, something much more.

It's actually quite funny how a single event or, in the case of Thomas A. Farrow, a single sentence can change the course of one's life. Tommy, he preferred this alias over Thomas, was just four days shy of his fifteenth birthday. At five foot eleven, big for his age, he sat in the North Reading High School lunchroom during the meal period he was assigned, his friends, thugs and bullies, the school toughs, assembled around him.

William Walcott was the oldest of this tight group, along with two younger boys, Ray Maxim and Carl Tunney. They huddled around Tommy Farrow with idealistic attentiveness. At seventeen years old, William had celebrated a birthday a month earlier in April. It was uncommon for a twelfth-grade student to mix with younger children, but not unheard of.

Farrow at fourteen, and both Ray Maxim and Carl Tunney, sixteen years old apiece, held the title, the *honor*, of being the toughest children in school, and they fit together like pieces of a complex puzzle.

Farrow, the youngest of the assemblage, was also the most respected, this being due to his size. He worked three days a week after school at the hundred-acre Paul W. Conley Container Terminal unloading cargo from cruise ships that docked at Boston Harbor. He was not afraid of hard work, and this particular work contributed generously to his bulk.

William started the proverbial ball rolling and with that, set in motion the career of Tommy Farrow.

"So what's the problem?" he asked. "You been brooding the whole period. Something bothering you?"

"It's nothing," Tommy said. "Nothing I can't handle."

"So, there is something bothering you."

"Not something. Someone."

This statement had taken William by surprise. Ray and Carl also leaned forward, spiked with interest. Someone was bothering Tommy Farrow?

"Who would ever think about messing with you, my friend? Messing with us?" said Carl. "Don't they know who you are? Don't they know the kind of friends you keep? Shit, I wouldn't want to mess with us, and I *am* one of us."

This made Tommy smile. "Oh, they know us alright. I just don't think they really care."

"Is this guy so bad he can take us all?" said Ray. "Is it someone from a different school? Someone at work maybe?"

"When I drop you off at the docks tomorrow, maybe we'll have a little chat with this fella," said William.

William Walcott was the only friend in this small group who legally had a license, but that didn't stop the others from driving when a vehicle was available or there was an absolute need. Even Tommy had snuck his father's Honda out a time or two, but they mostly relied on William to truck them around. He was Tommy's ride to work three times a week.

"Yeah, we'll fuck 'em up real good!" said Ray. "Fuck 'em real good! By the way, did I tell you guys I bent Jeanette Fitzsimmons over my dad's trunk last weekend? The bitch loved it."

Carl grinned. "Did you take your father's ride out again?"

"Hey, my parents were away for the weekend and I was real horny. I'll tell you, man, Jeanette, that bitch is crazy."

The group, including Tommy, smiled at this.

"So, my friend," William said, taking the conversation away from Ray's sexual adventures and back to the more pressing issue. "What's up? What's going on?"

"It's Mr. Baer," Tommy said with an almost embarrassed tone underlying his voice.

"Baer? What did that jerk-off do? I can't even believe that prick is married. I hear he even has a kid. Imagine that someone was hard up enough to sleep with that douche bag."

Edwin Baer, in Tommy Farrow's opinion, was the worst kind of asshole there was. New to North Reading just the year before last, and already had a reputation for belittling students with sarcastic remarks and making embarrassing examples of the kids just for the fun of it.

It was widely known that the small man, *the size of a woman*, William Walcott liked to joke, was a failed principal. Well, maybe a failed principal was the wrong choice of words. Baer, who had an administrative degree, was up for a principal job twice in the last of his eight years teaching high school, and was beat out both times by better-qualified candidates. This did not sit well with Edwin. His father had been a dean of students at Boston College and his brother a high school principal in Connecticut, sort of a family tradition. Three out of his four grandparents (though now all deceased save his grandfather on his mother's side) were also highly placed in the educational system, principals or assistants.

It seemed to Edwin that at various functions and summertime get-togethers, he was looked down upon by some members of the family. He felt he didn't measure up to them, and this had nothing to do with height. Edwin Baer was an ugly troll of a man. He stood just about five feet, six inches and maybe weighed 140 pounds soaking wet. The skin under his eyes was darkened, giving him a ghoulish appearance, not to mention a mouth that was far too big for his face. On the seldom occasions he smiled, he resembled a shark. At thirty-three years of age, he kept the hair on his head closely cropped to hide the fact that there was almost no hair on his head in the first place. He was the kind of man who was most likely teased and beaten everyday of his adolescence by schoolmates and neighborhood punks, and now that he was in a position of some authority, even if that position was *just* over children, he would, when it was feasible, make them pay.

Although the other teachers at North Reading High School said hello and goodbye to him at the appropriate times and involved themselves in small talk when cornered, Edwin Baer was not liked, and this consensus was unanimous.

"What? Is he failing you or something?" Carl asked.

"It's not like that," Tommy said.

"Then what is it like?" Ray this time.

"I guess it's like when someone is a short little jerk-off and they gotta show everybody how mean and tough they are. I think they call it Napoleon complex or something."

Tommy Farrow looked almost embarrassed to be having this conversation with his friends, the four of them close together now amidst the pool of students eating homemade sandwiches, studying in textbooks, and knocking off homework assignments early.

Now that a teacher's name had been brought out into the open, the conversation had turned secret. Ray and Carl, like sentries or scouts, looked around their small group at other students to see if anyone with wandering eyes or big ears might be zoning in on their little meeting. None seemed to be, but that didn't dissuade the boys from speaking with softer voices anyway.

"Okay," said William. "How is he laying on the grief?"

"It's just that . . . I don't know, it's almost as if . . . I guess it's because I'm so much bigger than he is, and the prick's an adult and all. He keeps making a fool of me, trying to show that he's not afraid of the 'big kid'," Tommy said.

"Example," said Ray.

"Yeah, an example. A lot of little things have been adding up. He'll say stuff like, *The bigger they are, the harder they fall,* while staring at me. Or, *Just because someone has muscle, doesn't mean they are strong,* then he points to his head meaning I'm stupid or something. This asshole's been riding me, and I'm not going to take much more of his shit."

"What can we do to help?" Carl asked. "Wanna egg the fucker's house? I know where the little prick lives."

"What's that gonna to do?" asked William. "This asshole has to be stopped. I've heard stories like this about Baer before."

"How does a grown man like Edwin Baer belittle children and then go home and face his wife and kid? Man, I'd be embarrassed to have him as a father," said Ray, who was now running a black plastic comb through his hair.

"I'm not taking anymore of his bullshit!" Tommy said again, looking at William who now saw something dangerous behind his friend's eyes, something waiting to be let loose, something that needed just the smallest of excuses.

"This last period," Tommy started, "just before I came down to lunch . . ."

The sun's rays from the large cafeteria windows seemed to spotlight Farrow, concentrate just on him.

". . . I slipped a note to Trish Morrison, I was trying to ask her to a movie. The theater in town, ya know the one that shows the old films? Well, it's playing a Clint Eastwood double feature this weekend and both movies are westerns. I heard Trish say she loves westerns. I mean, what kind of girl likes westerns, right? She's perfect for me. Anyway, I pass her this note, and Baer sees me do it."

"Oh boy," said Carl. "I know where this is going."

"He grabs the note from her desk, reads it to himself, and then says out loud, so the whole class can hear him . . ."

Tommy cleared his throat and conjured up his best Mr. Baer voice. " 'Mr. Farrow, if you intend to ask someone on a date, I would appreciate if you do it on your own time.' And then the bastard looks at Trish and says in a condescending voice, 'Ms. Morrison, I'm sure you can do much better.'"

"The fucking bastard!" William said, slapping a hard palm on the lunchroom table. "We have to finish this cocksucker off!"

Ray and Carl joined in with yeahs and nods of approval.

"You know what the worst part was?" Tommy said before continuing. "After Baer said that, Trish's face got all red, you had to see her. She looked like a tomato about to burst, and then the bell rang. When it did, she ran out of the classroom afraid to even look at me. I looked back at Baer, and the bastard was smiling."

"Son of a bitch! He's dead! How are we going to play this?" asked William.

"*We* are not going to do anything," said Tommy. "*I* am. I just don't know what yet, but it's gonna be big."

The group of four was silent for a bit among the drone of the cafeteria noises and conversations, and then a sly look registered across William's face.

"I got an idea," he said.

The sounds around the four friends seemed to fade away like the volume on a television set being lowered, and three of the four tuned in to listen to what William Walcott had to say.

"Well, it's not so much an idea, it's more of a bet. A bet with a prize at the end."

"And that would be?" Tommy asked.

"Your birthday's coming up in a few days, am I right? Gonna be fifteen?"

"Yeah, so?"

Looking at Tommy, William started, "My parents are going away this weekend. Correct me if I'm wrong, your birthday weekend."

He stopped talking and let that sink in and then here it came, the sentence that would change Tommy Farrow's life forever and put him on the path that would become his life's blood.

"You get up in class this Friday . . . just a few days from now . . . and punch Baer in the face, I mean really lay into the jerk. It would almost be like giving a gift to yourself." William speaking with more enthusiasm now, "You do that, and I'll throw you a huge birthday bash with a keg of beer and everything, all expenses paid! Fuck it, you knock the asshole down, I'll make it two kegs, your choice. Everybody will be there, I'll even invite Trish Morrison. Shit, man, you'll be a hero."

Tommy looked to Ray and then shifted his gaze to Carl, before settling his eyes back on William. They were all smiling, and without realizing it, Tommy Farrow smiled also.

Tommy didn't think too long or too hard deciding on a time in which the events that had been discussed in the school cafeteria only three days earlier would unfold. *What would Clint do at a time like this?*

Mr. Edwin Baer's ninth grade mathematics class and "sideshow" was fifth period and it ran from 11:45 to 12:30, right before lunch. *The kids at that time of their culinary delights are going to actually have something to talk about today,* Farrow thought to himself through a hidden half-smile.

He had decided on 12:00 for the main event between himself and Edwin; the perfect time, high noon, even though only one of them knew there was going to be an event. His eyes glanced across the face of the clock that silently ticked the time away atop the classroom door. 11:47. Thirteen minutes to party time.

Tommy sat in a desk three rows back and to Mr. Baer's right. His seating assignment was close to the windows on the west side of the building overlooking an expanse of green fields where the school football team,

The North Reading Hornets, practiced drills and tactical formations. He was sure big enough to play on the team and was asked no less than two times by the football coach, Mr. Hagler, to sign on, but he had no interest. He preferred to be banging beaver or bird-dogging some chick, rather than running around with a bunch of other boys wearing tight-fitting football pants. Besides, most of the team were pussies anyway.

He reduced his eyes to slits as Baer was handing out math exams to the first person in each of the five rows.

"Take one and pass it back," he said, an authoritative tone threading through his voice. Basically saying, *I'm in charge. You do what I say.*

Baer put his little hands behind himself as he patrolled the front of the classroom, his line of vision scanning over the students.

"Mr. Farrow, be sure to keep your eyes on your own paper during the exam."

Tommy, whose eyes had been looking down at his desk, felt like he'd been sucker-punched by Baer. He wasn't going to cheat, nor did he need to. This was just another of Baer's attempts to embarrass the big kid in class. The only difference was that on this day Mr. Baer was unaware of the two-ton weight dangling on a string above his head that was about to snap.

With that last comment, any doubts that Tommy Farrow may have had were erased like chalk markings on a blackboard.

"Yes, sir, Mr. Baer," Tommy said.

He wanted no suspicions to arise on the undercard before the main event.

Baer was surprised that Tommy actually answered him, but detected nothing sarcastic in the boy's tone, so ignored the response and continued to wrangle the front end of the classroom in his trademark, stooped posture.

"Keep your papers turned face down until I give the go-ahead to do otherwise. At that time you can begin the exam." His beady little eyes, two bullet holes, set deep in their sockets, flicked around the room.

Tommy, with pencil in hand, kept his gaze down and waited for Baer's command. His classmates were none the wiser to the historic event about to unfold. The twenty-plus students in the room were silent as they waited for Baer's signal to start. Finally he gave it with a slow, measured, "Begin now."

The students, including Tommy, turned over their tests in a crinkling whoosh; the sounds of graphite scribbling against paper filled the room as the exam began.

At five minutes to noon Mr. Baer pulled out the chair from behind his desk that was centered in the front of the classroom and sat down resting his elbows before him. He regarded the children, who were swimming in a sea of mathematical equations, not with pride, but with the intent to catch somebody cheating. Even someone just looking up from his or her paper would be reason enough for the failed principal to make an example. His hopeful eyes lingered over the student who was also the biggest. *Now that would be a real catch*, he thought.

Tommy Farrow, to Baer's dismay, showed absolutely no sign of cheating, or for that matter, shifting eyes.

At three minutes to noon, Baer folded his arms across his chest and sat back in his chair, his "throne". He was the king of this little world. He knew it, and he made damn sure the children knew this fact as well.

The sound of laughter coming from outside the large classroom windows caused one boy, Richard Liston, to look over toward the cheerful noise rolling around in the bright sunlight.

"Mr. Liston! Eyes!" Baer said with such a viciousness it was almost as if he had encountered the man who had murdered his family after a ten-year search. The boy immediately looked back to the exam paper and did not shift his gaze again. The test went on.

Mr. Baer wore an "It's good to be the king!" expression across his smug face.

A quick glance up at the clock told Tommy it was now one minute to twelve. In sixty seconds, high noon. The haunting soundtrack to *The Good, the Bad, and the Ugly* filled his brain. Eyes, now back on his exam, he started to count to sixty.

One, one thousand. Two, one thousand. Three, one thousand.

The classroom was absolutely silent except for the scratching sound the multiple pencils made.

Tommy kept his head down and counted off the last thirty seconds with his eyes closed. He let the yellow #2 he'd been holding in his right hand fall to the desk and roll across his answer sheet.

Fifty-eight, one thousand. Fifty-nine, one thousand. Sixty.

Time was up.

Tommy slowly pushed the desk that he'd been crowded against, away from himself with both palms; its legs made a long scratching sound across the tiled floor loud enough for Baer to target him with dangerous eyes.

"Is something wrong, Mr. Farrow?" said Mr. Baer.

Tommy said nothing as he stood up moving his chair away with the backs of his legs.

"Mr. Farrow!" his voice much louder now and peppered with distaste. He'd been waiting for something just like this to happen. "I asked you if something was wrong?"

Tommy stepped out of his row and took a step toward the front of the classroom where Mr. Baer was now also on his feet and pointing at the boy.

"If you don't get back in your seat you will fail the exam! Do you hear me? You will fail!" Then added, "I will also make sure you are a prime candidate for after-school detention!"

All of the other students were now looking up from their own papers to see what the commotion was about.

The black arms of the large clock above the door stretched upward reaching for the number twelve pinning themselves on that numeral forever in North Reading High School mythology.

Tommy Farrow was standing center stage as Mr. Baer came rushing around his oversized desk, his voice approaching rage.

"I told you to get back in your seat! Sit back down! Do as I say, right now, Mr. Farrow." Poking a finger into Tommy's chest, the pathetic little man had to look up to see the child's eyes. "Everybody else, back to your exams, this does not concern you! An important math test is still going on!" Baer was really shouting now. Most children obeyed, but curiosity got the best of several of the students.

"Mr. Farrow, you are on very thin ice!" Baer yelled, proving to himself, while at the same time showing the rest of the class he was not afraid of the fourteen-year-old Thomas Farrow who had more than half a foot over the smaller man.

"If you do not sit back in your seat . . ."

Then Tommy Farrow said a sentence that would follow him through the rest of his life, the rest of his career as a prizefighter. He spoke it loud and clear and by that afternoon the sentence had become legend in North Reading High.

"Get ready to rock."

"Huh?" said Baer. "What did you say to me?"

He stood on his feet before Tommy in the front of the classroom.

Tommy Farrow, his right hand at his side pulled into a tight fist, his knuckles seemingly bleached white, once again said, "Get ready to rock."

Baer neither saw nor expected the blow. Tommy brought his arm up from his side with lightning reflexes and swung with every ounce he had, his fist the needle, his arm the thread following it, a horizontal heat-seeking missile. There was absolutely no contest, or defense. Farrow's fist exploded, perfectly executed on the left side of Baer's trollish face. Tommy swung through, partially turning his body. He instinctively brought his left hand, also curled into a fist, up to his face as if to defend himself from return fire, but before both hands were up in a protective position, Baer was lying at his feet. The little man with the big mouth wasn't moving. Tommy bobbed for a second or two as if there might be something else for him to hit, but Mr. Baer did not get up.

After a long second or two, the math teacher stirred on the classroom floor moaning a bit. *That was good,* Tommy thought, *at least I didn't kill the fucker.*

The students in the classroom, slapping their desks and cheering, quickly drowned out the sounds that Baer made. The Torres brothers, Kevin and Paul, were actually on their feet clapping, a sound that only a few years later, Tommy Farrow would grow very accustomed to.

When the smoke cleared and all was said and done, no legal charges were brought up against Tommy Farrow, mostly because he was a minor, fourteen years of age, that and the embarrassment of Edwin Baer being knocked down and practically out by a student.

The incident was kept as quiet as possible. Except for the twenty-odd students, and Baer himself, no one else actually saw the event; in fact, only about six of the children in the classroom admitted to looking up from their exams when the punch was executed and the beer keg bet was played out to its full expression. Everyone had heard the loud smacking whump of fist against flesh and knew what had gone down, especially after seeing Baer lying at Tommy's feet.

The episode did become something of legend that would be talked about for years to come. Students, as well as teachers, whispered in the halls and behind Baer's back. He quietly left North Reading High in the middle of the following semester, and slit his wrists a year after that.

Just because you had a big mouth and knew how to use it didn't mean you should. If you were going to walk around like a big man and talk down to people, even if it was spent looking up at them most of the time, you had better make damn sure you could back up the shit you were shoveling. Baer had a mouth . . . and balls, for a little while, but no back up.

In the end, Tommy Farrow was expelled from North Reading High School and sent to nearby Wilmington High and, without realizing it, had started his career as a professional prizefighter.

His reward, as promised, his trophy for the one-sided bout against Edwin Baer was a birthday party featuring two kegs of beer, compliments of one William Walcott. Although the shindig that was to celebrate Tommy's fifteenth birthday did not happen on the weekend of said birthday, the day just after the Baer incident, his parents had grounded him for a month in addition to his expulsion. The party would be pushed back six weeks later to coincide with the beginning of summer vacation, and Tommy was okay with that, it was something to look forward to . . . and, yes, Patricia Morrison would be there.

Farrow had come out of this little bet mostly unscathed. He would still be able to attend school, albeit a new one just a few miles away. He had just about knocked out a prick of a teacher, and most of all, he would still get his party.

On the night of the incident, his father James, a big man in his own right, came into Tommy's lightless bedroom. Standing in the doorway, the illumination from the kitchen where his mom was cooking dinner leaked into the space framing his dad's huge shape. James Farrow stood silent for a moment before taking a full step into the room; the kitchen smells that came in with him were intoxicating. Tommy got up from the bed on which he was sitting and faced his father, the two almost eye to eye, fighters in the ring. James Farrow said nothing, just slapped his son across the face, once and hard. Tommy did not try to duck or block the blow. The thought of fighting or swinging back at his father never even crossed the boy's mind. He just absorbed the open hand, causing a single tear to leak down his right cheek.

James Farrow turned to leave, his body a black mass against the kitchen lighting that was rushing into the darkened space. Before his father stepped out of the room, he looked back to his son who was bathed in gentle slivers of twilight seeping into his window through the drawn shade partitions.

"Was it worth it?"

He looked at his father, the tear already drying on his cheek.

"He had it coming, Dad."

"Well, boy, that's one thing you're going to learn in life. We all got it coming."

ROUND FOUR

His first impulse was to turn around and leave what he had just entered. Farrow almost expected to see John and Keith standing side by side just outside the Hellmouth waving back at him. They were not.

The egg-shaped puncture hung silently as if on a dark canvas. The buzzing sound had stopped. It was almost as if someone had burned a hole on a giant piece of black oaktag and held it up to a summer morning sky, the light bursting in. He blinked his eyes and fought the urge to shield them. The illumination looked comforting, and he could sense its influence.

Farrow looked down at his wristband. 13:12. The digital numbers had started counting backward. This was real. It was happening. He was filled with a sense of urgency. He turned so that the light filling the aperture warmed his back as he continued to blink his eyes waiting for them to adjust, which they did rather quickly.

Before him stood a tunnel.

It will seem about a mile long to you, Keith had said.

Farrow looked down at the black work boots on his feet. They were the same style and brand as the ones he wore during his happy-go-lucky days of humping crates on the Boston docks during his high school years. He could see them clearly; they felt comfortable, broken in. He seemed to be standing on stone, or a hard landscape with similar rock-like qualities. He lifted his arms stretching them out from his sides, reaching. He could not feel the walls; he decided to think of it as a cave because that's sure what it looked like. The term Hellmouth reminded him too much of where he was going, where he would be soon enough. As his eyes adjusted a bit more Farrow realized he could now see walls, also made of stone, about five feet further than his outstretched fingertips. He looked left then right. *Plenty of elbowroom*, he thought. Above his head . . . nothing, just empty space.

He had learned long ago that someone his size should always mind his surroundings and especially the height of the room or area one occupied. He had many painful memories of head bumps to remind him of this. Standing up from a seat in an airplane was always fun; Farrow hit his head just about every time.

The passageway seemed big enough to accommodate an army jeep; well, at least there would be plenty of room to move around if he needed to do so.

Farrow brushed a hand across the right front pocket of his jeans. He felt the concealed Hellstick. It comforted him knowing it was there.

He stood still in the darkness listening. Nothing at first, and then maybe up ahead a bit, the sound of small rocks trickling, as if something had disturbed them while trying to move quietly by. Farrow realized he was cold, looking again from left to right; he rubbed his arms for warmth. His vision adjusted as much as it was going to, which was pretty darn good; he could see everything there was to see, stone and velvet blackness. *Wasn't hell supposed to be hot?* he thought, remembering the scene from the *The Exorcist*, the priests gathered over the little possessed girl, their breath fogging before them in the chill air of her bedroom. But then again, that was only a movie. He shook away the thought of a green-pea-soup spewing Linda Blair and listened a moment longer. Nothing. No small rock disturbances, no little red devils, and no demonic twelve-year-old girl having intercourse with a crucifix.

The tranquil blue read-out on his wristband now announced 13:09. *Shit, I better get moving.* The tunnel fell away before him in a slight decline, nothing too crazy or very steep, but he would be traveling a downward path.

Farrow felt for the Hellstick in his pocket for a second time in the last three minutes; it was still there and felt solid.

"Hello," he said, mostly to hear his own voice, or at lease a voice. "Scalia?"

He imagined the writer appearing from the darkness before him, like a ghostly apparition after hearing his name called. The two of them would then join arms and jump through the white light of the Hellmouth exit yelling "OOOOH SHIIIIT!!", like Butch and Sundance off the cliff in that scene from one of his favorite films of all time; but that didn't happen. Nothing happened. Everything was silent.

13:08. Okay, enough fucking around, it was time to save the world.

Farrow took a tentative step forward and then stopped. He took a second step. Fiery arms, smoking and charred, did not reach for him from the walls, nor did anything ooze up from the ground through the stone grabbing for his ankles. There were no other sounds save the rocks shifting he may or may not have heard minutes earlier. The climate did seem a bit warmer, though, and he had an idea things were going to get downright hot before this little journey was over.

He set out on a quick steady pace feeling confident, an emotion he had always conjured on his walk from the locker room to the ring. He had about a mile to go, that's how far it would be through the Hellmouth his "friends" had told him, until damnation.

His first impulse was to run the length of the tunnel, but a few factors came into play and stopped him. Although he could see well, say about as good as a darkened room splashed in bright moonlight, he could only see about ten feet ahead. Beyond that, zilch. Farrow didn't want to run into anybody or anything beyond his sight. He was pretty sure that nothing would be waiting up ahead in the dark to surprise him, not in here anyway, but if there was someone, he wouldn't be able to slow down fast enough before running into them. Another problem, he was not familiar with the topography, the tunnel's curves and contours. If he ran over an uneven patch of stone or a small crack in the ground, he could twist his ankle . . . or maybe worse.

Keith, or was it John, had said it would be about a three-hour walk once he exited the Hellmouth to where the writer was being held. If his ankle was twisted or broken, that wasn't a walk he thought he could make, let alone a return trip, maybe a running, fighting return trip. Farrow had broken bones before, and it wasn't something he wanted to worry about now. *If I did break a bone, what would happen? Would it heal itself? Would it stay broken forever?* he wondered. After all, he was dead. He didn't think the same rules applied here as they did elsewhere.

He continued on, the obscurity seemed to open up before him, parting like the Red Sea did for Moses. When he had advanced just about twenty-five or thirty paces, Farrow looked back once to the oval entrance from which he had come. It was all but gone; a hazy blackness hung there like a charcoal rain cloud moving over the misshapen face of a bone-white moon.

At the speed he was moving, Farrow projected it would take no more than ten minutes to complete this little part of the journey. On the happier side of things, he thought, he would have company on the return trip, someone to talk to when he came back this way. He and the writer would take a nice easy stroll back through the Hellmouth and get to know each other some before their memories were wiped away and they were put back into their bodies. They would have plenty of time to spare, maybe even share a few laughs.

Farrow couldn't have been more wrong.

As the minutes passed, he moved swiftly, listening to the only sound he could hear, his work boots below him on the stone ground. He noticed a considerable change in the climate. He was no longer cold. The temperature went from chilly to rather pleasing in just a short period.

He thought of a long-ago summer night with a beer in his hand, Ray, Carl, and William singing to Bob Seger on the radio, something about cowboys running against the wind, maybe a Clint Eastwood movie later on in the evening. *High Plains Drifter,* that would be a good one. Clint paints a whole town red and hangs a sign that reads "Welcome to Hell." Jesus, Farrow thought, he wished he didn't know now, what he didn't know then.

Please let it stay comfortable. I don't even mind it hot, but I'd have to draw the line at burning. He quietly smiled to himself. A hint of sulfur danced on the air. At first he though it was just imagined, but, as Farrow continued to trudge along, the smell grew thick and strong. *I must be getting close.* By his estimation he had been walking for just about seven minutes and the digital readout on his wrist proved it. 13:02.

In the distance through the shadowy darkness, and squinting his eyes the right way, Farrow could just about make out what he thought to be a small point of light. He focused on this area, assuming the tunnel would be shortly coming to an end. He imagined another portal ripped in the air that he would step into, step through. He had a very hard time holding onto the realization that he would voluntarily be going into hell, actually into hell, with devils and demons and such. Hell. What else could he call it to make it sound better? To maybe soften the harshness of the word? In his mind, if he used the words Purgatory, Hades, or maybe Perdition, would that make it any better? Would the fancier language ease his journey some? He thought not.

Farrow remembered a writing class he had to take in high school years ago. He didn't take much away from the course. He sure as fuck couldn't write anything that would coherently inform or entertain, but he did remember the teacher, a tall thin man with a calamity of black hair on top of his head and root-beer brown eyes. Mr. Canzonero, or Mr. Canzoneri, something along those lines. Anyway this particular instructor had once said: "Never substitute a complex word for a simple one just to sound more intelligent. The simplest way of writing something, or for that matter, telling something, is always the best expression."

Farrow was basically a simple man, and this one piece of advice had somehow stuck with him over the years, a piece of advice he used often. Simple was better; so hell it was.

The point of light in his vision, now the size of a silver dollar, remained. His palms were starting to sweat a bit. He wasn't sure if this was due to temperature change or perhaps nervousness. He didn't feel any hotter, so elected to choose nerves.

He pushed forward in a darkness that was now thinning out considerably. He could almost sense but not see his shadow that was sliding somewhere behind him on the stone ground.

I know it's not like I really ever had a choice, but what the fuck did I get myself into?

The path evened out for a few steps. He felt strong, like he could go on for days, the benefits of being a professional athlete.

His calf muscles adjusted as the ground before him started to arc upward a bit, climbing in a steady elevation. He could see the exit, manhole-cover sized, now growing larger, defining itself a bit clearer with every step, maybe fifty paces ahead.

Okay. This is it, almost there. The climate still did not seem to change much, if at all. Farrow was neither too hot, nor too cold. As the exit grew large in his vision, intense light covered his body in a baptismal radiance. The hairs on the back of his neck actually stood tall.

He cautiously walked up the last few steps; a mile of dark tunnel lay behind him. The exit was not as he expected it might be; it was an actual opening. He stepped into this space with a small sense of accomplishment. The warm intensity before him felt calming on his skin. The light wasn't coming from outside the channel; the sky seemed darkened out there.

It was as if the perimeter of the outlet itself was electrified, illuminated and blinding. Farrow closed his eyes and enjoyed the moment suffused in the tepid glow before slowly pulling them open again. The white radiance framed his large silhouette as he looked out into hell and what lay beyond.

When Tommy Farrow entered a boxing ring, the crowd cheering and stamping their feet, spotlights tracking his progression toward what would be a battlefield, and Brian Johnson's gravelly voice filling the venue with AC/DC's 1988 rocker "Heatseeker," there was always a feeling of nervous excitement.

On certain nights, when Farrow knew in his heart and soul he would be triumphant, there was an exhilaration that started in the base of his stomach and spread through his body like firewater. When he was unsure of an opponent, that anxious anticipation was different, a hint of pending doom hung around his neck . . . a feeling of giddy apocalypse.

This was how he felt now looking out from the cave's exit across the enormous landscape that was hell. The whole experience was surreal.

The scene could only be described as painted in a violent twilight. What could have passed for a thin orange sunset streak marked the sky to his left just above a darkening ground. Farrow knew there couldn't be a sun here. The bright light when he crossed the exit was no longer evident.

The land before him, while huge and seemingly unending, was basically, level ground. It looked to be hardened, cracked dirt, dust white in color like some sort of nuclear-war blasted wasteland. The air was dry and still, but nowhere near approaching the fiery temperature of countless books, movies, or dramatic preacher's sermons he had heard in church, an establishment he did visit, though rarely. The smell of sulfur was much stronger here than in the Hellmouth, but his senses had grown accustomed to it quickly. He actually found it kind of pleasant, almost like the after-burn scent from a match.

There were no people, or at least none he could see from this vantage point just a few steps from safety. As he traced his vision back and forth over the landscape, the sky seemed to darken a notch. The ground that had once seemed an almost sandy cracked white now had hints of orange infusing the thin fractures causing them to bleed more prominently across the region.

The colors reminded Farrow of the fall season, raking leaves with his father as a youth on the front lawn of their North Reading home and trick-or-treating on Halloween with his friends late into the cool holiday nightfall. Farrow always dressed as a cowboy, his head poking through a multi-colored poncho, a dirty brown hat upon his head, and, of course, a cigar sitting in the corner of his mouth. When asked exactly what cowboy he was, Farrow would answer from under his hat: "I have no name."

"Wow, no name? You must be the boy with no name."

To this he would meet his inquisitor's eyes, take the cigar from his lips, and in a hoarse whisper say, "I'm the man with no name."

The memory made him smile.

The only real thing he could see besides the sky and the ground, he just couldn't think of it as earth, was a lone tree about seventy yards away. It was large, maybe thirty feet from top to bottom, skeleton white in color and leafless. Its branches stretched upward, reaching and clawing as if to grab hold of the night. The tree placed on this landscape would have been the perfect cover for a horror novel or maybe a poster advertising some late-night spook fest. The only thing missing was a menacing, hungry full moon lurking behind it.

Farrow knew he would have to move past this tree and, although it projected a creepy image, he didn't think it could hurt him. He could feel the writer's soul beckoning from that direction, a long steady pull in the pit of his stomach, just as John and Keith had described. At first the sensation was more than a bit odd, but it was something he got used to rather quickly.

He wanted to familiarize himself with the bizarre surroundings, get acquainted with hell, this section of it anyway, but the unrelenting digital readout on his wrist told him he would have to start moving sooner rather than later.

Farrow looked back to the Hellmouth's exit, ten feet behind him in the quickly dimming light. He could see the slight hint of electric illumination that rimmed the opening and noticed large gray and tan stones haphazardly gathered on its sides.

He turned back to face the leafless tree and started toward it.

Three or four paces in, a vicious, high-pitched shriek, that of a woman in absolute terror, filled the air around him. The horrific sound didn't come from any one place; it was in the very atmosphere itself, flooding the area with dread, dismay, and pain.

The all-consuming sound stopped Farrow in his tracks as he fumbled to slip his hand into the right front pocket of his jeans. Both his hands, he realized, were slick with sweat. He felt for the Hellstick first with rushed fingertips grabbing, and almost at once he had it fully and tightly in his right hand. With no hesitation, Farrow pulled the item out and gave it a hard squeeze. The Hellstick extended immediately, the tip burning orange rage. Farrow held three and a half feet of deadly weapon in front of him, thin lines of smoke trailing off its length as it buzzed with white-hot energy.

He imagined it a baseball bat, and anything, anything at all, that came at him at that moment would be the ball. His muscles rippled and glistened in the dry air. His eyes shifted back and forth. The sound that had once been a scream, a gruesome, blood curdling scream, started again, but this time it was different. The noise he now heard, the sound that sung in the air around him was still female, but that of a much younger sort, perhaps a small child. This time what Farrow heard was not a scream, but a maniacal giggle, high pitched and absolutely chilling.

Goosebumps swallowed him whole. The sweat on his arms and body turned cold. The giggling now graduated to a child's high siren of laughter and swirled around him. Still, there was nothing to see, his eyes frantically searching. The nightmarish sound invaded every part of his being. It settled in his head and coiled around his brain. The Hellstick fell from Farrow's tightened grip and dropped to the cracked ground at his feet, receding back to its normal size.

The prizefighter threw his hands to his head and covered his ears yelling into the ever-darkening sky, "Stop it! Stop it! Stop it!"

That sound, that mad-house laugh, might have driven him absolutely insane if it had not stopped, which thankfully it did; and, like nothing had happened at all, Farrow was thrown back into silence.

He brought the hands away from his ears and slumped his arms to his sides, his eyes anxiously moving over the land. His breath previously coming in quick spurts, calming down now. He trained his vision on the distant white tree for a second or two. Nothing.

They're trying to slow you down. That's it. This is just a game, just a game.

He felt stupid, ridiculous actually. Farrow pulled himself together in a measured composure.

The Heavyweight Champion of the World. Yeah, right. Start acting like it, he thought in disgust. His behavior, his fear had surprised him. There had been a time when he had been afraid of nothing. Well, these were different circumstances, much different, and as it would be, times had changed.

Farrow bent down to retrieve the dropped Hellstick and made a note not to do that again, pussy out and lose his weapon especially when nothing was apparently coming at him. He scooped up the item and returned it to the pocket of his jeans. When it was safely there, he looked suspiciously around him. Nothing moved. A sense of harmony seemed to surround everything again. He focused his vision on the stark frame of the white tree in the distance and cautiously started walking toward it, and toward the beckoning soul of Robert Scalia.

If he had hesitated a second or two longer and looked to the ground just about a foot beyond where the Hellstick had fallen, he might have seen the Spitfire, his most powerful weapon, sitting on the hard, cracked surface. Small and shining bright red, it stood out against the orange and white setting. The tiny but deadly weapon had fallen from his pocket moments earlier when the Hellstick was pulled out in a fevered rush. It lay on the ground useless as Tommy Farrow walked away from it in the direction of the white tree and whatever lay beyond.

It didn't take him long to reach what he now saw was an abomination of nature. The tree stood out against the harsh and now completely black, cloud-covered sky, like an albino spider on a bed of tar. Farrow passed slowly on its right side. All the bark had been removed from its body, skinned, exposing the wood beneath its surface. A small crooked sign was nailed into the ropy and twisted body of the trunk. Printed in red lettering upon it were three words . . .

WELCOME TO HELL

He half expected the reaching branches to turn down and grab at him with wooden claws, but they did not. He stayed a good distance away from its base, about ten feet, just in case. Farrow guessed the tree stood as some sort of marker, one that he proposed to utilize on his return trip with Scalia.

Just look for the large white tree with the branches standing up like Don King's hair, he jokingly thought as he passed the damn thing.

He never stopped walking, but looked up into the tangle of branches as he passed below the tree. He thought of a spider's web, and if he got too close to that thing, he knew he would never get away from it, and then something *would* come for him. What that something might be, he didn't even want to think about. The branches appeared to glow, almost smolder against the pitch-dark sky and the tree seemed to be waiting, perhaps guarding something. Watching.

A few measured steps and the tree was quickly behind him. Farrow turned back to look at the thing one last time. It stood silent and menacing against all that black. In the distance, he could see the Hellmouth's vertical, glowing exit. It seemed to be saying, *Come again soon.* He intended to.

Focusing his attentions on the sensation of Scalia's soul pulling at him like a magnet, he left the tree and any thoughts of it swept from his mind. Farrow just wished he could shake the new feeling he had of being watched.

He'd been walking for the better part of an hour at an uneventful, steady pace before he came across, actually stumbled across, the first headstone and an endless wall that spanned his vision from left to right. He noticed the ground starting to smoke a minute or so earlier, a light mist that graduated to a thick, gray fog and hung six inches above the ground as far as the dark ambiance would allow.

The wall was massive in construction, twelve or fifteen feet high, old cobblestones piled on top of one other, thick and symmetrical. The cracking, filthy blocks looked hundreds, maybe thousands, of years old, but the wall looked strong. Farrow stopped in front of the headstone, taking in the huge continuous barrier before him. Pockets of ghostly light, not unlike lightning, flashed overhead revealing to him a large entryway twenty feet ahead. The epitaph that was advertised across the upper part of the headstone before him was all but illegible. Years of neglect had wiped away any evidence of identity or date.

The archway was ten feet tall and five feet wide, made of the same stone as the wall, with a semi-circular top. Farrow was a big man, but he could easily walk through that entry point with plenty of room to spare. He started forward very slowly as pockets of white light continued to pound above in various locations throughout the sky.

The space around him was silent except for his own breathing and footsteps. As Farrow approached the large entrance, his eyes scanned the grounds in the immediate area; he stayed sharp and ready, fist-wise. Nothing was going on. He almost expected to see a black raven perched on a branch somewhere, but sensed no life whatsoever. He passed under and through the aperture and everything opened up before him.

Just about ten steps into what he now saw was most certainly a graveyard, Farrow had a feeling, a sense of foreboding that the wall behind him had closed up, the cobblestones had grown together making exit impossible. He wouldn't be able to get out. The sensation was so strong that he stopped walking and turned around. Fifteen feet away the large doorway stood yawning, nothing had changed and the needling, dooming impression dissipated like smoke in the wind.

Poking up through the ground mist were large concrete crosses and more headstones, many more, standing like soldiers waiting for inspection. A crypt made from splintered, grizzled stone sat on a small hill off to his right. Clumps of grass and dead weeds were assembled around the small building.

With the mostly open space at his back, Farrow appreciated the change of scenery, even if it was deeper into hell and apparently a graveyard behind a monstrous, unstoppable wall. Unlike the earlier mostly barren landscape, these grounds boasted many trees all withered and dead with blackened leafless branches bent at tormented angles. The clouds had disappeared from the sky. A bursting full moon, fat and ripe, oozed light through the gnarled limbs illuminating the gravestones in a callous white glow giving the ground mist a spectral, almost living, pulsating quality.

The more his eyes danced across the scene, the more the images around him came into focus. Farrow could now see at least five or six crypts up on small hills decorating the vicinity, cement walls crumbling behind marble pillars streaked with filth and sinewy black ivy, each six-by-ten foot structure looking older than the next. *I wonder who's sleeping in there?* he thought, while tapping his fingers over the Hellstick in his pocket again, just to make sure the weapon was still there.

The colors here were all washed out, dry and dull, like a storm or perhaps many storms had washed away any life from the scene. Everything looked to be in black and white like an old horror movie. Blinking his eyes he realized that all color actually was gone from this place . . . this Hell's Graveyard.

When Farrow was a young boy he would watch television with his dad, a movie buff and an avid fan of westerns and the Universal horror films from the 1930's and 40's, especially the ones which featured the Frankenstein Monster.

The movies usually featured a single creature. For example, *Dracula* had, well . . . Dracula. *Frankenstein* had the monster . . . you get the idea. But on certain occasions in films like *The House of Frankenstein* or *The House of Dracula* you would be treated to several monsters in the same picture, including, but not limited to, mad scientists and hunchbacked people, who were usually assistants to the madmen.

In young Tommy Farrow's favorite, a movie called *Frankenstein Meets the Wolf Man,* the monster was portrayed not by Boris Karloff, but Bela Lugosi, who did an adequate job under all that makeup. He was nowhere near as good as the iconic interpretation that Karloff had mastered when he portrayed Frankenstein's creation, however.

The movie was filmed, of course, in black and white and began in a creepy cemetery. The scene was undoubtedly filmed on a soundstage somewhere in Hollywood, but that opening spectacle had given Tommy Farrow nightmares for weeks afterward, and it was that very same black and white graveyard in which he now stood.

Not stars, but luminous flickering white pinpoints sparked up in this area like lighters at a rock concert. They glowed brightly in the infinite black stretch overhead. The sky almost seemed to pull away from the ground giving it plenty of room to breathe. Farrow felt that this was it; this was where hell really began . . . and what better way to start the party?

He looked up at the paste-white moon that he knew was not really the moon but more of a circular spotlight that could have been a giant single eye watching him. It blazed down pupil-less, unblinking. He thought of it as the moon just to keep things simple and familiar in his mind.

Farrow could no longer see his work boots through the mist that stopped just above his ankles, but could feel the ground wetly sucking at his heavy soles. Something skittered below his line of sight about ten feet to his left, moving quickly away from him causing a mole-like disturbance below the white ground cover. He tried to track it with his eyes, but it disappeared into the night.

A cool wind now slipped between the old gravestones as dark angry clouds filled the sky and then choked it, covering the tiny, floating lights above and the fake moon. Farrow wrapped his arms around his body and thought, *Yeah, right, could be worse. It could be raining.* But it didn't rain, the night just threatened to. He thought of himself on the set of, or actually in, a horror movie and the progression of the night's events did little to disprove it. The ground fog in the graveyard and the crypts on the hills, the creepy trees; and the full moon, what was next? The Wolf Man?

A huge fist seemed to squeeze within his lower stomach as Scalia's soul pulled at him from within as if to say: "Stop messing around and come get me out of here." The pull was much stronger than it had been earlier and it got Farrow moving again rapidly through the cemetery and toward the writer.

Since there was no official path to walk on, he had to step between chipped and blemished gravestones and flat markers he could feel through the soles of his boots. He moved fast with his head mostly down. He elected to keep his hands deep in the pockets of his jeans for warmth, his bare arms taking the brunt of the chilly conditions. Farrow smiled to himself. *Of course, in the limbo area or whatever that was with Keith and John, I woke up on a beach. The beach where I had the most pleasant times of my life; so it would only make sense that in hell I'd be in the graveyard from a movie that had scared me so much as a child.*

"But you know what? I'm not a child anymore," he said aloud lifting his head to whoever may be listening.

This was all a game, an illusion to scare, tailored just for me. It's probably something different for everyone who passes through this way, some other makeshift horrific reality.

An uneventful fifteen minutes had passed when the mist started to sift away from the ground and grow thinner. The quiet walk had given Farrow time to think and collect his thoughts. He could now see his boots covered in mud and dirt. The amount of gravestones and splintered concrete crosses sticking up from the soft muck at odd angles was also decreasing. The sky that was once a dead-of-night black seemed a bit lighter, and that so-called moon was still no longer in evidence. It was either behind a cloud, or whatever was keeping it lit was off.

Up ahead about five yards or so, Farrow could see a path that seemed to be made from old cobblestones. Tufts of burnt grass and dead weeds stood up from between the large stones. It was bright enough around him now to see this clearly and in fine detail. The sky ahead was an almost purplish light blue and the smell of sulfur kicked up a notch. It was morning in hell.

The path before him fell away to the right in a gradual but steady descent. It was from this direction that the writer's soul beckoned.

Looks like I'm going right.

A lone grave marker lay ahead and Farrow concluded that it signified the end of the burial ground. As he reached the rather large stone, he saw that the path, now almost glowing a yellowish white, continued beyond. The prizefighter decided to stop at this last stone to scrape off the accumulated dirt and mud that was caked up into the bottom grooves of his work boots. Leaning an arm against the gravestone, he bent to remove the filth, working quickly on one shoe first and then the other, scraping his feet against the marker's large base. The mud came off easily enough in hardened clumps. Next he knocked the side of each foot against the stone to shake off any remaining grime.

When he was finished with the chore of cleaning his footwear, happy to know that he would now achieve better traction, his eyes fell upon the name and years that were deeply chiseled into the face of the black and gray marble stone before him in the new light.

The date stated year of birth and death, 1977-2013, and above the name was not the touching phrase "REMEMBERED ALWAYS" or "FOREVER IN OUR HEARTS." It simply said in hollow letters that seemed to jump out at him:

THOMAS A. FARROW

He was no longer cold as a hot flash washed over and then engulfed his body. The readout across his wrist read 11:46. Time was slipping away. Farrow pulled his eyes away from the epitaph and broke into a fast run down the cobblestone path. A run from which he did not look back.

ROUND FIVE

Like his pugilistic idols, Tommy Farrow trained old school. The prizefighter's workout today was much different than it was ten and twenty years earlier. In days past, roadwork was an absolute staple of a fighter's repertoire, four or five miles every morning. The new-fangled way, the hot shot up-and-comers for a new generation, ran intervals, 600 to 800 meters depending on how many rounds they were training for, monitoring progress on computers and injecting garbage into their veins. Farrow wanted none of the above; five miles of roadwork every morning, iron dead-weights, heavy bag, speed bag, jump rope, and sparring; but whether he was in training or not, he ran, and that was paying off now.

My name was on the damn marker. My name.

He sprinted away from the graveyard, but could feel it burning holes in his back, watching him, maybe waiting for his return, anticipating his return.

Have to get the writer and get going. No fucking around, in and out.

The sight of his name moments earlier, and the year he died, chiseled across and into that stone had shaken him quite badly. Although he felt very much alive, he knew he was not. He had crossed over, and this was not a place in which he wanted to *stay* crossed over. He didn't belong in hell, but he could not go back, not yet. He had to get Scalia. The writer didn't belong here either.

So Farrow ran, the cobblestones firm beneath his feet, orange and yellow sky in his peripheral vision. The strong smell of sulfur was hanging on the air. Sweat poured down his back and greased his forehead.

He grabbed a few quick glimpses of black smoke turning upward from small holes spread out amongst the landscape, spirals of thick pollution spinning into the air.

What were they cooking down there? He didn't want to know.

His lungs felt good, strong, like he could run for miles if he had to, but something, an oblong object appearing in his vision a few yards ahead told him that wasn't going to be the case. He had been running for less than five minutes.

He slowed down before coming to a full stop on the pathway, his chest rising and falling. His hands wiped his eyes and he blinked to make sure he was seeing things correctly. He was.

The color had returned to his vision, it had snuck up on him. Everything was clear and crisp, almost like watching a movie on Blu-ray. Farrow regarded the mix of colors in the sky as if seeing them for the first time. The black and white portion of tonight's feature had ended just before he passed by the grave marker with his name cut into it he now realized. Everything looked, for want of a better word, beautiful.

Not ten feet away from the spot he now stood, was a doorway. Maybe eight feet high and four feet wide, bigger than the average household sort, and again, much like the Hellmouth, it was ripped into the air, another plane of existence leading to a deeper section of hell.

The large rectangle stood nighttime black against a mostly bright sky. It looked cold within that doorway; Farrow could feel a chill air seeping up through it and winding around his body, pulling him closer, icy fingers holding on. It took him a minute to realize that it wasn't the suggestive cold pulling at him, it was Scalia's soul, and it was in there.

When Farrow was a child, maybe eleven or twelve years of age, he and his friend Peter Hagler, older by three years and shorter by an inch, were playing hide and seek in his uncle's Long Island home; his uncle and father long gone into town to buy feed for the lone horse that patrolled the fenced-in backyard.

The two boys left to housesit were quickly bored and decided on a game of hide and seek. It was determined that Tommy would be IT, meaning that Peter would have to hide somewhere on the property and Tommy would have to find him. A small amendment to the game's rules kept the hiding locations within the confines of the house. It was decided that the property was just too vast and there would be too many spots to hide.

"I could look for hours and still not find you. I wanna get a chance to hide, too, you know," Tommy had said, so Peter agreed and the game began.

There were only two floors to the small farm ranch; one level the basement where the boys seldom ventured being that it was haunted, or as haunted as every basement was to small boys with active imaginations. The other, the main floor, was where Tommy started to look for his friend and he intended to make easy work out of the five rooms, praying that Peter *was* in one of the five rooms. He did not want to descend into the basement alone.

Tommy tiptoed into certain areas, while barreling into others, in search of Peter, to no avail. He checked in dark closets and under beds, behind large chairs and in cabinets. His friend could not be found. He searched the upstairs thoroughly and then went over it a second time for good measure. To his dismay, Tommy realized that Peter was not on the main floor, as a disquieting feeling seeped into his body. *The basement.*

A small tapping sound coming up through the floorboards confirmed that a restless Peter was in fact below him hiding somewhere in one of only two rooms the downstairs housed. Tommy closed his eyes to collect himself and draw strength; then with eyes wide open proceeded downstairs to find his friend.

The old wooden staircase creaked and groaned under his weight as he tried to slip quietly into the darkness. There was no light switch at the top of the stairs as was traditionally common in most houses. The basement's lone bulb sat below him in the ceiling's center, a two-foot string with a loop on the end, not unlike a noose, needed to be pulled for incandescent illumination to take place. Tommy focused on this fact. When he got to the bottom of the stairs he stood still for a bit while his eyes adjusted. As they did, he made out the light string silently hanging directly in front of him and went for it.

"Peter? I know you're down here. You can come out now."

Silence.

"Come on, the game's over. You're IT. It's my turn to hide."

Silence again, but now maybe a stifled giggle. Standing under the bulb, Tommy looked all around himself and into the dark corners of the basement. He could make out nothing but inky shapes and piles of boxes, anyone of these things could be Peter waiting to spring out at him with a yelling scare. Things were still quiet, but Tommy could sense his friend nearby.

He pulled the string and there was a small click above his head. The bulb wasn't very strong, but it did throw enough brightness for him to see the shapes huddled around the walls. As he had deduced a second earlier, they were a bunch of old crates that dripped shadows onto the floor like leaking black paint.

There was a small room to his left that was actually more of a closet. Tommy could see directly into this empty space, immediately crossing it off his short list. Peter was not there. A single room lay before him now; it's where his friend had to be. He stood before the doorway just about ten feet away, fear flooding his body as he braced himself for Peter to spring out and scare the shit out of him.

He did not want to step through that door, but he had to face it. He stood for a second longer, his heart rate elevated and his breathing coming in quick silent gasps. He walked slowly, his hands, not for the first time even at this young age, were clenched into fists. He remembered something he once heard his father say: *Face your fears to get by them*, and that's what he intended to do, face his fears.

Tommy walked up to the murky doorway, the only other room in the basement, took a deep breath, and facing his fears stepped through.

He now remembered that long ago day, stepping into that basement room, Peter jumping out and screaming "GOT YA!" His fist rushing toward his friend and knocking him down, the first of his many one-sided fights. He had faced his fear and came out on top. He smiled at this thought. He stood looking at the doorway before him, this doorway into hell; it was time to face his fears again.

The door, or maybe a better word was passageway, was not at all unlike that of the Hellmouth. Running along the length of its sides and across the top was a thin streak of red and orange electricity, with hits of ice blue bouncing intermittently.

He took a step closer and was surprised to actually feel the cold air from within and maybe the sound of wind howling. Well . . . something howling.

It was just like being back in that basement all those years ago, knowing somebody, in this case, probably something, was waiting to scare him. *Face your fears to get by them, right?* In so doing, Tommy Farrow took a deep breath and stepped through the doorway.

He immediately rubbed his bare arms. It was suddenly very cold, in his estimation about thirty degrees. Farrow was surprised to see he stood atop a stone staircase that reminded him of the one in Dr. Frankenstein's laboratory in the original 1931 film. Some quick calculations told him it was about eighteen or twenty cracked and rotted steps to the next level. He looked up, out, and around the landscape from this perch with his breath fogging before him.

At first he heard nothing at all, and then as if his ears popped from the altitude, he heard the screams. Sounds filled with absolute terror, shrieks of suffering, pain, torture, and death. This was it, he decided, he was really in hell.

Oh yeah, he thought, *this was hell.* It was a funny thing, but as of yet, he could see no people to match with these sounds of horror.

He slowly looked around the massive, never-ending landscape. It seemed to go on for miles, maybe even years. The ground holes he had seen after his quick trek through the graveyard, belching up black smoke, were in evidence here by the hundreds, maybe thousands. They were bigger than the ones he'd witnessed earlier, but still pouring the same shadowy pollution that littered the air above. Dark ash was falling from the sky in abundance like an angry wet snow; the smell it emitted was sickening. This, Farrow now realized, accounted for the nighttime appearance he had seen within the doorway before entering it.

It was bitter cold where he now stood in his thin t-shirt and jeans, but at ground level it looked hot, and why shouldn't it? This was, after all, hell.

The terrain was the same he had seen upon his exit from the Hellmouth. A glowing, heated illumination seemingly generated from the ground filled the considerable area in a gaseous manner. Swarms of large black flies moved around the sky in a hissing madness among the falling ash.

The screams, shouts, and yells continued. For a chilling second, Farrow thought he could hear the terrible sound that filled the air earlier, the female child's laugh that had constricted his brain and squeezed, that menacing playful giggle. Then it was gone, maybe not even there at all. He never wanted to hear that laugh again; it had gotten into his head like an infection. He felt to endure it too long, recovery would not be possible.

Farrow kept his arms close to his body to preserve heat and moved down two cracked steps, pebbles and gray concrete dust dribbled off the sides. The steps, about three feet wide each, descended to the bottom level in an unbalanced slanting fashion, so he stuck to the center. He wondered what would happen if this staircase crumbled. There would be no way out, the doorway would float in the air about ten or twelve from the surface, out of reach. He doubted he would find anyone willing to help them to it.

He turned around and looked at what would be their exit, their back door out of hell. The rectangular rip in the air stood humming. He could see the cobblestone path lying within it like a long serpent's tongue.

The setting around and past the exit-rip was more of the same; a sky, if this *was* really a sky, packed with flies and black smoke reached upward and spread out across his vision.

The screams of people in pain and terror continued. The prizefighter didn't want to know what was happening to them, but, hey, if they were in hell they deserved it, right? Maybe so, but that didn't mean he wanted to see it. Farrow had the feeling he was going to have a ringside seat.

He looked at the digital display on his wrist. 11:06. He had been traveling for just over two hours. He should be reaching his destination before long. He turned back around keeping his eyes low on the staircase as he slowly descended them. The climate changed almost immediately, just six steps from the top and he was no longer cold, quite comfortable actually. The screams of agony were all around him now, assaulting him from every direction, but he still saw no people. Small loose rocks crunched beneath his work boots as the ground level grew closer. He thought for a second or two he could almost feel the staircase quiver under his feet.

This thing is not going to take people moving over it much longer. Just one more time, that's all I need. Two people and one more climb. Up and out.

Beads of sweat formed on his brow, his arms no longer hugging his body were slick causing his muscles to shine. He could feel the Hellstick heavy in his pocket.

The bottom, only three steps away, ended before another cobblestone pathway. The gray stones here were symmetrical and gleamed as if they had just been polished. Unlike the path that led away from the graveyard, these were even and had no clumps of grass, yellowing or otherwise, poking up from in between, nor did any stretching weeds litter the path's sides.

The screams were much louder at this lower level. The black smoke, he now saw, was pouring from the holes amid the dry ground. These mostly dark cavities seemed to be about five feet in diameter; they looked to Farrow like the gopher's hole he had seen in the movie *Caddyshack* some years ago. That movie had made him laugh hard, but there was nothing funny about this.

Up ahead he saw the path, which was anything but a yellow brick road. It ended with some sort of large structure that stood out against the black backdrop of ashen sky and pollution, maybe a half mile away. It reminded him of the castle he had once seen at Walt Disney World when he was about six years old. It was the only real vacation he could remember his parents taking him on; except for the week they spent at the Grand Canyon. He didn't remember much about the Disney park except for that magnificent castle, not to confuse that magical castle with whatever the structure up ahead might be. Taking a better, longer look at it now, he thought it seemed to be made of glass. It was almost shining.

Glass holding cells, wasn't that where John and Keith said they would be holding Scalia?

At this realization Farrow felt a huge pull, almost like a slim hand reaching into his stomach, grabbing hold and dragging him down the last few steps. The writer. It was Robert Scalia's soul calling to his, pulling him, and he knew it was saying: "Hurry up, prizefighter! Come get me out of here!"

The screams around him sounded more horrific than ever, more blood curdling, almost as if the real pain and torture was about to begin. He could not imagine an eternity of this, he couldn't even imagine a few more hours.

Farrow had grown accustomed to the smell of sulfur that was so thick it seeped into his mouth and he could taste it, but now there was the addition of the ash. While the scent of sulfur was somewhat pleasant to him, the aroma of the ash was nothing but sickening. He had an idea what it was, but didn't want to admit it to himself just yet. He tapped the Hellstick lightly with the palm of his hand; it was still safely in his front pocket. He started walking to where the writer was being held.

Time to face your fears, Tommy.

Six steps into his quest and a rumbling vibrated up from the soles of his boots. The ground was shaking. Black smoke spun next to him. He looked up, slits of purple and a menacing gray sliced between the pollution while something resembling lightning started to fire off to his left and above the glass structure. Bright sizzling flashes now zigzagged across his vision. Farrow looked down at his feet; a dark chalky mist was surrounding his boots. *More ground fog? Here?* Then he heard the crumbling. Rocks were falling, quiet at first but filling his ears quickly, and edging above the screams momentarily. He spoke out loud.

"No! No! No!"

He realized what was happening, had happened. It wasn't ground mist that had covered his boots; it was concrete dust. The staircase behind him had collapsed. His doorway out of hell was gone. Farrow slowly turned around for confirmation.

He stood there before a pile of rubble, the black ash dumping around it. The flies swarming overhead seemed to jitter excitedly. About twelve feet above the heap, the rectangular doorway floated like the monolith in Kubrick's *Odyssey*, almost as if saying: "How're ya gonna get up here now, big boy?"

The pieces of shattered concrete lay silently below the door almost mocking him. As the ash came in contact with the useless staircase, Farrow heard a burning noise not unlike bacon sizzling in a frying pan, and then gray smoke started moving upwards from the wrecked stairs.

The pile was dissolving before Farrow's eyes. The derelict staircase was disappearing. The ash was acting like acid rain against the ragged surface of the stone. He looked down at the cobblestone path on which he stood; the ash seemed to have no effect there or on his skin for that matter. But for the horrible smell, it was harmless. *This puts to sleep any ideas of piling pieces of concrete and broken stair to reach that door*, he thought.

The game was fixed; hell was playing with a marked deck, adapting to the situation, working things out in their favor. What would Clint do in this situation? He ran through the catalog of Eastwood movies in his head. Nope, nothing about being stuck in hell with a doorway out of reach. Sorry, Charlie. Clint did escape from Alcatraz though.

If he really needed something, he would get it, that's what John and Keith had said to him. Well, he really needed a way up to that door. He guessed, he hoped, when the time came, what the two odd men with the British accents had said would ring true.

Farrow turned back around toward the large glass structure that lay before him at the cobblestone path's end. A moment ago the land was barren, but now, like a sleepy village coming to life, turning its lights on one by one, things were coming into focus, appearing before his eyes. The screams of damnation that filled the air finally had a home.

The first things he saw clearly were the men in the black and blue suits. They were walking on the stone path before him almost like people going to work on a large city street. Farrow had assumed they were men because they were tall and thin with short, close-cropped black hair and wearing what seemed to be designer suits, either all black or all blue. Several walked just passed him close enough to touch; they seemed not to be aware of the prizefighter at all.

Don't involve yourself and you will remain virtually invisible.

He was shocked and amazed by the things he was seeing and all but forgot about the Hellstick and Spitfire in his pocket. The men, at least as big as Farrow, had no faces. It was as if the defining features had been erased, almost like in a reality cop show when someone wants to remain anonymous and the face is blurred out. The result was chilling, to say the least.

These people held weapons: whips, maces, chains, and knotted ropes, items for torture. Beyond and around the men on either side of the path, scenes of persecution lit up and came to life like gnarled roots punching up through the surface of an endless field of death, the ash floating around like a dead winter's black snow.

To get to the glass structure where Scalia was being held, he would have to walk past the horrors spread out before and around him. He would see everything in full detail. The screams continued and Tommy Farrow thought he would never sleep again.

The men in the black and blue suits were going off to different activities, different settings of maltreatment, helping out or joining in. As far as Farrow could see, torture of inquisitional proportions was being cruelly administered. He started to walk tentatively along the cobblestones toward the writer's location, taking small cautious steps. His hands were balled tightly, a reaction he was accustomed to when a possible opponent was close.

It was almost like walking through a pay-as-you-go Halloween house. Farrow remembered as a child his parents taking him to a haunted firehouse in the city of Boston. It was long after the sun had set, pulled below the city skyline. The firehouse, just about three miles west of Fenway Park, was turned into a ten minute walk-through spook show every weekend in October.

You would purchase a ticket out front from a member of the Boston Fire Department wearing a rubber Halloween mask, in this case a vampire, and then join the mobs of people on line outside of the firehouse's red brick facade waiting in the crisp October night. The moon sailed high above the city and the smells of hotdogs, sauerkraut, and baked beans wafted through the air, compliments of the corner vendor.

Farrow remembered not being the least bit afraid anticipating what scares might await him inside, but as he and his parents crept closer to the attraction's entrance his hands pulled into fists.

Walking through the makeshift "Firehouse of Horrors" you were led by, no doubt, another fireman wearing another rubber mask. This time Freddy Krueger's image was fitted around the tour guide's head. Farrow just knew it had to be a firefighter because he was big and looked strong, something the boy admired, and the guide seemed to know the lay of the land, every niche and alcove.

The spook-show consisted of walking and stopping at different scenes of imitation torture and horror. People, mostly scantily-clad young girls chained to walls with noticeably rubber-looking shackles, yelling Help! Help! and scenes of mad doctors working in smoke-filled laboratories raising their arms in the air and laughing wildly in a controlled environment. Dracula and the Frankenstein Monster also made appearances. Every now and again somebody dressed in black clothes and white face paint would spring out from a dark crevice shouting BOO! to achieve a maximum scare.

Farrow stayed between his parents and thoroughly enjoyed the fright fest in the dim lighting of the firehouse . . . but what he was seeing now was a different animal all together. The torture before him this time was the real thing.

He told himself to stay focused on the glass structure, the luminous holding area, about a half-mile away. His eyes, however, betrayed him as he came to the first scene a few feet ahead and off to his right. He took a quick glance, and could not look away.

A naked woman, maybe twenty-five years old, was laid out on an old medieval torture rack. The device looked very sturdy, easily strong enough to hold this young woman in place. Locked around her wrists and ankles were heavy bands made from unforgiving metal that boasted years of rust. Iron chains led from these harsh bracelets and were attached to a pulley system connected around two barrel-shaped rollers, one at the head of the table, the other at the foot. A large wooden crank was attached to the menacing barrels, and when turned would stretch the woman and pull her arms and legs out of their sockets. Not a very nice death.

No less than four of the large faceless figures in the black and blue suits were assembled around this torture device with the writhing woman upon it. Her body was slick with sweat and her breath came in quick rabbit like gasps. Nothing happened for a moment; the four figures just stared down at their victim. The anticipation of pain could almost be worse than the actual sensation.

One of the faceless demons wearing a black suit, reached down and started to apply small two-inch cuts to the woman's body with what seemed to be a sharp box cutter. He started out slow, but quickly gained momentum furiously digging into her flesh. Her screams were incredible. In a matter of seconds her quivering form was wrecked, covered from the top of her head to the soles of her feet with angry red slashes. Next, one of the blue suits began to pour a liquid from a red container over the helpless woman. Her instantaneous reaction when the liquid seeped into her many raw wounds was strong causing convulsive fighting movements against the iron shackles holding her there. The ungodly screams of pain were the sounds of nightmares. The strong smell that quickly reached his nostrils confirmed that gasoline was now being used on this woman to season her body in a very nasty manner.

Farrow was sweating again. *Don't involve yourself, she's meant to be here.* He noticed needle marks amongst the slashes tracking up and down the inside of the woman's right forearm. *These people didn't inflict those*, he thought, *she's a . . . well, was a drug addict.* The woman gyrated against her bonds, wrists and ankles leaking blood from behind the tightly locked metal bands.

"Please, stop this! My God! Help me! Not again, no more. No more, it hurts!"

Not again? Had Farrow heard correctly?

A faceless black suit rotated the lever on the barrel-shaped roller by the woman's wrists. A few cranks and the slack in the chain quickly became taut, the screaming woman pulled into a position from which she could scarcely move any part of her vulnerable body. Her arms stretched out above her head, fingers like frozen talons, her legs unable to shift even an inch. The woman was at the breaking point, one more crank of the lever, one more rotation of the barrel, and her limbs would start to leave their sockets.

Her body quivered as though maybe a chill was washing over her as more small cuts were applied, followed by a second gasoline dowsing.

"OH MY GOD! DON'T DO THIS! IT HURTS! IT HURTS! I'M SORRY! OH GOD! OH GOD! OH GOD! STOP!"

To Farrow's shock and absolute disgust, he witnessed a faceless black suit lean over the woman, hovering by her face, close down, almost as if he were looking into her pleading, begging eyes. A small hole ripped into the lower section of the horrible featureless skin. Slowly the small rip widened black and cavernous. Strings of moist flesh pulled and stretched over this crude opening before tearing off and hanging loosely from this makeshift mouth that pulled itself into a grin. The black suit's head shook up and down. The thing was mocking her, smiling, and maybe, Farrow thought, laughing.

"PLEASE, NO! NOT AGAIN! NOT AGAIN! NO MORE! NO MORE! NO MORE! I'M SORRY! GOD, HELP ME! I'M SO SORRY!"

The faceless black suit that seemed to be the leader of this party, nodded at the blue suit, a small "go ahead, proceed" motion, and without hesitation, the blue suit bent over and started to crank the lever causing the wheel to complete another rotation.

The woman's body convulsed as it was slowly pulled apart. Her fingers and toes spread as her head threw itself from side to side in a panicking, rejecting manner.

Farrow now saw the lead black suit point at a faceless blue suit across the torture rack over the woman's extended torso, and with a slight tilt of its horrible head, the blue suit touched a lighted torch that Farrow had not seen earlier to the woman's gasoline-slickened body. While continuing to be pulled apart, the woman now burst into flames. Red and orange quickly spread across and then engulfed her. The screams were incredible as the woman's body blackened, spitting twisting funnels of smoke upward before spreading out joining the polluted sky.

"OH GOD, IT HURTS! IT HURTS! KILL ME! PLEASE KILL ME! LET ME DIE, JUST LET ME DIE!"

After a short time, that still seemed much too long to Farrow, the woman stopped screaming, stopped making any sounds at all. The metal bands around her wrists and ankles were unlocked from her burned and smoldering limbs. All four faceless black and blue suits lined up along the far side of the rack like soldiers. They placed their hands on her smoking form and shoved the woman onto the ground where she broke into pieces like a dropped porcelain figurine on stone. The burning barbecue smell, as Farrow had suspected earlier, was indeed human flesh.

He stared at the small wrecked sections that were once an attractive woman. They seemed to sizzle before bubbling and then disappeared into the ground, as a four-foot hole simultaneously pulled itself open with a groan and vomited forth a trainload of thick black smoke into the waiting skies above. Falling ash continued to pepper the area in abundance.

Jesus, he thought to himself, *what the fuck did I get involved in? This is a mad house. This is a fucking loony bin for sinners. What am I doing here?*

He now saw beyond the torture rack, thousands more just like it, people were being burned, others stretched and ripped apart; the one common denominator, though, was they all were screaming. Men, women, and, yes, even children, were crying and begging for forgiveness. He heard many pleading sounds. Cries of "MY GOD!" and "HELP!" sang all around him, floating in the air like a rolling tempest. He had to get moving, he had to get Scalia and get the fucking hell *out* of hell.

Farrow was about to start walking, not at all anxious to see what the next scene might be, what this very real haunted house had in store for his viewing pleasure, when something appearing on the torture rack caught his eye and stopped him dead in his tracks. The woman, the same woman, who had just been slashed, stretched, and burned, was spread out completely intact, naked, and painfully shackled down. She had materialized out of thin air, writhing in the same chains. The men in black and blue assembled around her again, ready to go to work.

Please, no. Not again, she had said, screamed in fact. To his horror, Farrow realized that this was the woman's eternity. It was going to happen to her all over again, every few minutes, every day, over and over and over. Every time would be just as painful as the last, and she would remember every bit of it. Her nerve endings would remain working a hundred percent so she could suffer to the fullest effect every single countless time forever and ever.

"Please, not again. It hurts! Help me! God, please help me!"

He wanted to help her. He had to stop this. Farrow uncurled his hands that had unconsciously evolved into fists and started to reach for the Hellstick.

Don't involve yourself in anything, Tommy. Get the writer and get out. She's there for a reason.

62

He hesitated for a moment before pulling his eyes away, not wanting to watch the scene again, or for a second longer.

"MY GOD, IT HURTS! HELP ME! PLEASE!"

Farrow moved onto the cobblestone pathway and off to the next display of horror and degradation, closer to the glass holding structure and deeper into the "haunted house".

He felt like he might be sick, and that was strange he thought. *How could someone who was already dead, suffer?* But that was probably the whole basis of hell; make 'em feel as much as they can, and none of it good.

The smoke shooting upwards from the ground holes, that now looked more like pus spewing wounds, continued to fill the sky with an apocalyptic, menacing presence. Farrow stared down at his boots while Scalia's pulling soul reeled him in, and the shining glass structure grew closer. The screams around him begged to entertain his gaze, but he stayed focused, exercising a prizefighter's willpower.

About eight months after he turned professional, an event promoter presented Farrow with two tickets to see Bruce Springsteen at New Jersey's Giants Stadium. He and a date, a woman named Ashley Walker, who wore a very short skirt and really high heels, had field seats about thirty rows from the stage. He remembered the enthusiastic screams and yells for "The Boss" all around him.

That was how he felt now, like he was on the field in the middle of a Springsteen concert, save for the fact that the screams around him were not that of excitement and pleasure, but of absolute terror.

A muted banging to his left caught his attention and then his eyes, as he was once again drawn into the horror before him, and like before, he could not look away.

Standing upright were rows upon rows of what seemed to be oblong water tanks, maybe three feet wide and nine feet tall; in other words, plenty of room to hold a single human body within its confines. The front part of these tanks was constructed of thick smooth glass so perhaps someone who might happen along could watch the show. Each of these tanks, and they were too numerous to count, held a human body, all makes and models, hell did not discriminate. The bottom, sides, and top were made of solid, rusted steel, and like the torture racks, looked centuries old.

The banging sounds again. Multiple instances. In the tanks within his immediate line of vision, two men and a woman were contained, hitting the heavy glass with balled fists in a panicking fury.

"Help me! Help! Help us!"

They were looking at him. They could see him. Farrow took a step back.

"Unlock the latch!" one yelled to Farrow.

All three human fish tank residents were pointing upwards to what seemed to be a small hooked clasp on the outside top portion of each tank.

Don't involve yourself.

Farrow quickly saw what was meant to happen. The tanks would fill with water and when the level was high enough, depending on each person's height, they would drown to death, death for the already dead. Around the ankles of the three people in the tanks, iron shackles were locked and connected to large O-rings that sat at the tarnished bottom between their feet preventing them to rise with the water level and perhaps gaining exit from the glass enclosures. All three people were now staring at Farrow with wide panicking eyes the size of saucers. They started up again banging on the glass, their shouting muffled voices coming in loud and clear.

"Help us! Unlock the latch, please! Get us out! Help me! Help! Please! God help us!"

Don't involve yourself. They are meant to be here, they deserve to be here, he repeated to himself.

Farrow now saw fluid rushing into the glass and steel enclosure through a small two-inch pipe positioned low on the bottom section of the rear wall.

"There's still time! The latch! Please!"

Real terror inhabited the muffled voices now as the water level increased rather quickly. It was up to their knees and then chests in no time, the water sloshing violently within the tanks due to furious attempts at escape. Breath fogged the inside of the glass from distressing gasps. All three sets of eyes were burning into Farrow, arms held high, fingers pointing at the clasp, water spraying and tinted pink due to the unforgiving shackles cutting into the flesh and bone around helpless ankles.

Farrow took yet another step back from the scene, almost to the center of the cobblestone pathway. His body was shaking, eyes filling with tears as he mouthed the words "I'm sorry. I'm sorry. I can't help you."

Some hero, he thought, *some fucking hero. Why send me here if I can't do anything to help anybody? Yeah, I'm gonna save the world; they send a fucking angel with broken wings.*

The water was chest, then neck high. It wouldn't be long before they were below the water. It would soon be over. The liquid in the tanks was a deeper scarlet now as chained ankles leaked blood in profuse amounts from the thrashing captives. The fists drumming on the seemingly unbreakable glass continued as the cries for help twisted into bellowing weeping and dreadful screams.

The three people before him lived almost a full minute after their heads were consumed and overtaken by the rising level. The shape of their wide bloodshot eyes matched their bubble-spewing mouths in a horrible circle. All three died staring at Farrow as their lungs filled with water and each soul's living spark was extinguished like a candle's flame. The worst was the woman, whose long hair floated around her bloated face in an almost ghostly manner.

He stood motionless and silent a moment before speaking out loud to himself.

"What the fuck did I just see? What did these people do to deserve this? To be here?"

The water was now draining, being sucked backwards through the pipe from which it came. To where, Farrow did not know, as he saw no plumbing. The process only took a minute or so, ending with a sucking sound not unlike that of a straw trying to get the last of a delicious beverage.

When the tanks were completely empty, which was almost instantaneous, the three people who had just drowned in a horrific panic moments earlier, reappeared coughing up water and standing once again, ankles chained. The incessant pounding on the glass and the muffled calls for help began all over again.

Wow, he thought, drowning every few minutes for eternity. Farrow didn't know what was worse, the horrors inflicted at the torture rack or this one? He knew he didn't want to find out one way or the other. Another step backwards and he was turned around once again by Scalia's pulling soul.

"I know, buddy, I know. I'm coming."

Shaken up, and with great reason, Farrow pulled himself together and cleared his mind, a routine that always helped before a bout, especially the big ones, the ones he was unsure of. The sky seemed to darken a bit before intermittent bursts of white light started to shoot behind the dense smoke filling the sky. Maybe a storm was coming.

The black-and blue-suited figures that were in short supply at the last attraction, scurried along the cobblestone pathway as if late for work or an important meeting. No attention at all was paid to Farrow and he appreciated that.

Up a bit to the right side of the walkway, hundreds of severed, living human heads were sitting atop spiked wooden posts, screaming as hungry insects filled their mouths and ears.

Farrow looked around and beyond the glass holding structure up ahead, and then to his left, right, and rear. Not a single space was unoccupied by some sort of terror being inflicted upon damned human bodies . . . well, human souls, masquerading as bodies. Hell was all around him, and Tommy Farrow, standing among falling black ash and hordes of swarming flies, was smack dab in the middle of it.

The screams of terror, the begging and the yells of pain continued. The sounds, if he didn't listen too hard, were not unlike those at a prizefight or maybe a rock concert. Farrow was certain of one thing though as he moved closer to the writer and the approaching field of staked human heads, the people around him were anything but happy and he was almost sure that there was no one chanting "BRUUUUUCE".

"I'm coming, Robert. Hang tight, buddy. I'm coming."

A large cluster of faceless black and blues were about fifteen yards away from him off to the left side of the cobblestones. They were raising their arms with what looked like large flaming wooden clubs and bringing them down in a thunderous manner on a crumpled body below them. Guillotine blades rose and fell, severing heads into metal buckets of twitching maggots that bore hungrily into the still living decapitated flesh. Farrow looked away.

"I really hope you guys were right," he said silently to John and Keith. *"I don't want to remember any of this shit."*

Naked bodies were hanging upside down by bleeding ankles from harsh-looking barbed wire, arms tied behind their backs. Nothing else seemed to be happening to them, no beatings, cuttings, or burnings, they just hung there like slabs of meat; but be that as it may, not a very pleasant way to spend forever.

Nobody Farrow saw was not screaming, crying, begging, or whimpering. On many occasions, people looked at him and yelled for help. They could see him. Even under extreme fatigue and torture, and it was *all* extreme. People cried to him for help, to save them. This was a very unsettling equation added to his problem.

Why didn't the faceless black and blue suits see him or come for him? Of course they had no eyes, but that didn't stop their torturous ways. Farrow remembered the twenty-four hour rule that John and Keith had explained, how nothing would touch him or anyone else during the first twenty-four hour period they were in hell, as long as they didn't involve themselves in anything.

Still, he thought, things seemed a bit too simple so far, too smooth going. He was allowed to enter hell easily enough, but there was that laugh, that child's laugh he had heard twice now. It had an almost mocking "I've got a secret" quality to it. He remembered driving into Jersey to see that Springsteen show, Ashley sitting next to him turned sideways, her high-heeled shoes freshly off, her bare feet high up in his lap, the long, warm toes with the nails painted devil-red playfully wiggling into his crotch, his jeans tightening. It was free to enter the Garden State, but if you wanted to leave, you had to pay a toll to get out. *Was hell like Jersey,* he wondered? *If he wanted to leave, was he going to have to pay?* He thought probably . . . *yes.*

He continued toward the holding structure. It grew larger in front of him with each gaining step. The glass walls were defined clearly against the black-as-smoke backdrop in a sky that continued to spit ash. As the screams and cries around him intensified.

As he made the final leg of his journey, maybe twenty yards to go, he thought of Superman's Fortress of Solitude. Everything on the building before him seemed to be constructed from ice. A low, white mist hovered above the ground at the foot of the structure that was maybe as big as Fenway Park. It was full of gleaming right angles, sharp points, and smooth, shining platforms. The design was a sprawling electric white. If it wasn't for the fact that this building was in hell, and the presence of the spreading black smoke above that resembled rain clouds threatening to ruin the picnic, Farrow may have thought it beautiful.

Boy, if that place crumbles, he thought, *somebody's going to lose a leg.*

Along the front sides of the building, on either side of what Farrow believed to be the entranceway, maybe twenty faceless beings in the black and blue suits, ten on each side, stood lined up like soldiers awaiting instruction.

The pull from Scalia's soul was so strong now, and, yes, painful; it felt to Farrow like an invisible arm had reached into his chest, snaked its way around his rib cage and grabbed hold of his spinal column pulling him forward in a hurried rage.

"I'm coming, I'm coming. Give me a few minutes."

Three of the faceless demons stood blocking the entrance to the holding area just a few feet before him now. Two in black suits and the other in blue. Farrow looked back and forth along the wall on either side of this small gathering. The others stood there in a line at attention, but the three he was most concerned with continued to crowd the doorway behind them.

The entrance was inky and stuffed with shadows. Beyond the suits, he had seen several pairs of blood red, silver-dollar-sized eyes staring out from the black doorway at him. He blinked and they were gone.

Farrow had once ventured into a "Funhouse of Mirrors" at the 1998 Massachusetts State Fair. He was twenty-one years old, just eighteen months after he had turned pro. It was one of the last times he would see Ray Maxim and Carl Tunney alive, the two would die in a car accident in Salem just about a month later.

Standing before the glass structure, Farrow had a sneaking suspicion he was leaving a haunted house and stepping into a fun house. He didn't think, however, much fun was going to be had.

As he approached the faceless suits blocking his way, Farrow slipped his hand into his pocket retrieving the Hellstick that was still compacted to the size of a roll of quarters; it felt good in his hand. Solid. One squeeze and he'd be holding a deadly weapon, some kind of God Sword that would cut these fuckers in half, but he liked to think of the extended version of this now small item as a baseball bat.

He remembered a time, not too long after he had emerged from that house of mirrors in '98 unscathed and laughing with Ray and Carl, hitting each other on the back, all smiles. A woman named Teresa Lewis, who would eventually become his wife, stood with a friend, both teetering in high-heeled shoes, by a popcorn vender a few feet away. The smell of butter floating heavily in the night air and the sounds of people laughing amongst the amusement-ride noises was palpable.

It only took one look and time stopped. He was in love, but what he was most concerned with right now was not his future wife, but how their first date together had ended, after he dropped Teresa off at her Back Bay apartment on Riverway Drive. That situation could have some relevance. That situation also involved three men that were in his way . . . and a baseball bat.

Meet the new boss, he thought, *same as the old boss.*

ROUND SIX

It's too bad Teresa lives so far away, Farrow thought. She was funny, smart, and beautiful, not to mention that body he'd be giving up. *A serious girlfriend at this time would be too much to take on . . . or would it?*

He was deep into training for a fight, one in which if he would prove victorious, just might kick him up a notch, get him some real bouts against the big boys. He'd finally be swimming in a pool with some genuine contenders, make a name for himself.

Farrow had some thinking to do. A woman like this could knock him down for the count and keep him down, but in a good way. Teresa was a once-in-a-lifetime shot.

Their first official date together had gone very well. Farrow kept it simple. Keeping things simple was always the best route. Simple was better. The conversation during dinner progressed smoothly. The two had gone to an eatery at "The North End," Boston's Italian district, a place called Giacomo's on Hanover Street. If the joint had been a bit too loud, that annoying fact was more than compensated for by the intoxicating smells of garlic and marinara that swirled about the place.

Teresa had actually acted a bit shy at first, admitting she had never been out with anyone famous before.

"Well, I don't know. I really wouldn't say I was famous," Farrow said, "just a couple of fights. I mean I'm not Rocky Marciano . . . or Ray Robinson."

"Yeah, but you were on television and everything," Teresa said, referring to an ESPN undercard bout that had been televised a month earlier. Her cheeks reddened as she looked up at him smiling.

"I think if I really were famous, we wouldn't be able to enjoy our night together. People would keep bothering us," Tommy said.

Teresa had liked the way he'd said "our night" and "bothering us," including her.

"Maybe one day if I make it to the Boston Garden, or maybe even Madison Square, and I get to headline, you know, the main fight, then maybe I'll be famous, but until then . . . I'm just your date."

Farrow did notice that Teresa was getting more looks than he was and it was killing him, because even at this early hour in the evening with the whole date still ahead of them, she already had a good hold on his heart. But the fact was, the travel distance between their homes could be a real problem with his scheduled fight preparation regimen. His trainer, Johnny Laguna, wasn't going to go for it either. He had high hopes and big ideas for Tommy Farrow and would not let some "chippy" get in the way. He had promised Farrow there would be plenty of women, and plenty of time for those women in the future, but none of those women, he thought, would be Teresa.

"Did anyone ever tell you that you look like Robert De Niro? You know, when he played that fighter? Except bigger and with better hair."

"Yeah, you mean Jake LaMotta from *Raging Bull*. No, I had never heard that before," he lied, now it was his turn to blush. "I just think I look like myself."

Teresa smiled at him over the flickering candlelight with her mesmerizing cat-like green eyes locked on his. She was beautiful, and he was in trouble.

Motioning to the menus before them, Farrow said, "Any idea what you might want, my dear?"

Blushing again, Teresa said, "Yeah, and I can't believe I'm saying this, but I think I do know what I want." She wasn't looking at the menu.

Yes, Farrow was in trouble.

The movie they had seen after dinner was at the Coolidge Corner Theater on Harvard Street in Brookline. The movie house was independently owned and specialized in showing old black and white films. This week's feature was *King Kong*, the original 1933 masterpiece. The film happened to be one of Farrow's all-time favorites.

After the movie's final line "It was beauty that killed the beast," and the final image of the giant ape lying dead at the bottom of the Empire

State Building, he was relieved to see Teresa smiling wistfully and still staring wide-eyed as THE END flashed on the screen.

"Oh, my God, that was so good. I haven't seen *King Kong* in years. I used to watch it every Thanksgiving with my father. This night just keeps getting better and better."

Farrow had the impression that it could have been any movie the two had seen and she would have given him the same reaction. He had a suspicion that she was just as into him as he was her. *There was nothing wrong with that,* he thought, *nothing at all.*

"Oh, yeah? Well, I got one more trick up my sleeve," he said smiling, taking her hand. It felt warm in his. "Our chariot awaits, milady."

They walked slowly to Farrow's '92 Toyota Camry parked three blocks south of the theater, the two smiling contentedly.

Looking at Farrow's big arms Teresa said, "You got more than tricks up those sleeves."

The final leg of the night ended in the heart of the Boston Common in front of the frog pond where the reflection of the three-quarter moon bounced off the surface of the softly stirring water.

"I really had a nice time tonight, Tommy," Teresa said, with a voice so soft and inviting, Farrow wondered if the date was almost over, or maybe it would go on for another hour or three. "You made, and *make*, me feel special."

"Hey, a guy's gotta do what a guy's gotta do, right?" Farrow said smiling.

"So, Tommy, what's your secret, huh? What's the thing that makes you want to fight for a living? Don't get me wrong, I think it's very noble . . . and sexy."

"Are you sure you really want to hear this? I mean some of it's not all that pretty. You might not think much of me, but I want to be honest. No secrets."

"I want to know everything about you, and it's a deal, no secrets from my end either."

Farrow looked around the park motioning his arm in a "look at all this" manner.

"Did you know the Boston Common is the oldest city park in the United States? In the winter they have ice skating on this frog pond, not to mention the swan boats in the summertime," he said pointing to the body of water before them, the traffic noise from Beacon Street filtering down around them.

"Yes, Thomas," she said. "Stop procrastinating. I know those little tidbits of information. I've lived around here my whole life. So tell me, what's your big bad secret? Why do you fight?"

"Okay," he started, "when I was young, maybe five or six years old, I used to stutter . . . real bad. I guess I didn't like taking shit from people, even at that young age, you know how kids could be . . . they used to call me 'the stuttering punk'. I was always big for my size, so I learned to fight . . . and, man, I was good at it. Soon, nobody made fun of the big kid who talked funny, and by the time I was nine years old, I guess I outgrew it, spoke just fine after that."

He stopped for a second and let this part of his story sink in before he continued. Teresa was listening intently.

"When I was in ninth grade, just before my fifteenth birthday, I was kicked out of North Reading High for hitting a teacher." He stopped and let her absorb that last part. "I mean the guy was an asshole and he was really riding me . . . my friends made me this bet . . . I guess I was like A-Rod, taking steroids, young and stupid. Not that I took steroids or anything, just the young and stupid part."

"Like A-Rod, huh?" she said through a smile. "Speaking of assholes . . ."

"Yeah, yeah, I know. Anyway, I was kicked out of school, expelled, and transferred to Wilmington the following year. I actually made some good friends there. We heard that teacher I hit killed himself a few years later."

"Really? Geez." Teresa thought about that a moment. Then she said, "You used to stutter? You hit a teacher who later killed himself? That's why you box? That's why you became a prizefighter?"

"Well, in a manner of speaking, but there's more to the story."

"Do tell," Teresa said, looking like she was enjoying this. "How do you top punching out a teacher?"

"Easily. My first year in college, the University of Virginia, only about three months into the first semester, right before Christmas, my buddy and I, this guy named Timmy Johnson, tough son of a bitch . . . we used to call ourselves TNT, ya know, for Tom and Tim, get it? TNT."

"Yeah, I got it," she said through a wide smile. "Very clever of you two, ever think of writing for television?"

Looking down at her, half smirking, he continued, "Well, me and Timmy were speaking to these girls one night, it was on a Saturday, and the next thing you know this big meathead is telling us we can't talk to them anymore, how we are not allowed to talk to his sister. At first I thought the guy was protecting his actual sister, until I realized he meant his fraternity sister. Timmy and me figured screw that! We'll talk to whoever we want to talk to. So that night we waited for him outside his fraternity house to have a little chat, the only problem was there were four of them when this guy returned. One thing led to another and me and Timmy are fighting four guys."

"My God, were you hurt?"

"We were actually doing okay against the four. Like I said, this guy Timmy was one tough mother, and I know you know I'm no slouch either."

Teresa nodded her head enthusiastically.

"Suddenly the whole fraternity house empties out and we're fighting like twenty-five guys. We held up all right for about a minute; it was almost like Batman and Robin, the old 60's T.V. show? Except this was TNT and we were explosive . . . that is until we weren't. They overtook us easily, and I took a beating like never before. Needless to say, Timmy and I, we were both expelled from school. I had bruises for months after that."

"My god. You badass."

Teresa was laughing and she playfully hit him on the arm.

"Do you think you could take me?" she said smiling.

"Not in those shoes," he said pointing at the pencil-thin heels she was wearing on her feet. "One good kick and you could pierce my heart." And then in a quiet voice, "And I think you already did."

"What?"

"No, no, nothing, I was just rambling."

Teresa looked at him suspiciously.

"So, is that it? Is that how you became a fighter?"

"Well, my dad had enough of me getting kicked out of places like school, so a friend of his at work had a friend who knew this trainer, now my trainer. His name is Johnny Laguna, a real good guy with an absolute bellow of a laugh, and a great fight trainer. He's trained a lot of big names. You might even know some of them."

"I'm not stupid, you big hooligan," she said almost laughing. "I bet I know more about boxing than you think."

And Farrow did bet that she knew more about boxing than he might think, she was funny and smart. She was the whole package; he had to work something out with Johnny. He couldn't lose this one.

"My dad figured it would be good for me to channel this anger somewhere positive before I got myself in real trouble, so about a year and a half ago I turned professional."

"When's your next fight? Two months from now?"

"It's actually just under two months, and it could be a slight problem, it's something I'd like to talk about. I want to get everything in the open, no secrets. This is only our first date and my heart is skipping beats, and that's not easy to do to me. I think we really might have something here," he said, getting serious quickly.

"I think you're right, Tommy. I don't want the night to end, and I don't think we *might* have something, I think we *do*."

He liked hearing her call him Tommy. That voice was something he sure could get used to.

"I'm fighting this guy named Christopher 'Tree Trunk' Kearns. They call him Tree Trunk 'cause he's short, only about five-foot eleven, and his body is wide, you know, like a tree trunk. He's real ugly, too; small, beady eyes that are too close together, pointy nose, and a Marine haircut. Always wears an expression like he's trying to figure out a math problem. Anyway, him and his trainer, another asshole named Jack Leeds, have been talking shit about me all over the news, and 'Tree Trunk' is ranked much higher than me. If I can beat him, and I have no doubt that I will, I'll move up in the rankings and finally face some real contenders, not just big thugs and palookas. I'll start making some money too. Real money."

"You guys are like little kids with these nicknames. Do you have one?" she said.

"Yeah, as a matter of fact I do."

"Well?"

"Promise you won't laugh?"

"I promise. Scouts honor." Teresa was holding up three fingers together, pinky and thumb pressed to her palm.

"Heatseeker. Tommy 'Heatseeker' Farrow."

"You know something, I actually like that. Can't wait to see your missile," she joked. "Oh my God, I can't believe I said that!"

"My fists . . ." he said holding his hands up before her, hiding his laughter at her embarrassment. "My fists are the missiles." Farrow's face was turning bright red for the second time this evening. So was Teresa's, he noticed. *God is she cute!*

"I actually got the name from a horse, an Arabian mare, I used to ride out on Long Island. I'd spend summers at my uncle's farm. Those were some of the best times in my life. I'd ride her on the beach with the waves crashing next to us. That horse was really something. Right before we would take off, I would pull back on the reins and say 'Get ready to rock!' The horse would rear up on her hind legs, almost like she had a purpose, like I was the Lone Ranger or something . . . and then I was flying. I never felt so powerful in my life than with that mare under me. She was my first love. Heatseeker was a beautiful animal."

"You know, you're not so bad yourself."

"Okay, sweetheart, stop making me blush, fighters don't blush. Do it again and I might have to spank you."

"Promises, promises. So . . . what happened to the horse?"

"I went back one summer . . . and she was gone. My uncle said he sold her to someone in Arizona. I later found out she died. I must have cried for a month." He sneaked a quick look at Teresa and then looked down, wondering what she was thinking.

Farrow stayed quiet for a few moments, then said, "It's a funny thing, my line 'Get ready to rock', before the horse would start to run, you see AC/DC has a song called 'Heatseeker' and the first line is . . . you guessed it, 'Get ready to rock'. When I hit that teacher, I said that same line. It's also the song that plays when I walk into the ring before a fight. The name Heatseeker kind of went full circle . . . it's my salute to her, you know, like my own little tribute."

The two were silent for a few minutes. Teresa was waiting to see if Farrow had anything left, anymore of his soul to bare.

"Anyway, love," she secretly liked him calling her 'love', "for the next seven weeks I'll be in training, and it might be a bit hard to see each other . . ."

"Tommy, say no more," she cut him off.

"I could probably swing it maybe twice a month until the fight, but I have to stay focused . . ."

"Listen, my little missile," pet names already, "I have exactly two months of school left until I graduate, so this works out perfectly. We'll see each other when we can, taking it slow for a few weeks, and then at the end of June we can pick this up where we leave off tonight. How's that?"

"You don't know how good that sounds, that sounds like sweet soul music. I was worried to talk to you about this. Everything feels so right between us."

"Just one thing, though, one small condition," Teresa said, pausing for effect.

"And that is?"

Smiling again, she said, "I want ringside seats to the fight."

And with that last statement, before he could answer, she went up on tiptoe. Her bare heels popped out and cleared the back of her shoes, and she gently kissed his lips. With his right arm around her waist, Farrow pulled her closer, while his left hand playfully moved her long hair out of her eyes. He kissed her back deeply, while the two stood embraced like that for some time.

A warm breeze wrapped around their bodies and cut across the mirrored surface of the duck pond disturbing the moon's perfect reflection.

After dropping her off at "The Fens" apartment complex in the Back Bay area of Boston, and another small make-out session at Teresa's front door, the headlights of Farrow's Camry cut into the night before him as he sailed toward Route 93 heading back to North Reading. On the radio, Mick Jagger was singing about the Midnight Rambler.

The Fens.

He kept saying the name in his head. It was a fifty-minute ride from his doorstep to Teresa's. He could make it work. He had to.

He didn't know, maybe the stars were aligned tonight, something nuts like that, because Farrow was on cloud nine and it was a cloud that he didn't want to get off.

He laid out a potential plan that was charging up in his mind. He took stock of himself and, with an imaginary pencil and pad, made notations in fictitious graphite, checking off what needed to be done. On the radio, the sounds of The Rolling Stones continued to growl and bleed, crunching guitars through the car's sound system.

First things first, move out of my parents' basement. Then I gotta get some new wheels, but maybe new is not the way to go. Maybe some new "old" wheels, a Charger or a Mustang, something like that. Farrow had always loved those old muscle cars, especially the one Steve McQueen drove in *Bullitt;* the '68 green Mustang, that vehicle was something else.

He broke his thought patterns for a moment. *Where am I?*

Looking around, unfamiliar street signs hurtled past in streaks of green and white. He couldn't be too far off track, so he wasn't worried. Getting back to it, *Okay, I beat "Tree Trunk" Kearns first. Gonna chop that asshole down like the piece of wood he is. Next, the car, maybe if things move along like I think they will, I can even have Teresa pick something out with me, something we both like.* Farrow was having fun fantasizing and thinking long term. This was unlike him, he had never been this smitten before, but there it was again, the image that kept filling his mind. Teresa.

He reflected over the evening. Everything about the preceding night had warmed him from the inside.

"Please call me," was what she said to him after their last kiss and before she turned and closed the front door to her apartment. Farrow promised to do so, would in fact do so the following evening. He could hardly wait. They had set a date for two weeks, fourteen days, two Saturdays from tonight. A plan had been put into motion to see each other every two weeks until the fight, where Teresa would sit ringside for the first time of many.

One day at a time, Tommy. You can get everything you want, just take it slow, Johnny Laguna's voice, methodical. *Take it slow, until it's time for the speed.* And Farrow had the speed. He had the speed, the muscle, and the heart.

He would be up every morning and run farther than his normal five miles, maybe tack on an extra two or three before he met Johnny at 7:30 inside Conn's gym. The owner Jimmy Conn, was also Tommy's cut man, maybe the best in the business, classic good looks and a sparkling sense of humor. The three of them together would be unstoppable.

Conn's Gym was in Charlestown, a run-down building riddled with old fight posters that decorated the walls and a thick smell of sweat always hanging in the stale air. Nowhere else in the world did Tommy Farrow feel more comfortable.

He planned on getting down and dirty, he felt he could beat Kearns easily, even if the bout was in two days, let alone seven weeks. He watched plenty of tape on "Tree Trunk" and would be surprised if the fight went any longer than three rounds. He didn't plan on getting hurt. He felt invincible.

Farrow was thinking of Teresa's eyes now, an exquisite, luminous green when she had looked up at him at the frog pond before their first kiss. Those eyes had a hold on him and he saw his future. All that black hair piled on top of her head and framing that perfect face, her stretching up on tiptoe reaching for his lips . . . he lost himself in the memory, completely lost himself before his ride turned rough.

He was bouncing over the pothole that flattened his right front tire before he saw it; the top of his head hit the Camry's inside roof, hard. Farrow heard himself shouting "Fuck!" followed by the rubber grinding pavement, a faint sound of whump, whump, whump was added to the car's soundtrack, the Allman Brothers "One Way Out".

"C'mon, give me a goddamn break."

The night had been so perfect.

Where the fuck am I? Too many things to think about, too much shit going through my mind.

Nothing around him looked familiar, rows of dark houses off the central road with moonlight spilling across the front lawns. The skeleton-white moon was now much too high for romance.

Whump. Whump. Whump.

Shit. The rim was going to be messed up if he didn't stop and repair the flat tire, a chore he had done many times. Let's get it finished and keep things simple. That was always best, fast and simple.

Farrow didn't see any police cruisers, or anyone for that matter who might be willing to help. The place looked like a ghost town, hopefully without the spooks. He stopped the car at a red traffic light in front of a small drug store that was nestled between an empty building and a pizza joint that also looked vacant. The sign on top read Roxbury Drugs in large red letters.

How the fuck did I wind up in Roxbury? With a flat tire no less? Great, he thought, *the ass-hole of Massachusetts.*

He briefly considered driving on the tire the few miles it would take until he was on more familiar ground, in a better, safer neighborhood, but that would likely worsen his situation, completely destroying the rim and stranding him. Fuck that, he was a professional prizefighter, he wasn't running from anyone or anything. He would stop the car and change his tire.

The light turned green and Farrow crept the car slowly along the road before choosing a block on the right side of the street to turn down. This appeared a bit brighter than the others. The road was lined with small run-down houses similar in size and shape, quiet and ominous.

Three street lamps, with a fourth just flickering along the small road's curbsides were illuminated, two on the left and two on the right. The other six or so he could see were either sabotaged, or had no electric current being fed into them.

He still saw no people. *This is good,* he thought, *and thank God Teresa's not with me.* He pulled the car next to one of the working lamps on the left side of the street; this would make it easier for him to change the right front. The Camry was bathed in a vaporous mustard glow from above. He pushed the gearshift into park before fishing through the glove compartment in search of the flashlight he knew was there.

In the mid to late 1800's, Irish immigrants settled in Roxbury, including the family of John L. Sullivan, a bare-knuckle fighter who was the first recognized Heavyweight Champion of the World. This small piece of history actually thrilled Farrow; it was Roxbury's present reputation that he had a problem with. Farrow knew he had to be quick, in and out. Looking around through his car windows he sensed eyes on him, predatory and watching.

Upon exiting the vehicle, the first thing he noticed was the heavy smell of garbage resting on the air. It was almost as if Roxbury was built on a refuse dumpsite. He had been through here a time or two in the past in the daylight, most recently about four years earlier with his father on their way into Malden to pick up a lawn mower he had gotten a deal on from a co-worker. Farrow, even then, could remember an unpleasant aroma floating around this area, so much so he had closed the window of his father's car to keep the smell out, but that was nothing like this overpowering presence. It almost seemed like a living entity, probing and seeking.

He stood under the street lamp and looked back and forth along the dark road, any thoughts of Teresa now banished from his conscious mind. He wouldn't let her into this place, didn't want to taint the thought of her with Roxbury.

A television was being played loudly several houses from where he stood; he could hear the laugh track clearly, some late night sitcom. Across the street and maybe two houses over, Farrow thought he could hear hushed voices quietly conversing, and then nothing. Was someone watching? He couldn't shake the sensation of unseen eyes boring into him. He saw no one, though.

Back to the task at hand, the flat tire. For good measure he looked around and listened for a second longer, a dog was barking a few blocks over. *The natives are getting restless,* he thought. *Keep it simple, in and out.*

Farrow walked to the rear of the Camry, minding his surroundings. He no longer saw the moon in the sky. *Probably covered by rain clouds.* It was noticeably cooler out now and a slight breeze forced upon him a nice helping of au de garbage. How quick the night had turned from one extreme to the other.

He slipped the key, which went in easily enough, into the small hole located in the trunk's rear above the license plate. He turned it and it hit home with an audible click that told him the lock was released. The trunk popped a few inches before Farrow helped by extending it to the fully open position. He put the keys in his front pocket and turned on the flashlight, fanning it across the inky contents within. He trained the light's glowing beam on a large round mass in the trunk's inner depths, the tire. He poked it with a finger. Full. *Thank God.*

A bit more relieved now, Farrow clicked the flashlight off and laid it down next to the waiting hunk of rubber. The soft burn that simmered off the street lamp was more than enough to get the job done. He located the tire iron and jack under the trunk's black mat and retrieved both items along with the fully inflated spare that he now saw had plenty of tread left. "That will do just fine," he said under his breath.

He put the items on the ground near the right front side, looked quickly around one more time, and listened. Nothing. Farrow got down on one knee before the flattened wheel and pushed the jack under the car until it was properly positioned. With the rusted tire iron in reach, he got to work.

The task, when completed, took him just over eight minutes and, with the exception of stopping to look up at an airplane that had marked a few seconds of time slipping past way up overhead, its buzzing mechanical drone almost comforting, Farrow had stayed focused.

He stood up grabbing the wrecked tire in a single, dirty hand and the jack in the other. He deposited the two items in the still-open trunk and realized there were no sounds to be heard at all, not even the television laugh-track that had almost seemed like company. There were no human bodies he could see, but the sense of being watched, that overpowering feeling, was still there and much stronger now.

He rubbed his hands together back and forth quietly to discard any filth that might have been there, then proceeded to wipe his palms across his pants legs. He didn't want the Toyota's steering wheel decked out in grime. He remembered the tire iron still on the ground by the car's right-side front. *Shit.* He walked back to the area and scooped it up.

A police cruiser, red and white lights swirling furiously on top, quickly rolled by the corner passing the street with a blur of colors, its siren blaring. Something was going down close by. Roxbury. Time to get outta here.

Farrow dropped the tire iron in the open trunk before closing it down tight without making any unnecessary loud noises that may wake people and draw any unwanted attention. With that done, his mind immediately focused on the keys in his front pocket, his ticket home. He tapped several fingers against the waiting lump, proving to himself they were still there. They were.

Okay, let's get the fuck out of Dodge.

He walked slowly to the driver's side door, the keys already jingling in his right hand, and unlocked it. Farrow put the fingers of his left hand under the handle grip so as to pull the door open, but a voice from behind him stopped this motion.

"What yo doin' here, white boy?"

Farrow turned.

Emerging from the night. Three youths were approaching him from across the street, pimp rolling their way in his direction. The one out front was holding a baseball bat hung low, pointed toward the street; but a baseball bat was a baseball bat, and unless the three wanted to play ball, no good would come from it.

"I said, what yo' doin', white boy?"

Farrow couldn't see anyone else in the immediate area but the three young men. The two behind the leader didn't seem to be brandishing any kind of weapons, concealed or otherwise.

"What yo' got there?"

The one out front was pointing down at Farrow's right hand, now arched and obscuring the car keys.

"No thanks, guys, I don't need any help. Had a flat tire, but it's all fixed now," Farrow said through a smile, realizing he had been watched the whole time. These lazy assholes waited for him to do the actual physical work, letting him change the tire himself, and now they were probably going to try to rob him and most likely take the car.

"We ain't ask if yo' need help. I said, what yo' got there?" still pointing at Farrow's right hand.

He quickly put the keys into the right front pocket of his jeans. Something told him he'd need both hands free.

"You boys want something? I'm not looking for any trouble, I had enough of that tonight, and I just . . ."

"Who da fuck yo' calling 'boy'?" Voices were elevating now.

Wonderful, Farrow thought now holding his hands up with the palms turned toward them. He said, "Look, gentlemen, I'm not here to cause you any trouble, and I don't want any trouble. I just stopped to change a flat tire and now I'll be on my way."

"You not goin' nowhere. What you got in yo' wallet? We take da car key, too."

Farrow lowered his arms. He wasn't getting out of this without a fight. He looked at the three figures before him. Two of the men had on ball caps turned sideways, fucking New York Yankees no less. He wondered what bullshit gang these three assholes belonged to.

"You not looking fo' troubles, but troubles find you," the leader again. "Dis are town, are place."

Farrow took a step away from the Toyota minding his surroundings. Always mind your surroundings, Johnny Laguna had taught him. What's around you can become an important factor in any fight. How level the terrain may be, potential obstacles to stumble over, stuff like that.

The ground looked level, he wasn't too close to the curb and there was plenty of room for him to move around if need be.

"Hey," Farrow said, standing tall, talking to the one out in front. The other two, silent so far, moved sideways away from him spreading out a bit. "This isn't your town, dis ain't *yo'* place," mocking them now. "This town belongs to John L. Sullivan, and tonight I'm taking it back."

"John L. who? What da fuck yo' talking 'bout? Le's get dat wallet now. I don't likes to repeat myself," said the leader.

The night was quiet around them and the air was still. He had a sense that others not willing to get involved were watching the event play out from a distance. The large circle of light on the ground from the street lamp's beam would act as the ring, and Farrow was standing at its center.

He tucked his chin into his chest and bent his knees slightly before bringing his curled, tightened fists up out front in a prizefighter's stance.

"John L. Sullivan was a bare knuckle boxer and this used to be his town, but tonight it's my town," Farrow said.

"What, yo' think yo' wanna box or something? Gots me a baseball bat right here. Yo' gonna fight a bat? Who you think yo' are? Yo' just some motherfucker punk," the one out front said through a smile, his teeth bracketed by gold.

The word 'punk' brought back memories, unpleasant childhood recollections. Farrow waited for them to come. He felt that once he dealt with the leader, he didn't think the two behind would give him much trouble. Everything seemed frozen, a snapshot in time. The smell of garbage was recycled freshly in his nostrils.

With the baseball bat held the way a ballplayer would, both hands tightly around the base, the big man up front, the leader, wearing an oversized Celtics jersey, took a step forward. Now with just about two or three feet between them, and with Farrow's head the intended target, he swung the bat and said again, "Who you think yo' are, motherfucker punk?"

Farrow stepped into the blow. In boxing everything is backward, instead of retreating from a punch, you move into it. He turned sideways to the left because there wasn't a lot of space between the two men; the velocity from the bat's swing wasn't much, no room to hit for the fences. Extending his arm and intercepting the bat's vertical arc lessened the blow even more. He caught the solid piece of wood in his left hand and held on to the thick rounded end, in turn, keeping the unfortunate leader held standing in place for a second.

"I'm the punk with the stutter," Farrow said.

He dropped the right side of his body slightly and with a tremendous adrenal burst, shot his tightened fist in a vicious uppercut into the thug's ribcage, the full weight of his body behind the blow. Two hundred and twenty pounds of blunt force and the sound of ribs cracking broke the night's silence, the ghost of John L. Sullivan fueling his mind and running through his veins like lit gasoline.

The leader went down to his knees quickly, the baseball bat now in full control in Farrow's left hand. The mugger wrapped his arms around his torso to protect his ribs, looked up, eyes registering surprise and shock as he saw a fist the size of a frozen turkey hurtling toward his chin. Farrow, bending low, followed through with the punch. The loud *thwack* echoed up the street as the man crumpled to the floor unmoving.

Farrow stood up straight now and flipped the baseball bat, twirling it in the air. He caught the appropriate end and said, "Are you guys serious? The fucking Yankees?"

The man on his right came at him now; Farrow saw his left hand was wrapped around a box cutter. He heard Johnny Laguna's voice in his head: *When he throws the punch attack the arm.* Farrow put his free right hand up in a protective position in front of his face. He bent and bobbed slightly. The third thug was off to the left somewhere, not involving himself yet.

The man on the right came quick, swinging the blade in a side-to-side slashing motion. Farrow stood his ground in the lamplight's center. A siren from a police car or maybe an ambulance whirled and screamed off in the distance. *We're gonna need the latter here in a minute,* he thought. The youth shoved the blade toward Farrow's head, and when he did, Tommy stepped to the right and punched the man's left bicep with such force the box cutter fell to the ground almost on impact and the man grabbed the bruised area with his right hand.

"Ohhh man, you crazy or sumpin', what yo' tryin' to . . ."

He saw Farrow standing before him, the baseball bat now being held in both hands like a samurai sword. The corners of Farrow's mouth were drawn down into a snarl, his eyes lit up, blazing . . . crazy.

"Hey, c'mon, man, we just foolin' round. We jus' playin' and all."

Farrow swung the bat and almost took the youth's head off. There was a wet, bone-crunching sound as the solid piece of wood hit the man's skull, immediately dropping him to the ground next to the leader who was still not moving. The New York Yankees cap was several feet away in the gutter where it belonged.

Farrow dropped the bat on the floor next to the two would-be muggers with a loud clamor. He watched it roll for a second before lifting his eyes and locking them on the third man.

"Two outs, you're up."

The third youth took two steps toward Farrow, who was not only not breathing hard, but also back in a boxer's defensive position, arms raised, knees bent, and leading with his left arm.

"Come on, shit bag, you want my wallet? You want my car? Come and get it."

The third man, completely unarmed, took another step closer before looking at the bodies of his two friends assembled at Farrow's feet. He then turned and ran off into the night, disappearing into the smell of garbage that was still thick in the air. The kid's pants were so oversized and low hanging, Farrow was amazed he didn't trip and kill himself.

"Anybody else?" he said quietly at first and then much louder. "Anybody else want a piece of me?"

He waited for an answer. Silence. Farrow knew they were watching him. He stalked back and forth in front of his car like a lion in a cage anticipating prey.

"Come on, who's next, ya bunch of pussies?"

The two youths on the ground before him slowly writhed around in blood, piss, and filth.

Good, I didn't kill anybody.

The third man was long gone.

What kind of scumbag leaves a friend in trouble like that? Fucking stupid gang members. The street was silent.

"Yeah, that's what I thought," Farrow said loud and clear before slowly climbing into the Toyota. He deliberately took his time getting into the car to show he wasn't afraid and not running from anyone or anything.

John L. Sullivan would have been proud.

He pulled out of the road slowly. *Come get me, assholes, I'm right here.* No one did. All it took was a left hand turn and two miles to put Roxbury behind him.

Farrow clicked on the radio. Roger Daltrey was growling about not getting fooled again. In a few minutes, Farrow's heartbeat sank back to a normal rhythm and before he knew it, he was singing along with the radio as thoughts of Teresa seeped back into his head.

ROUND SEVEN

Farrow remembered that long ago triumphant night, how elated he'd felt on the ride home singing with the radio and bragging the next morning to Johnny Laguna after his roadwork was complete.

Things were different now, though; the smell of Roxbury garbage was replaced by the stench of burnt human flesh, and the three men before him, if you could call them men, were not imitation street punks with their pants hanging below their asses and wearing oversized basketball jerseys, this was the real deal. If he lost this fight, he lost everything.

Now just about ten paces away, the three black and blues stood tall, their backs to the holding area doorway. If they had visible eyes, Farrow thought, they'd be looking right at him. He contemplated squeezing the Hellstick, releasing its fury and cutting the suits down, being done with it. *Would that cause a commotion? Would others come running to join the fun?* Farrow didn't think these beings would leave their friends in a fight. This wasn't Roxbury.

Okay, let's think this through, Johnny Laguna again, *always consider your next move, don't jump the gun, stay calm, think about your options, slow is fast, until fast is fast, and believe me, brother, you got all kinds of fast.*

Farrow put the Hellstick back in his front pocket remembering the hand wraps around his knuckles. He couldn't see them, but John and Keith had assured him they were there. *If you hit something, you will hurt them,* Keith had told him. He was a prizefighter; he wasn't going to walk around this place yielding some half-assed sword. A fighter used his fists and if he had to fight that's just what he would do, he'd go out like a man, not like Luke Skywalker.

The black smoke above gave the illusion of thinning out, but Farrow chalked that up to the angle from which he was looking. *God this place is huge.* The burning ash smell was dissipating some as well; it was nowhere near as strong as a few moments before. He looked back to the sky, the part of it he could see on top of all that glass. The smoke was definitely thinning. It seemed the closer he got to the structure, the less bedlam was around him, or the less its effects took hold.

What a strange fucking place this is.

He brought his eyes back to the problem at hand, the three faceless black and blues. Just seven paces away, but now they were facing each other, almost as if in deep conversation. And just like that, to Farrow's complete and utter amazement, the three faceless beings dispersed. They walked away in three different directions. None of them regarded him at all. The ten on either side of the entrance stood unmoving, unconcerned.

This was either very good or very bad, he thought.

He moved forward. The unguarded entrance was just a step or two away now. The rectangular doorway with its glass walls was inviting, almost calling to him, "Come on inside, Tommy, your friend is waiting."

The pull from Scalia's soul was unparalleled now. Farrow thought about breaking into a slight jog just to keep up with the unyielding magnetism, the commanding force of the damn thing, or maybe *damned thing* was a better choice of words he thought through a smirk, and then remembered where he was, and the cocky smile receded back into his face.

"Okay, buddy," he said out loud. "Here I come."

Tommy Farrow stepped into the darkened entranceway of the glass structure.

The first thing he noticed were the levels, maybe thirty or forty of them going up as high as he could see. People, human bodies, seemed to be floating in the air; all the glass that surrounded him brought on this illusion. Farrow looked around in awe. The place was unbelievable. His mind hit a speed bump and he couldn't think straight, just flashed his eyes around in silence, up and down and sideways. He saw people below him also. Seemingly hovering in little glass cubicles. Waiting, he assumed, for their twenty-four hour holding period to end and damnation to begin.

He took an uncertain step forward, afraid to put his full weight on the glass floor; he had visions of the ground shattering, falling through, and millions of pointed shards cutting his body to pieces over and over again. *That would be a fuck of a forever,* he thought. Farrow bounced his foot slightly, and then harder. The floor seemed sturdy and he concluded it would take something a heck of a lot heavier than him to cause the glass ground to splinter, crack, and blow apart.

Everything looked so fragile and delicate; the thickness of the glass was maybe only a quarter of an inch, but held sturdy. Farrow passed by each makeshift cell slowly regarding the people locked within. Most were not looking at him but huddled in terror, or curled into a fetal position on the clear floor weeping. The ones who did see him, cowered and backed away. He understood immediately, these people didn't know who he was; he could have been some demonic freak coming to snatch them up for whatever horrors their perpetuity held.

He walked slowly still looking around; this place was something out of a fantasy novel, all the glass, the perfectly carved right angles and edges . . . it was almost beautiful. He thought, if this structure wasn't being used, well, for what it was being used for, it might be a feature of paradise, anywhere but here. The people, men, women, children, black, white, and every other color and nationality you could think of, were all present; young and old, fat and skinny, everyone was welcome.

Farrow looked up through the glass ceiling, beyond the many floors. The twisting, black smoke moved like rain clouds, the view from this vantage point gave the smog a thick elucidation, while outside close to the structure, he remembered that hadn't been the case, it seemed to be thinning out some.

Now, past the people seemingly floating in their clear cells, he looked through the walls, and could see the depraved acts of the faceless black and blues: beheadings, burnings, flaying, cutting, stretching, the whole nine yards. The large ground holes, continuously coughing forth the ominous smoke, looked like fat lifeless eyeballs staring blankly into the sky.

The pull from the center of his body was now taking him much deeper into the complex and by way of a clear staircase three levels higher. He kept his hands low, but ready in case any surprises lurked around a given corner. The hallways before him maintained a faint almost tired light. Two more times he saw those large red eyes he had seen earlier. They seemed harmless, almost curious for the moment before retreating back into the darkened portions of the corridors.

He was getting close. Scalia's pull, almost painful now, was causing him to quicken his pace. The glass under his feet vibrated. He sensed it wouldn't be much longer. Glancing down at his wrist for the first time in a while, the digital readout displayed the time they had left. 08:56.

It had taken him nearly four hours to get to this point. He had to be quicker about things. Getting out would be faster, much faster. He knew the way and there would be no bullshit, no stopping to look at the grisly attractions. His mind stopped the full-ahead charge, instead remembering the doorway about twelve feet high in the air they had to reach atop the old and now defunct staircase. There had to be a rope or a chain somewhere he could snatch without causing too much attention, this place seemed to be based on ropes and chains . . . and screams.

I'll figure that out when I have Scalia. We'll figure it out together.

About seven or maybe eight cells ahead on the right side of the crystalline hallway, a soft blue wedge of light was discharging from one of the small chambers. The soothing radiance fell onto the floor and reflected off the other cells. Farrow slowed his pace, walking the rest of the way. It had to be him, he felt it in his mind and heart, but most of all the tremendous pull in his chest told him it was so.

He approached the lighting with equal parts excitement and trepidation. Four cells away now, three. Nothing shone out from the other enclosures, no blue glow or otherwise.

Farrow saw Robert Scalia's feet first. White sneakers pressed close together laced up nice and tight. As he moved completely in front of the small room that was maybe six feet by six feet, he saw that Scalia was sitting on the floor, deep into the right corner of the chamber. His legs drawn into his chest with his chin resting on his knees, his arms encircling his legs.

He didn't look up, didn't see Farrow standing there, not yet. The writer, about Farrow's age, had been crying. He looked to be a lost soul; except he wasn't lost, he was stolen.

Farrow hesitated for a moment before tapping on the glass with a single knuckle. Scalia's head shot up, his eyes registering absolute terror seeing the large man standing there. He quickly stood and pressed his body against the back glass, the wall furthest from Farrow, one hand held out in front of him as he retreated in an angle away from the huge prizefighter.

"Stay away from me! Stay away. Get back! I've done nothing wrong. I've done nothing to you. Just keep away!"

His voice, slightly high-pitched and cracking with fear, was somewhat muffled through the quarter-inch of glass between them.

"I've done nothing to you people, just stay away from me!"

Farrow noticed the blue shine he'd seen earlier was no longer in evidence. It must have been a tag from Scalia's soul marking his holding location. The writer now had both hands pressed against the back glass wall. He seemed to be trying to push himself through, away from Farrow.

"Please just stay away." Scalia was visibly crying, approaching sobbing now. "I've done nothing wrong. I've done nothing wrong."

"Robert," Farrow said loudly. "Robert, I'm not here to hurt you."

Scalia stopped all the noise he was making at once, almost like a switch had been turned off, and he stared at the prizefighter.

"That's better, just calm down, Robert." Farrow paused, then said, "You are Robert Scalia, is that correct?"

He waited for an answer. After a few seconds of suspicious contemplation, Scalia slowly nodded his head looking up at Farrow.

"Okay, good . . . you're a writer?"

"What in God's name does that have to do with anything?" Scalia said, clearly agitated, raising his voice a bit now. "Anyway, how do you know me?"

Farrow not liking the tone in Scalia's voice figured he'd have a bit of fun.

"Well, if you're locked in there, I guess your books aren't all that good. I mean, I've never heard of you. What, do you self-publish?"

"What, is this how my torture starts? You come in here and insult me? Assault me mentally? A kind of psychological torment?"

Scalia was starting to cry again and Farrow could tell he was not far from the breaking point.

"Robert, stay with me. I'm not here to hurt you."

Nothing.

"Robert, listen to me. My name is Thomas, Thomas Farrow, and I'm here to take you out of this place . . . fuck, to take us both out of here."

Through tears now, a step or two closer to Farrow, "Take us out of where? Where . . . are we, Thomas?" he said using Farrow's name for the first time.

Good, he's starting to trust me. Before answering, Farrow looked up through the glass ceiling and past the other souls seeming to float in their small glass prisons, the black smoke above, spreading over them like a death shroud.

"We're in hell, Robert."

It seemed to Farrow that ten minutes must have passed before Scalia spoke again; he was now standing at the glass wall with only inches between the two.

"What do you mean we're in hell? What could you possibly be saying to me?"

"It means just what it sounds like it means Robert. We've died, we're both dead . . . and this is hell. I'm here to . . ."

"What are you talking about? How can we be dead? I feel fine. I was driving to meet my wife, being driven . . . we were going to have a late dinner . . . we're alive. We're both alive. I was in the back of the limo and then I . . . I . . . woke up in this insane asylum."

"Robert, please, let me get you out of there, and I'll explain everything as best I can. Just stay calm, stay focused, and stay with me. I'll tell you everything I know . . . I'm actually hoping you can help me fill in some of the blanks."

"How can this be hell? How can we be dead?" shouting through the glass wall again.

"Robert, for fuck sake, calm down." Farrow motioning with his hands now. "Look at all the shit going on around you. Look at it out there. Does this look like any place you've ever seen before? It sure isn't Disney World."

Scalia's eyes searched frantically around the glass, through the walls, his eyes dancing up and down. The scenes of pandemonium continued and, from their location, he could see it all. The screams of horror and pain, though a bit lessened through all the glass, were still there, and Robert Scalia had a box seat.

"Do you see what I'm talking about? You have to trust me. I'm here to take you away. We're leaving together, and a lot more than just *our* lives depend on us getting out of here."

"How the hell can our lives, let alone anyone else's life, depend on us getting out of here if we're already dead?"

"Robert, can I ask you something?" Farrow said in a voice on the verge of elevating to something not so pleasant.

"Sure, what do you need?" Calming down a bit.

"Are your books overwritten? Too many words, you know, too long?

"Why would you ask that?"

"Because you don't shut the fuck up! Listen, Scalia . . . Robert, I'll explain everything to you that I can. I'll tell you everything I know, but I have to get you out of here first and we're sort of on a time limit. We don't have . . ." He didn't want to use the word eternity, so he finished off the sentence with, "We don't have long."

Scalia, quiet now, stood at the glass partition staring at Farrow.

"Okay, good. I have your attention. Just stay calm and you'll be fine, we'll both be fine. Now, how do I open this door? I don't see a handle or any kind of latch," Farrow said looking up and down the smooth surface of the glass. With the exception of a small hole, maybe an inch in diameter and about waist high where a doorknob might have been, there were no other markings in evidence.

Farrow bent down to inspect this hole. He saw it did not go all the way through the glass; it was more of an imperfection than anything else he decided, just a small rounded indentation. He brushed several fingers across the odd spot. Nothing happened.

"I don't know how it opens," Scalia said. "For a while now, those . . . things with no faces have been coming in and out of here, bringing people back and forth. A few times I heard a kind of grinding noise. That could have been the glass somehow moving, but I haven't actually seen it."

Farrow considered that for a second, his eyes still moving up and down the door. He pressed his hands on the cool surface of the glass and tried to slide it. Nothing. He gave it a little bouncing shove; it vibrated some but did not come open.

"Stick your finger in the hole."

Farrow looked up at Scalia not recognizing the female voice he had just heard.

One cell over, a woman was standing in the center of her glass enclosure, holding up a single index finger.

"Stick your finger in the hole," she said through a mouth glazed with cherry-red lipstick.

The woman in the cell next to Scalia's looked to be maybe thirty years old; she was perhaps a bigger escape risk. Locked around her right ankle was an angry looking two-inch wide band of metal. Coming off this band was an old rusty chain maybe five-feet long that snaked across the smooth glass floor and was attached to an iron ball, three times the size of the bowling sort. Boldly stenciled across this ball in white print was 300 LB.

The woman was wearing a classic medieval ball and chain. Farrow thought it was kind of overkill, she couldn't have weighed more than 120 or 130 pounds tops, that iron ball had to be more than twice her weight. He saw she was also wearing red, four-inch high-heeled shoes with her toenails decorated in purple paint poking out the open front part of the shoe.

Hooker, he thought immediately.

The woman was slim and fit with a tiny waist and under the circumstances wasn't bad looking. Maybe five foot eight with the heels. She wore black jeans that seemed to stop mid-calf and looked like they were spray-painted on, and a black sleeveless T-shirt that stopped just short of her stomach exposing a silver hoop attached to her bellybutton.

Farrow could almost imagine her chomping on a piece of bubble gum and hanging in through a car window reciting what she would do and how much it would cost. Her brownish-blonde hair was thick and loose on her shoulders and he was not surprised to see she had been crying, the black makeup around her eyes was smeared giving her the appearance of a battered raccoon.

Farrow, with a quizzical look on his face produced a single index finger and pressed it into the small, waist-high indentation in the glass wall. He noticed that Scalia was standing far back away from him; maybe afraid the glass would shatter. Nothing happened. Both men turned toward the woman wearing the ball and chain.

"The pad of your index finger," she said. "Press the pad of your index finger into the hole. It works like a button. I saw them do it a few cells down."

Farrow quickly adjusted the position of his finger and pressed into the circular dimple. The glass wall shivered slightly and then slowly started sliding downward in a shrieking whine, causing both men to noticeably flinch.

In less than thirty seconds the wall was no longer between the two. With the partition gone, Farrow noticed that the writer was not a very big man, maybe five foot six or seven, and a lean hundred and sixty pounds at most. His brown hair was cropped short and his thin face resembled that of a young Richard Gere. Like Farrow, Scalia was wearing blue jeans, but instead of a t-shirt, he wore the collared golf kind.

Farrow held out a meaty hand.

"Let's go, writer, we have to move."

Scalia hesitated for a moment before giving in and offering a cautious grip to the bigger man. When the two touched, both felt a slight electric jolt, before Farrow pulled him out of the now open cell and into the glass-encased hallway.

Far behind Scalia in the darkened shadows, several sets of large red eyes, blinking curiously, watched the two men, before retreating back into the murky blackness.

"I think we're being watched," Farrow said.

Scalia turned his head quickly, looking up and down the hallway.

"What are you talking about? I don't see anything."

"Trust me, they're there. We're being watched. We best get going. Like I said earlier, we're on sort of a time limit here, we don't have all day." Farrow glanced down at his wrist to prove it to himself.

"Hey, guys, don't forget me."

It was the woman standing in the cell next to Scalia's. "Take me with you. Open my wall." She stopped talking for a second and then added, "Please."

Scalia was looking at Farrow now.

"Absolutely not," the prizefighter said.

The writer continued to stare.

"Robert, we can't get involved. If she's here, locked in there, it's for a reason. Look at the size of that ball attached to her leg, for Christ's sake, are you gonna carry her?"

The woman was now at the front of her glass cell close to the two men. The chain locked around her ankle trailed across the floor to the iron ball.

"Please, I don't belong here, it's a mistake. They made a mistake. I was snatched and brought here by accident. Please! You have to get me out of here and get this damn thing off my leg." She motioned to the suffocating band locked around her ankle and the oversized ball. Her eyes, now locked on Farrow's, were brimming with tears.

"Please, I'm not supposed to be in here, someone made a mistake."

Farrow lowered his gaze in deliberation.

"I don't think I have much longer before they come for me." Her voice stronger now with a hint of authority, the red gloss covering her lips, glistening. "I don't belong here, the same way you two don't belong here."

"Farrow, come on," Scalia now. "Let's figure a way to take her with us. Three of us would have a better chance out there than two, am I right?"

"Another body can also slow us down, didn't you hear me about the time limit? I'm sure I mentioned it."

"I've seen what happens to people out there, and so have you. If we don't do anything, it's almost like we passed sentence on her ourselves."

Farrow saw that the writer was much calmer now and a hell of a lot more rational. His voice was composed, he could see Scalia's mind going to work behind his eyes, figuring things out.

"Robert, you don't understand, I'm not allowed to take out . . ."

"Hey, Heatseeker, stop fucking around and open my gate! Get me the fuck out of here! I'm coming with you!"

Farrow's head snapped in the direction of the woman.

"How did you . . . how do you know I'm called Heatseeker? That's my nickname when I fight," he said.

The woman started right in.

"I was . . . seeing a guy who was a big fight fan. He had plenty of cash to throw around, so I let him. I saw him on and off for maybe two years, but Saturday nights after we finished . . ." She paused. "You know . . . he would make me stay and watch whatever fight was being televised like on Pay-Per-View, or whatever they call those stations. I saw you a bunch of times, always rooted for you, too. I even saw you live once, ringside, on his dime. Boy, can you throw a punch."

"Wait a minute . . ." it was Scalia's turn now. "You two know each other?"

Farrow was shaking his head as the woman answered before he could get a word out.

"No, we don't know each other. He's a fighter. A professional prizefighter," the woman's muffled voice shouted through the glass. "If I'm not mistaken, he's the WBO Heavyweight Champion."

Scalia just stared in awe at the bigger man.

"I thought you looked familiar. That's right, Tommy 'Heatseeker' Farrow. I've heard of you."

Scalia extended his hand a second time; Farrow gave it a quick pump.

"Would you like an autograph?" he said sarcastically.

"Wow! Tommy Farrow. I've seen you on television a few times also. Wow, man, you're real good. I can remember about a year ago . . ."

"Okay, guys, listen, this is not the time and place for this stuff. I'm thrilled that you are both fans, I really am, but we have to get the fuck out of here."

Quieting down, Scalia now said, "Why would they send a boxer to come get me out of here?"

"Robert, because . . . I died a few seconds after you did. Please, there's a lot to explain, and I promise, when we have the time I'll tell you everything I know, but we have to go now. Trust me, everything depends on us getting *you* out of here."

Scalia was silent again, but now the woman standing in the ball and chain started to bang her closed fist against the glass before them.

"Open the fucking cell! Please, I don't belong here! Just open my fucking wall!"

Farrow put his hands up and showed his large palms to the woman as if he were a beaten man, someone in retreat.

"Okay, okay, just stay quiet and stop making so much noise."

As he finished the sentence and the woman stopped yelling for her freedom, all three of them noticed the glass floor beneath their feet bouncing, heavy with tremors.

Someone was coming.

"Fuck," Farrow said. "It sounds like the opposite direction from where I entered. We have to be fast."

Scalia huddled close to him; the two men were now directly in front of the woman's cell. Farrow pressed the pad of his index finger into the circular indentation; the shrieking whine again, thirty seconds and the glass partition was down and out of sight.

"Okay, let's be fast. Come on!"

The woman actually started to move forward before the cruel band, locked around her ankle, and chain connected to the iron ball stopped any progress. Her right leg was off the ground behind her, pulling the rusty links taut.

"Oh shit, my leg. I forgot about my leg. Farrow get this thing off me," she said.

The vibration on the glass floor intensified. Whoever it was, was getting close.

"Farrow, do something!" pleaded Scalia. "They can't see us standing out like this. They're going to figure something is up."

"I don't believe this. We should be halfway out of this loony bin by now. We're not supposed to get involved. I told you that."

Pointing to the woman, Farrow said, "Okay, get in there with her, curl yourself into a ball in the back corner, hug your knees and keep your eyes closed."

Scalia did as he was told. The woman put her chained, extended leg back onto the glass floor; her high-heeled shoe clicking as she did so. Next she retreated back to the center of the room standing in front of the writer. Farrow hurried into the cell that Scalia had occupied only moments earlier and sat on the ground hugging his own knees.

Whoever was approaching was almost upon them, just a few seconds away, but now, another disquieting sound overtook the progressing sound of heavy feet, a whining shriek. Both glass cell walls were sliding back up.

Before Farrow could stand, both ramparts were locked back in place, sealing the three souls within. Scalia and the woman sang out a chorus of "OH MY GOD!" and "OH NOOO!"

The two men looked at each other through the glass separating them from one another. The woman was crying, black mascara was leaking down her cheeks.

"Oh God, oh God. I'm so sorry. I'm so fucking sorry," she said, afraid to look at either of the two men. "This is my fault. I didn't mean for this . . . I'm so sorry."

"Listen," Farrow said. "Just be quiet, okay. Be quiet until they've gone. Let them do whatever it is they do and we'll figure this out."

He looked over at Scalia who had his head down between his knees again and noticed his body shaking. *He's crying*, Farrow thought.

The woman, silent now, walked over to the large iron ball, the chain attached to the metal band jangling as she did so, and sat down on top of it. She rested her arms on her knees, put her head down and stared at her long toes that were jammed out from the front part of her shoes.

Three of the faceless black and blue suits blurred passed the two cells that held Farrow, Scalia, and the woman. There appeared to be business at hand.

The marching and rattling vibrations stopped about a minute later, and the groaning hum of a cell wall retreating into the floor reverberated again. Screams of "Oh, God no!" "Help me!" and "Please save me!" assaulted the present hallway, swirling about and joining the muffled ones outside the glass holding structure. Someone's time was up.

"Everybody stay calm. Clear your mind and breathe easy. We got a big fight before us now. We're going into the ring soon. Slow your heart rate and we'll do just fine. Slow down until it's time for the speed and, brother, you got the speed."

Farrow spoke these words of wisdom out loud to Scalia and the woman, the way Johnny Laguna spoke them to him before each and every bout. Scalia slowly lifted his head and looked over at Farrow.

"I'm going to get you out of this place, I promise," Farrow said, and then smiled through the glass at the writer, while the woman just kept her head pointed down.

"OHHH MY GOD! AHHH! OH NOOOO, PLEASE NOOO!"

Shouts of absolute horror now filled the glass hallway outside the cells. Farrow, the woman, and Scalia all looked up to the front of their respective holding areas.

"PLEASE, I'LL DO ANYTHING! PLEASE, SOMEONE, HELP ME! IT HURTS, IT HURTS!!"

The floor tremors were gaining momentum again. Farrow concluded the black and blues would be passing by directly with their prisoner, getting him outside to begin whatever depraved eternity they had in store. Scalia looked at Farrow and then to the front cell wall.

They saw the man first. An overpowering, four-inch band of metal was clapped around his throat, smoking and red. It had been heated. A five-foot iron pole was attached in the rear, at the center of the man's neck, and held by two of the black and a blues, pushing the screaming man forward. His hands were tied behind his back and his ankles were lashed together with barbed wire, making walking impossible. He hopped and slid in unmitigated horror.

"SOMEONE, PLEASE! OH MY GOD!"

The third faceless suit, a black, followed close behind as if seeing a project to its fruition. The four bodies drummed along quickly, passing Farrow, Scalia, and the woman without so much as turning their heads. The man's screams faded with a bit of time and no one spoke to each other for the better part of five minutes.

When Farrow finally turned his head to the right, both Scalia and the woman were standing at the side glass wall dividing the two cells.

"Okay, Farrow, let's go. What do you got? How you gonna get us out of here?" The woman spoke quickly and with purpose. "I can't end up like that. Please, if you know how to get us out . . . let's do it now. I can't be tortured like that. My whole life was torture, I can't do it anymore."

Behind the woman, Scalia looked anxious, his eyes gave him away. *Come on, Farrow, I'm with you. Whatever you say, I'm with you. You want to leave the girl . . . that's fine, please let's just go.*

He stood slowly and faced the two souls. His face was expressionless.

"Back up a few feet," he said, a quiet tone to his voice. "It's time to leave."

Farrow reached into his right front pocket and produced something that looked, to Scalia and the woman, like a roll of quarters.

"I said back up a few feet."

They did. Farrow held his right hand out a bit to his side and applied a little pressure to the four-inch item he had concealed there. Instantly, three and a half feet grew from his enclosed fist, the tip glowed an almost blinding orange, smoke drifted off the length of the thing. Without having to repeat himself, Farrow saw Scalia and the woman back up even further in their small enclosure.

He held the long wand up like a baseball bat, looked Scalia in the eyes, and with a sly grin on his face said, "Nothing like a good piece of hickory."

Farrow swung the Hellstick into the glass wall. It went through like a heated knife going through butter. By the time he had completed the swing and brought the Hellstick back around his twisting body, he saw the glass spider-webbing and cracking. It stayed that way for a second or two before shattering and raining jagged shards between the two cells. Robert Scalia was actually jumping up and down clapping his hands.

Farrow pointed the still extended Hellstick to the ground and entered the adjoining cell looking at the woman.

"What's your name?"

"Cherry," she answered immediately, "Cherry Moore."

"That's your birth name?" he said smiling.

"No, oh I'm sorry, God no. It's Paula, Paula Yannicelli."

Farrow held out a big hand.

"Glad to meet you Paula Yannicelli." The two shook. "Now let's get that shackle off your leg and get the fuck out of here."

Scalia was at the bigger man's side in an instant.

"What do we have to do?"

"Okay," Farrow said, "bend down by Paula's ankle and pull the chain coming off that band . . . tight, I don't want to cut her foot. We may be dead and everything, but apparently we still can feel pain."

"Yeah, apparently," said Scalia, who was now holding the chain tight about eight links away from the band locked around Paula's slim ankle.

"Before I do this," Farrow started, "is there any way you can take your shoe off and slip that band from your leg, wiggle your foot out?"

"No chance," Paula said. "It's locked around my ankle too tight, nice and snug. I guess it's going to be with me for a while."

"Why are you even wearing that thing?" Farrow said.

"I kicked one of those fuckers in the blue suits right where his balls should be. Guess he didn't take too kindly to that," she said smiling. Farrow saw for the first time a beautiful smile. "When I'm cornered, I can fight, honey."

"Well, it's a good thing you're coming with us then. Okay, I'm going to cut the chain now. Hold still, I don't want you to lose a foot. Nice toes by the way," Farrow said looking at the purple nail polish and motioning to the front part of her shoe.

"Yeah, well, this guy once paid me $200.00 to suck my toes for a half hour; the world is full of freaks, but they pay well."

"Tell me about it."

Farrow gently brought the side of the Hellstick down on the old chain about three links from Paula's foot. It snapped instantly amidst a sizzling display of smoke and a powerful smell of sulfur. At once, she pulled her leg into her body finally free of the large iron ball but wearing a permanent ankle bracelet.

She thanked Farrow with a quick kiss on the cheek. "Wow, you can go a few rounds with me anytime," she said through a smile.

The prizefighter looked at her sideways, his eyes narrowed, and he gave her a slight nod.

"Okay, what next, Farrow?" Scalia said in a hurried voice.

Bringing his attention to the writer, "I want to cut the chain where it meets that iron ball," he said pointing to the round abomination before them. "That should be almost five feet of strong chain, and we're going to need it."

"Need it for what?" Scalia said.

"You'll see, just trust me. Once we are out of here, I'll tell you everything. I also have some questions for you."

"Ask away."

"Let's get out first. Once we're safe, there will be plenty of time for questions and answers."

"Farrow?" Paula said.

"Yeah?"

"I just wanted to thank you, you know for what you did for me, for taking me with you guys."

"Don't thank me," he said, "thank your friend over there." Pointing to Scalia, "He's the one convinced me, but we're glad to have you. Gives me something nice to look at in the middle of all this shit."

Paula smiled up at him, and Farrow heard Keith's voice floating in his head, "*Only two can come out*," and wondered if he had done the right thing.

After the section of chain was cut away from the ball, Farrow picked up the assembly of links with his free hand and held it out measuring it against his body. He estimated its length to be as he had guessed earlier, just about five feet or maybe a shade longer. In any case, it would be enough.

"Great, this should be good." Looking at his two new friends, "Robert, I'm going to need you to wrap this chain around your waist like a half-assed belt. Make a knot with it best you can in front and pull your shirt over it."

"But what if . . ."

"Please, just do it. We're going to need it. I promise you I have an idea."

Paula was sitting on the iron ball again rotating her ankle and inspecting the metal band that still graced it. The three links of chain hung down the right outside part of her foot and the band seemed to be a continuous piece without a hinge or keyhole. It was a problem she would attend to when they were safe; and if a new, irremovable ankle bracelet was the worst thing she had to endure, she guessed she could deal with it.

With the remaining piece of chain wrapped and secured around Scalia's slim waist, Farrow extended a hand and pulled Paula up from her sitting position.

"Okay, guys, I'm going to bust us out of here now," he said, still holding the Hellstick pointed at the floor. He could see someone, another prisoner, below him, looking up through the clear glass. "Just stand back from me as far as you can . . . and maybe shut your eyes in case any small pieces of glass or debris fly back at us."

Farrow held the Hellstick up like a baseball bat once again, smoke pouring from it now, feeding off the energy of this place. The smell of sulfur filled the cell.

"Hey, Robert," Farrow started, "have you ever been to Fenway Park?"

"Yeah, actually I was in Boston for a book signing, ya know like on tour, and this crazed fan gave me two tickets. Kerrie, that's my wife, and I went to the game, but the messed up thing was the fan had seats right next to the ones he'd given me. He and his girlfriend bothered us the whole time . . . through the whole game. He even brought with him some more books for me to sign."

"I know, the life of a celebrity right. Anyway, do you know that seat way in the outfield? The one painted red that Ted Williams hit on a long fly ball?" Farrow said.

"Sure, I have a photograph on the wall in my office of Kerrie and me sitting with that seat between us. We took it before the game started and not many people were in the stadium yet."

Farrow looked back at him and smiled before he swung the Hellstick at the glass wall. Both Scalia and Paula saw the muscles in his biceps and back ripple as he bent his arms and followed through with the swing, a repeat performance of his first time at bat minutes earlier. The results were the same.

After Farrow pulled the Hellstick from the horizontal slit he created in the glass wall, smoke pouring from its length, the smooth surface spider-webbed before breaking into a thousand sharp pieces bouncing at their feet with a glass-on-glass clinking sound. Their escape route was now wide open.

"Time to go, just keep your heads down and follow me," he said, taking charge at once, and for Scalia and Paula, that was just fine. They fell in behind the prizefighter.

It didn't take long to wend their way through the long hallways. Some of the residents were standing curiously at the front part of the glass walls, while others begged to be let out and join them.

"Now, when we get outside, we're going to walk as one. Stay close together, don't look at anybody or anything. It's about a half-mile walk to where we're going, and then things might get a bit tricky." Looking at

Scalia, "That chain you have wrapped around your waist is going to come in handy."

Next Farrow turned toward Paula who was clicking close behind in her four-inch 'fuck me' pumps.

"How long have you been here? Do you know when your twenty-four hours might expire? I heard you say before that your time was almost up. That's all they give you, you know, before they come. That time limit could come into play if we don't get through that first doorway I mentioned."

Their feet drummed and clicked on the glass floor as people screamed all around, inside and out. Distant red eyes continued to appear before them in spontaneous bursts, before receding back into the shadows. The unending black smoke continued to fill the sky above their heads.

"She was here before me," Scalia said. "When I woke up on the floor she was standing in her cell looking over at me."

"Yeah, I was here a while before him. If I had to guess I'd say almost a full day. That's why I panicked back there and got so out of control. I think my time might be up soon, real soon." She started to cry again. "You can't let them take me, Farrow. You have to get us out. I can't be tortured like that, I can't be here . . . forever."

"Paula, listen, you're with us now. Like Robert said earlier, three is better than two. As long as we can get up and out through the doorway before your time is up, I think we'll be alright. Just keep one thing in mind, though, it's Robert who is most important, not me and not you, *he's* the one we have to protect, we *both* have to protect."

"Hey, big guy," she said, calming down some. "You protect me, and we'll protect him. Deal?"

Farrow smiled down at her before he agreed.

"Deal."

"By the way, what doorway are you talking about?"

"Oh, you'll see," Farrow said.

A rectangular square of bright light now stood before them at the hallway's end, the exit from the holding area. Farrow stopped walking and put his arms out blocking Scalia and Paula from passing him.

"Okay, that's the exit. I'm not going to lie to you, it's pretty messed up out there. Just stay close and keep your eyes on the ground. Don't look at anyone. There's some fucked-up shit happening every few feet, and trust me it's nothing you're gonna wanna see. People might call to you and beg for help." Looking at Paula now with narrowed eyes, "But don't listen. If they're here, they're here for a reason."

Farrow dropped his arms.

Both Robert and Paula looked at the prizefighter and then each other before nodding their heads in understanding. All three slowly walked to the holding area exit and stepped through the doorway out into the light that consumed them at once, and completely.

It took a few seconds for their eyes to adjust. Robert and Paula pointed their heads down as they were told, but Farrow was gazing out over the gaseous landscape. He could see powerful sections of blue cutting through the black smoke above. The smell of burning flesh was still in evidence, just not as strong. Farrow expected an assault on his nostrils when they moved away from the holding area.

Even with the falling ash filling their line of vision, he could just about make out the doorway far off in the distance hanging in the air, outlined in electric light. Different though were the scenes of torture and degradation. They were gone, replaced by a new kind of insanity.

The faceless men in the black and blue suits stood in pairs huddled around terrified human souls whose naked bodies were sodden with perspiration, their wrists and ankles lashed together with wire. On the ground directly in front of them were dozens of gaping openings. Unlike the ones belching forth smog nearby, these openings, about three feet deep, had jaws and were filled with rows of razor-sharp teeth.

The souls were pulled along struggling against their bonds, and one by one shoved into the large carnivorous mouths. Eaten alive. As they were cut down, usually at the knees first, they sunk further, writhing into the gullets of whatever lay just below the cracked surface. Blood, in a crimson, rhythmic arc fountained from the chops, bathing the person next in line.

The screams of pain and terror were unlike anything Farrow or any of them had ever heard before.

"Okay, we're going now," Farrow said. "Stay close and hold on to one another, and for God's sake, don't take your eyes off the floor. You do not want to see what's going on here."

They quickly started walking, favoring the center of the cobblestone pathway, Farrow in front. Both Paula and Robert's bodies were quivering; the writer, holding onto Paula's elbow, had his eyes closed. The screams around them were incredible and almost insisted on a small peek, but taking Farrow's advice, neither did.

The punctures in the ground that weren't eating people continued to push out thick pollution that cannoned upwards, and the smell of human flesh cooking that was faint just seconds ago, once again became the dominant aroma in the air.

Scalia made an effort at conversation, an attempt to take his mind away from the horrors around them.

"Why are you here?" he said to Paula, his eyes still tightly shut. "What did you do to deserve all this?"

Neither he nor Farrow thought the girl would answer his question as she continued to walk next to him in a contemplative silence, but after a few seconds Paula started talking like she had known the two men for years.

"My mother left me when I was just a baby. You know the story, probably heard it a million times." She continued to look at the ground as she walked with ease in her high-heeled shoes, the sounds of terror spinning around them. "My father raped me every chance he got starting when I was nine years old." Her voice low, Paula wiped away tears and neither man said a word. "We needed money, and I knew how to fuck. Shit, my father said I was good at it, real good. So when I turned fifteen, he pulled me out of high school . . . did I mention I was on the track team? A great runner, the top in my squad, but that would have been a different life . . ."

She stopped speaking, almost as if searching for the right words to continue. "Once I was out of school, that's what I did, sold my body to any scumbag that wanted it, and believe me there were plenty. We had no choice, we were broke. I used the name Cherry Moore, that's how people knew me on the street. They'd come for a piece of Cherry's pie."

The trio kept moving at a quick pace, the depravity around them was unrelenting. The enormous jaws in the ground continued to chomp open and closed on the unwilling human souls.

Red mist sprayed and colored the air in obscene, explosive currents.

"My father never had a real job," she continued, "he just sat back while I worked on mine. He'd help himself to a piece of my ass anytime he wanted it. The man was a pig, a disgusting alcoholic. He died from liver failure just before I turned twenty-eight and, believe me, I was glad to see him go." Paula was openly crying now, the sounds she made fit right in with everything going on around them. "But then there was this man, a pimp, his name was Donell Mosley. He took me under his wing, and you probably heard this story, too. He beat me and kept a large percentage of my earnings. It took almost three years before I had enough of his abuse. This one night he was actually whipping me with a belt. Welts were rising from my body, these long angry-looking marks . . . he didn't stop swinging until I was crying . . . cowering on the floor like a child. The asshole enjoyed doing it . . . the fucking sadist. So that night I killed him. I slit his throat with a box cutter while he slept."

She paused for a second trying to find the right words before finishing her story. "But as it turns out there was someone else in the bedroom I hadn't seen, someone with a gun. There was a bright flash and a loud echoing bang. Next thing I know, I wake up here surrounded by those assholes in the suits. I started fighting and kicking immediately, earning myself the excessive, if not sexy, ankle jewelry. So, to answer your question, Robert, I'm here for murder."

"Doesn't that count as self-defense?" Farrow said. "I know he was asleep and everything, but you were trying to prevent yourself from getting beat . . . prevent him from hurting you anymore."

"You would think so," Paula said, "but I guess whoever is in charge of this stuff felt differently. So here I am in hell." She was crying again. The black makeup around her eyes was an absolute mess, and her lipstick had long faded. "I don't belong here, please get me away. Take me with you."

"We're gonna do our best," Farrow said, as he stopped walking and held his arms out slightly to his sides preventing the rest of his party from moving onward any further.

"That's it, we're here," he said. "We're through the worst of it anyway. If your eyes are closed you can open them now, but only look up," he was pointing into the air. "That's where we're going. That's our way out."

Robert, his eyes now open, and Paula were amazed to see an electric-lined doorway that was actually more of a crude hole cut in the air hanging about twelve feet above the surface on which they stood.

"That's where I came from. There used to be a staircase, but as soon as I reached the ground it crumbled behind me and dissolved when this floating ash touched it," he said motioning to the black snow littering the air around them.

Neither Robert nor Paula spoke; they both seemed to be deep in thought, maybe deciding whether or not they would go mad and just run back the way they had come.

"How . . . how are we going to get up there? Even if . . . even if you lift both of us, we can't reach down to pull you up. You'd be too far below, and . . . and probably too heavy," Robert said, stuttering to a smiling Farrow.

"That's why I had you bring the chain my friend," he said tapping the writer's stomach, feeling the tangled metal bulge waiting to be set loose.

"Of course, the chain, the one from my leg," Paula said looking down at the band locked snuggly around her ankle. "It could work, if you lifted us both up to the doorway, we could lower the chain and pull you up. With both of us . . . we could do it, I bet we could do it!" Excitement was now growing in her voice.

"That's the plan I had, and I think it'll work, but Robert goes up first."

"Why, for the love of Hemingway's ghost, should I go?" His voice getting back to normal now, "Haven't you ever heard of 'ladies first', Farrow? Paula should get to safety before either of us; didn't you listen to her earlier? Her time is almost up."

"Listen, Robert, I don't have time to argue, you're going first. You're most important. Paula and I have already agreed to that. We'll be quick, I promise. We're not the ones that are going to save the world, you are."

"Another thing, what do you mean by that? How am I going to save the world? You said you would answer all my questions, now I want to know . . ."

"Robert, please," Paula speaking now, "listen to Farrow, okay? He's gotten us this far. He keeps telling you to trust him . . . so shut the fuck up. Keep your damn mouth closed and trust him."

Scalia put his eyes back on the ground.

"Okay, I'm sorry . . . it's just that . . . sorry. What do you want me to do?"

"Simple," Farrow said clapping his big hands together and rubbing them back and forth. "You're going to get on my shoulders and stand up. I'll push you up to the doorway and you're going to climb through, then I'll repeat the process with Paula. When you are both safe, lower the chain down and pull me up. Once on the other side of that thing we should have a few minutes to spare, and I'll answer all your questions . . . okay?"

"Yeah, sure," Scalia said in an agreeable voice. "Let's do this . . . fast."

It only took a few seconds to lift the writer until he was in a standing position on Farrow's shoulders. Reaching, Scalia was actually able to rest the palms of his hands on the ground surface inside the ripped doorway above. The prizefighter took his hold from Scalia's ankles and put his hands under the soles of his feet and straightening his long arms, pushed him upward.

"Pull yourself in," Farrow said, his voice a bit louder than he wanted it to be.

They saw Robert's legs kicking in the air as he fed himself through the doorway, and then a quick glimpse of his ass crawling before he quickly turned around and poked his head back out from a seemingly different dimension of hell.

"What do you see?" Paula said.

"There's no one up here. It's quiet, nobody is screaming, just some of those holes blowing black smoke, a lot smaller though. There's a cobblestone pathway, too, like the one down there." He was pointing his finger past them, "But it's not as well kept." He said, smiling now, "Guess there's no gardeners up here, no one with sharp tools anyway, thank God."

"Robert," Farrow said, speaking up to him, "I'm going to toss you the Hellstick, try to . . ."

"What's a Hellstick?"

"It's the thing that rescued us before, remember the roll of quarters that extended into a . . ."

"Of course I remember, just didn't know it was called a Hellstick. Kind of silly, don't you think?"

"Yes, it's very silly, very James Bondish, but that's what it's called. I didn't name it. Someday if you meet John and Keith you could complain to them about it.

"Get ready," Farrow said. "Here it comes."

He tossed the small item up through the doorway and Scalia caught it on the first try accompanied by a huge smile. He then placed the item on the ground just to the right of the doorway.

"Whatever you do, don't squeeze it. When that thing opens it can cause a fuck of a lot of damage. It will cut down and slice through anything."

The climate seemed to get a bit hotter around them and a shrieking wail pierced the air. Farrow and Paula brought their hands up to cover their ears. Above, Scalia seemed unaffected.

"What's going on?" Paula said, absolute terror flooding into her eyes.

Farrow turned around to see no less than thirty faceless demons in black and blue suits pouring toward them like the tide at a beach, lined up in a semi-circle and closing fast. The mouths on the ground seemed to have disappeared, as well as any and all scenes of torture. Now there were only the suits.

"Fuck! Fuck! Fuck!"

"What's happening?" Paula shouted.

"I think your twenty-four hours are up."

"Oh God! Oh, my God! No, it can't be! Just a few more minutes, it can't be!" Her eyes were frantic, searching back and forth along the line of approaching faceless suits. They were all holding something: rope, wire, chains. They came on strong and in force, all to play with Paula.

"Take your shoes off, quick! Get on my shoulders!" Farrow yelled at her.

Paula wiggled out of her high heels and started to climb with a rushed fury onto Farrow's back.

"Come on, hurry . . . hurry! Stand up! Reach up to Robert. Stand on my shoulders!"

Scalia, now well aware of what was going on, what was happening, was reaching down, stretching his arms and extending his fingers out to Paula. The look on her face was that of a thousand nightmares from which one could not wake.

"Paula, grab my hand, reach up a bit! Quick!" She attempted to go on tiptoe, standing on Farrow's shoulders, her long toes digging into the fighter's muscles. For just a second her fingers brushed against Robert's, and then all was lost. In her haste, Paula fell backward landing on the ground behind Farrow, next to her discarded shoes.

From above, Robert watched in terror as the semi-circle of black and blues tightened around them like a noose.

"Robert," Farrow, now in a fighter's stance, was yelling up at him, "take the path through the graveyard and find the cave beyond the white tree."

The first suit to reach Farrow crumpled under his blow, a powerful shot to the faceless face. The demon went down hard. Now there were two more suits on him and Farrow took them both down, a single blow each, an uppercut and a roundhouse. He remembered the Spitfire, if any situation called for the Spitfire this would be it. He dug his hand into his front pocket, his fingers searching frantically.

The little pill-shaped item was not there.

"Damn! Damn!"

Now both hands were searching all of his pockets.

Where is it? Where the fuck is it? Must have dropped it somewhere! Fuck me!

In horror, Robert saw Paula on her back being dragged away by the links of chain still attached to the band around her ankle, she was screaming and flailing her arms.

"Robert, get to the cave! Follow it to the end, you have to make it out, everything depends on it! You have to make it out! Just beyond the white tree!" Farrow was screaming up at him now and throwing blind punches. "Everything depends on you, Robert . . . everything depends . . ."

And then like an army of red ants covering a piece of meat slathered in syrup, they were all over him. Scalia could no longer see the prizefighter. He was gone, covered in a mound of black and blue suits, and the soundtrack to this main event was that of Paula screeching as she was dragged away to be tortured for eternity.

For just a second within his head, Scalia thought he heard a little girl laughing, a terrible high-pitched cackle that chilled him and filled his body with a dread so deep he himself started to scream.

111

ROUND EIGHT

It's actually quite funny how the mind works . . . depending that is, on the particular situation at hand. Negotiating right and wrong or perhaps just turning north or south on a dark, barely moonlit road with the windswept rain pinging off your automobile's hood can have many different outcomes.

One path, or slick paved road, can lead to a skidding accident. While the opposite direction may produce a rain-soaked hitchhiker, so grateful for the ride that she agrees to dinner the very next evening and you eventually marry her.

Life, as well as death, is full of decisions, subtle choices, and an assortment of final actions that could harvest the conclusive aftermath.

The crazy shit you think of at times like this.

Robert Scalia, on his hands and knees, slowly drew back from his peek hole twelve feet above the madness below. His head and the front part of his body quietly slipped deeper into the rectangular portal in the air, orange and blue electricity sizzling around its perimeter.

Nothing on the ground beneath seemed to be paying him any mind. His heart was rapid firing, punching through his chest as he sucked in small quick breaths that filled his lungs momentarily before expelling the air back out. His eyes were bulging.

His first instinct, the thing his mind told him to do, commanded him to do, was retreat, get away, hide. This thought, this decision was paramount.

"Oh God. Oh no. Oh God. Oh no. Oh no."

For a writer, Scalia had a way with words.

Now in a sitting position, he pushed his butt off the cobblestones and kicked both legs in and out before his body, crab walking backward away from the ripped doorway. The black ash cascaded down in turmolic swirls concealed within its edges, darkening, as the electric-lined rectangle grew smaller in his vision.

When he was a good distance away, maybe twenty feet, he stopped and without realizing it pulled his knees into his chin while cradling them with his arms and started to cry.

He could still hear Paula screaming. *They had dragged her by a single ankle, probably were still dragging her.* In his mind, he could hear Farrow's commands. Farrow yelling up to him.

"Take the path through the graveyard . . . Get to the cave . . . Go past the white tree . . . You have to make it out . . . Everything depends on you."

What did all that mean? Why am I so important?

He had never gotten a chance to ask. Well, had never gotten an answer. Lifting his head he saw the thing that Farrow had called a Hellstick laying on the ground just to the right of the floating doorway. At least he had that; all the prizefighter had done was squeeze it to produce the vicious electric sword. If he were going to make it out of here he would have to retrieve the weapon, and he planned to do so. He was no fighter; he would need something to protect himself.

His friends, if that's what he could call them, were gone now. He was on his own.

The fighter came for you, he got you out of there. You can't leave him . . . or the girl.

He could only imagine what horrors were in store for them. This thinking he knew was irrational. He was safe. He made it out. It was Robert Scalia who was meant to escape, not them. It all depended on him, that's what Farrow had said. He had to survive.

What depended on me?

Farrow was just a prizefighter . . . and the girl a hooker. Farrow himself had said that Paula belonged here . . . was here for a reason, wasn't that what he had said?

But he rescued you. They both rescued you. Paula had originally told Farrow how to open the cells before he did it 'action-hero style'.

Scalia stared at the electric vibrations that framed the doorway down to hell's lower level, hell's worst level. Sitting silently on the pathway he looked around himself. The view above was open and clean. Endless.

There were no trees in the distance not to mention any snow-capped mountains or picturesque scenery. The sky had been washed in dark purple and stars seemed about ready to pop at any moment. The black smoke firing up from the small ground holes continued, but there was no smell of burning flesh, they seemed harmless and the smoke dispersed before it got too high. Aside from a slight hint of sulfur, things were pretty okay.

Scalia tried to form a coherent line of thinking, piece together the things Farrow had been yelling up at him amidst the bedlam. He was supposed to travel through a graveyard . . . *Great,* he thought . . . cross a field with a tree in it, a white tree, and then head for a cave. Sounded easy enough, plus he'd have the Hellstick.

He would be just like the sword-carrying vigilante, Martin D'Cutta, who inhabited the three published novels he had penned. Scalia was not a brave man, but with a weapon, not unlike the one his literary creation carried around below a dark trench coat, maybe, just maybe, he could walk proud for once in his life and be something more than the coward he knew he was. If he could light up that sword thing, the Hellstick, or whatever it was, he could become Martin D'Cutta.

You have to go back for them. You can't leave them.

That was nonsense. Farrow had done what he was supposed to do. He got him out and gave him directions. He knew the risks.

"I'm here to take you out. We're leaving together. A lot more than just our lives depend on it." That's what Farrow had said to him.

Leaving together.

Scalia brought his eyes down to the spot just to the right of the doorway; they fell upon the waiting Hellstick. He would grab the item and go. He didn't owe Farrow or the hooker anything. His eyes began tearing again. He would save himself.

Together.

A triangle of light from the doorway's rim covered the Hellstick in a spectral tinge marking the weapon for easy retrieval.

The fighter saved your soul.

Scalia brought his hands to his waist. The length of chain Farrow had protected there was still with him, secure and intact. He remembered that chain was once attached to a large metal ball locked to Paula's ankle; he wondered even now what they were doing to her? He started to shake as a fevered hot flash slowly worked its way over his body.

Scalia stood and looked around himself again. Everything was quiet. The cobblestone path led in an upward direction from his current position before leveling out.

He walked to the doorway, sure to stay clear of its center favoring the right side of the rectangular tear before him. He quickly retrieved the Hellstick, scooping it up with a fast, one-handed motion. He secured it in the right back pocket of his jeans.

Standing that close to the doorway, he thought he could still hear people screaming from below and, for just a second, a hint of burning flesh reached his nostrils. He moved quickly back to his position of about twenty feet away. A position he felt was a safe one.

Scalia's heartbeat and breathing rhythms were now back to somewhere around normal. He closed his left hand on the chain around his waist working his fingers around the links and gripping tightly. It felt good and strong and, he realized, could also be used as a weapon if needed. He brushed several fingers against the Hellstick in his rear pocket. It was still there and he could sense its power, feel it through his jeans.

He was locked and loaded. He created Martin D'Cutta and now he would become him. He would no longer be a coward or be afraid. He would finish this little journey alone. *The pen wasn't mightier than the sword; the sword will fuck you up.* The latter part his fictional hero's tag line. It was something Martin D'Cutta said before he killed a bad guy, almost like Bruce Willis' "Yippee-ki-yay, motherfucker!" from the *Die Hard* movies.

D'Cutta would go back for his friends, not leave them.

He shook this thought away. He couldn't go back anyway, he didn't know where they had been taken. Almost as if on cue, he felt a pull from the center of his body, a heated, grasping feeling, and knew at once he was connected to the boxer, and if he wanted to find him, he could.

Hellstick or not, he wasn't a fighter; he wasn't built to rescue and save. He was no Martin D'Cutta, why even try to fool himself. Robert Scalia was a coward; deep down he knew this. He looked out for number one, and maybe Kerrie. He had to save himself, Farrow had said so, had yelled it up to him. He was the one who had to come out of this thing on top.

They saved you, your soul. They both saved you. They put you before themselves. You have to go for them.

Scalia faced the doorway. It stood out black and rectangular, framed against the twilight. He turned his back and took a single step away from the portal. He paused for a moment.

They saved you.

He took another slow, deliberate step on the stone pathway, before graduating his pace to a full-out walk. His once warm blood was now chilling in his veins.

Robert Scalia did not see the white circular section of sky open behind him, high up and distant. If he did, he would have been reminded of the moon just as Farrow was earlier. No, he didn't see the so-called moon bearing down on him, nor did he see it blink just a single time, but open and close it did, just like the shutter behind a camera's lens . . . or a giant watching eye.

Scalia decidedly came to the conclusion with sudden resolution that it would be best for everyone if he saved himself. No need to screw up some half-assed rescue attempt. There was no need for them all to be stuck in this place for eternity. Tortured forever. After all, he was the important one.

He felt a pull from the center of his chest again, almost like a hand grabbing and trying to hold him back. His eyes brimming with tears, he elected to ignore the sensation.

It's actually quite funny how the mind works . . . depending that is, on the particular situation at hand.

When Robert Scalia was eight years old, he and his parents lived on the first floor of a two-family apartment building in Queens, New York. The building, an old brownstone construction with four windows as bright as watchful eyes, two on the top and two on the bottom, was nestled comfortably on the street corner standing tall and proud. Across from his family's apartment, contained by rusty metal fencing and running the length of the block and beyond, was a graveyard that Robert had vowed never to venture into, especially after dark.

Frank Duran, a friend born out of convenience more than anything else, lived in the residence upstairs from the Scalia family along with a sister and his parents. Frank was a year younger than Robert, but a bigger boy. The two often played on the black tar rooftop where, after a good rain, water would pool and reflect the sun off its smooth surface.

On a Saturday morning in mid-summer, Robert's parents, Nancy, a stay-at-home mom, and his father Michael, a firefighter, were having breakfast together. Robert, who had eaten earlier, was up on the roof playing with Frank.

A firefighter worked rotating tours, so when the opportunity for some time together showed itself, the two took advantage.

Michael would die in a chemical explosion in the line of duty along with six other firemen in just over seven years, but no one knew this then.

Nancy had prepared a feast indeed: pancakes, bacon, eggs, sausage, and toast slathered with butter. A steaming cup of coffee sat before each of them. Light washed in from the kitchen window announcing what a magnificent day it would be while the other of the two windows, the one that shone into their bedroom, still had the shade pulled down.

The conversation during the morning's meal was the same subject as always, the future: a much bigger house somewhere out on Long Island where Robert would go to school, all the friends he would make, and how Michael's commute would not be so bad. The two felt very comfortable talking about these things and about the life they had as well as the one they would make, the better one, for them and for Robert.

Breakfast was nearly finished; it was just before the clean-up stage where Michael would take over the reins and let Nancy relax a bit before the two, along with Robert, got on with the day's events. There was a trip to a nearby park planned and maybe a late afternoon movie.

The morning was shattered when Michael and Nancy heard the screams coming from the floor above, except maybe a little further away, like from the roof. It was Robert. The two dropped everything and raced to the stairwell and proceeded upward at a fast pace. The screams continued and grew louder the closer they got to the source. Frank's mother, Christine, joined them on the staircase in pursuit of the noises.

Michael was in the lead and all but kicked open the heavy door that would let them out onto the roof. He took charge protecting the people behind him and would be first to see whatever it was beyond the door between them and the unknown.

When the three adults burst onto the top level of the apartment building, the sight they saw was something much different from what any of them had imagined.

No one was hanging off the roof's edge, no one was bleeding or had been stabbed, but for Robert Scalia, in a sense, what was happening, was much worse.

Frank Duran was lying on top of him. The two boys were fighting; well, the word fighting would be an overstatement. Frank was fighting. The bigger boy was all arms and legs. Punching, swinging, and kicking. Robert lay cowering, trying to cover himself from the onslaught of blows. The smaller boy screamed as if his arms were being pulled from their very sockets.

Both women, Nancy and Christine, brought hands up to cover their mouths, as Michael attempted to break the two children apart, repeating the single word "Boys!"

The one-sided rumble continued for a moment allowing Michael to realize that his son was not fighting at all, not even trying to defend himself. He was taken aback. A sick, embarrassed feeling filled his body, a combination of anger, pity, and disgust. The word pussy seeped into his mind, and not wanting to, directed it at his son.

After another minute or two of struggling with the boys, all three parents finally got them untangled. Christine Duran apologized for her son's behavior several times before pulling the bigger boy through the doorway by an arm and down the stairwell.

Robert slowly got to his feet crying uncontrollably with his arms outstretched in search of his mother for a hug, anticipating immediate reciprocation. Michael held out a single arm between the two blocking the act of affection from occurring, and instead spun the boy around and smacked him several times on the backside, hard. His father's voice could be heard a block over yelling at the boy.

"If someone hits you, if someone fights you and wants to hurt you, you fight back. You stand up for yourself!"

The spanking from his father and the punishment that followed, a day confined to his small bedroom, confused the boy. His father had never taught him how to fight or defend himself, nor did he attempt to over the next eighty-four months before the chemical explosion.

It was this single incident that Robert Scalia had always traced back to his cowardice and the reason he shied away from situations and confrontations. If things had gone differently that day, maybe if he had stood up for himself, or at least tried to, he might have grown into another kind of man, a different person, a better one. Instead, he developed a sense of humor, did very well in school and college, and became a writer; a career he absolutely loved.

In time, he created the character Martin D'Cutta, someone he wished he were more like, but D'Cutta was a fictitious hero; Robert Scalia remained a coward for real.

Unlike the glass structure where Scalia was held earlier along with thousands of other souls waiting for their handpicked fates, Farrow and Paula were being kept together. Detained in the same space. The room was underground and had only a single glass wall, the other three were made from old dungeon stones, thick unforgiving blocks, dry and filthy.

Paula would be tortured and Farrow would be made to watch.

The prizefighter stood with his hands tied behind his back to a section of the right wall. His wrists, lashed together with a piece of cord, were attached to a large iron ring that was embedded deeply into the stone. He was able to shuffle from one foot to the other and move a few inches forward, but that was all his bonds would allow. The invisible hand wraps around his clenched fists were useless to him. He pulled at the iron ring, his muscles contorting, but the menacing iron circle would not budge.

Continuous back-kicks did not give Farrow enough leverage or power to weaken or pull the solid ring from its cemented station on the wall. Time had passed, he didn't know how much for he could not see the digital display on his wrist, but was sure that soon enough, it would no longer be in his favor. There was still a three-hour trek back to the Hellmouth and, right now, he wasn't going anywhere. Scalia had to make it, he willed him to make it.

With the exception of the uncomfortable position Farrow was left standing in, he was basically unharmed. Paula, who shared the small room, was another story altogether. Her twenty-four hours had expired and she was fair game. She would now be made to experience the full vehemence of hell; all its attentions could be directed upon her and whatever depraved eternity waited.

The position she was left in was one for the books, it made Farrow's tight stance seem like a Hawaiian vacation in comparison. The position was made to hurt, cause humiliation and absolute agony and, from the look in Paula's eyes, Farrow thought, it was succeeding on all levels.

Scalia stopped dead in his tracks from a slow jog when the large gravestone rose in the path before him. The sky was now a deep bluish swirl with hints of fading purple and a daub of yellow and orange. There was still enough brightness to clearly see everything in his surrounding area, he was just not sure he wanted to. The object that was seemingly a full moon, looming and fat at Scalia's rear, was no longer in evidence, gone from its post up high.

He bent down in a squatting stance, his forearms resting on his knees as he drew huge gulps of air into his lungs. *How could I be out of breath so easily? How could my soul be sucking wind like this?* Being dead was just like being alive; you apparently felt the same sensations.

After a few moments he stood up as his breathing calmed down some. He placed the palm of one hand on the large flat stone before him to steady himself. The marker was cool in temperature, the contact made him feel not so alone.

It stood about four feet tall and had flat sides with a semi-circular top. He recognized it right away to be a grave marker, although larger sized than the ones that crowded countless cemeteries he had seen throughout his life.

He thought of the old, two-family apartment building of his youth.

He removed his hand from the large stone and took a silent step backward. Beyond, he could see other gravestones, normal-sized, peeking up from a thick white ground mist that covered the area. The markers closest to him seemed to be placed haphazardly, sporadically. Looking beyond these, the gravestones gathered in abundance as his eyes traced the cobblestone path into the cemetery and the mist, before it disappeared completely.

The sky darkened, but Scalia could still see everything. He listened and thought he could hear a thin wind passing around the gravestones and burrowing under the blanket of mist.

Farrow rescued you; both he and the girl had a hand in getting you out of there. You left them.

"Hey, every man for himself, right?" He spoke out loud, his voice small and far away in the open space.

Farrow practically commanded me to run . . . to get out. Scalia's mind was working now, thinking and doubting his decisions. Left or right? East or west?

They were dragging Paula by her ankle, she was screaming.

Scalia touched the belted chain around his waist.

They covered Farrow like syrup over pancakes.

The Hellstick in his back pocket hummed.

"Cut the shit, Robbie!" he shouted to himself, using the nickname Kerrie was fond of. It was time to go before the light ran out altogether. The last thing this writer wanted was to be stuck parading through a graveyard in hell with limited vision.

Robert Scalia collected himself, took a deep breath and stepped around the large gravestone that was blocking the path, kicking with his left foot what seemed to be a small mallet. The tool had a four-inch wooden handle with a large iron head. Next to that, he also saw, was an eight-inch chisel . . . or some kind of metal spike.

He spoke aloud again. "What is this stuff doing here?"

Almost as if on cue, Scalia looked up at the face of the large grave marker and read what was freshly cut into its smooth surface.

Paula lay on her stomach four feet off the floor upon a small stainless steel table in front of Farrow. She was facing him about three feet away, just beyond his reach. Outside the room, two faceless sentries, one wearing a black suit and the other dressed in blue, stood guard, unmoving, with their backs to the prisoners.

Because of Farrow's height, he had an absolutely perfect view, looking down onto Paula and what she was being forced to endure.

Her wrists were crudely lashed behind her back with enough wire to hold two women her size. The metal band that was until recently locked around her ankle, had been removed. Now both ankles were tightly tied together with the same wire that bound her wrists. The wire was wrapped around her ankles, vertically first and then horizontally through her bare feet and pulled tight, jamming them together as one. Next the wire led from her ankles and was snaked through her bound wrists and connected to a thick wire noose that was secured around her slim neck. The whole package was pulled together tightly so that the curling soles of Paula's feet were just about touching the back of her head. Her wrists being held in place at the small of her back were useless. An evil hogtie with virtually no play in the length of wire. If she tried to straighten her legs that were bending back to her head, even a little bit, the wire noose circling her neck would tighten as needed, first strangling her, before slowly cutting into the flesh in her throat and sawing her head off.

Paula was being pulled back into an upward position so that her pleading, begging eyes were locked on Farrow's, who stood just a few feet away helpless. Her body was arched in such a way, such an impossible position, that he didn't see how she could last much longer. Her terrified expression spoke to him, though she said nothing, only made rasping and choking sounds.

Farrow could see the filthy bottoms of her bare feet shaking and straining, arching forward to stay as close to the back of her head as possible. A battle she was losing. Her face was a dark, bursting crimson, and Farrow thought he could maybe see a thin red line of blood starting to circle the top of the wire that was now almost assuredly cutting into her neck.

The prizefighter balled his hands into murderous fists and pulled furiously at the iron ring holding his hands in place behind his back.

"Motherfucker! Son of a bitch!" he yelled out into the room, while he kicked the wall behind him, 220 pounds of blunt force. He thought he felt it vibrate slightly, but only in a mocking fashion.

Scalia put a single hand to his mouth as he read the epitaph that was carved into and across the stone's surface.

A fighter came to rescue a writer
and take him out of hell.
The writer ran, a cowardly man
now for both, the toll of the bell.

Without realizing it, Scalia's hand had found its way to his back pocket, his fingers brushing against the concealed Hellstick.

The sword will fuck you up, he thought.

When he read what was written under the little poem he actually reached in and grasped the deadly item, his breath quickening again.

Kerrie Scalia
1990-2013
Suicide

My God. Suicide. Oh, my God.

He remembered a scene from the film *The Exorcist.* The older priest telling the younger one not to listen to the demon, that it would mix lies with the truth. Was that what was happening here? Scalia's heart was racing.

What could he do? What should he do? What would Martin D'Cutta do? Didn't Scalia himself tell Farrow earlier that there was strength in numbers when he was trying to convince him to rescue Paula? He had to go back and get them. He knew this now. How could he have not known this all along? What kind of man was he? It wouldn't be right to leave them; it was never right to leave them. He had to at least try. Alone he knew he was dead. He would stay dead. The mocking poem all but told him so, but now Kerrie's life was at stake also. How could he have been so stupid?

Be a man, he tried to reason with himself, *for once in your life, be a man. No more hiding behind the written word. Become Martin D'Cutta, or as the street thugs and villains in your novels referred to him as Martin the Cutter. Go get your friends. Yes, they are your friends, and save your wife.*

Robert Scalia left the Hellstick safe in his rear pocket, and instead bent down to pick up the mallet and the eight-inch metal spike on the ground before him. He held the two items in his right hand and brushed the chain around his waist with his left, it was still there waiting to finally play a part in the day's events.

The beginning of an idea formed in his mind. He outlined it like a scene from one of his novels, and actually thought it could work. He categorized the things he knew for sure and sifted through and shifted them.

There was that pulling sensation within his stomach, Farrow's soul pulling his. It's how he would find him . . . or them. If Paula was not with the prizefighter, he would know or at least have an idea where she might be. He silently went over the rest of his plan; it was almost like a rescue scene three-quarters of the way through a good book.

It could work.

Scalia felt different. For the first time in his life he refused to be scared. He would not let that emotion devour him here, because if he did, then hell had already won the battle. He would fight for the first time in his life. He had stayed under the radar long enough, hiding behind jokes and the written word, buried in chapters and prose. Robert Scalia was finally going to fight for something, for his friends, for his wife, and for his soul.

He turned around and faced the cobblestone pathway that dropped away from him back in the direction of the portal leading further into hell. A sensation of anger washed over his body. He felt alive for the first time in his life . . . well, death. A strong jerk within the core of his stomach pulled him a step forward; it was Farrow, he knew.

"I'm coming, prizefighter. Coming to repay the favor. I'm coming to get you out of here. We're leaving together. You, me, and Paula."

Scalia, with his shoulders thrown back, stood tall and started to jog down the pathway. The smell of sulfur that he didn't notice a moment ago seemed a bit stronger now as the sky continued to darken.

"Motherfucker!"

Farrow continued to back-kick the wall, his heavy boots not making so much as a chip in the thick concrete. His bound wrists continued to pull at the metal ring keeping his hands in place behind his back. It wouldn't budge an inch. He was strong, but the unyielding metal circle was stronger. He pointed his head up and yelled, "John? Keith? Can you hear me? You guys said I could ask for stuff that I really, really need."

Silence.

"I need my hands untied. I need to get free. They're killing her."

Silence.

"Are you fucking there?" Farrow's head swung back and forth from left to right. "Oh, fuck! Come on, guys. Help me! Fucking, help her!"

Paula's face was puffed and swollen now, its color graduated from tomato orange to a bruised purple and her tongue was peeking out from the corner of her mouth. Her bent back legs were quivering furiously but continued to hold their position. The soles of her feet were just inches from the back of her upturned head. Her pleading, begging eyes, filmed with tears, were still locked on Farrow's.

He could see veins ripe and bursting blue, mapping through the skin on the tops of her feet due to the lack of blood flow. The single thick vein up the side of her confined neck seemed ready to explode and spray the room in a stream of crimson.

The prizefighter saw the first hints of defeat, the first hints of giving up in her eyes now. *It wouldn't be long,* he thought, *before her legs could no longer hold that position and straighten out some. The wire would cut into her neck and eventually slice off her head. What then?* he wondered. *Would her head grow back or be reattached to her neck, only to have the whole experience repeat again and again?* He thought probably yes, from what he had seen so far, the incredible acts of perversion he had witnessed; he thought that's exactly what would happen.

Farrow saw Paula trying to move her fingers and her pinioned hands some; she opened and closed them making small helpless fists. She continued to curl her feet forward and her neck back. She was strong and determined. A quality he could identify with, one he admired.

"Hang on, honey, this is all a bad dream. We're both going to wake up any minute now, wake up and get out of bed. We're going to be okay." He tried to keep his voice at a calm level, but after he said those few sentences to her, even he didn't believe his own words.

"John! Keith! I need you now! I need you right now!"

It took Scalia maybe six minutes to get within sight of the portal that acted as a passage down to the main stage of hell. He easily spotted its electric-infused outline standing out amongst the recently blackened night sky.

He held the mallet in his right hand and the metal chisel in the other. His hold on both items was firm. When he got within five feet of the doorway, Scalia dropped to his knees and proceeded to crawl, still holding the tools in his bunched fists.

When he was just about a foot away, he tossed the mallet and the chisel to the right of the doorway where the Hellstick had waited earlier, and flattened out onto his stomach. The cobblestones felt cool and his heartbeat sped up a bit.

The writer inched forward very slowly, digging the tips of his sneakers into the grooves between the stones. The smell of sulfur, and now death, thickened, and Scalia realized his eyes were closed.

He could sense an open space before him and knew with just a quick flick of his eyelids he would soon be looking down onto the mayhem he had fled from earlier. He stayed like this for a moment before taking in a single deep breath, and then Robert Scalia opened his eyes.

The location, twelve feet hanging in the air was the same, but the view, the things he was looking down upon, were different from before, much different.

Scalia was not only looking out onto a barren city street, but an entire metropolis that went on for as far as he could see. The towering buildings and brick structures closest to him seemed familiar, but nothing stood out as an exact replication. It almost resembled Manhattan, but without the trademark staples, no Chrysler building or Empire State standing proudly along the skyline.

In this city, or facsimile of one, Armageddon had recently been played out. The recurring color was a thick, smoky gray. Heavy ash covered everything in a powdery mist. Buildings were cracked amongst turning clouds of fog, and, in some instances, lying completely across intersections. Small fires danced among the profusion of abandoned cars throughout the quiet roads. Smoke spiraled up from manhole covers and the sky was filled with pollution that thrived with a spectral illumination.

Scalia slowly looked around this horrific interpretation of a nuclear war, or he assumed that was what it was supposed to be. He was wide-eyed and holding a scream just inside his throat. Where were all the people and the instruments of torture? Where were the screams and the faceless assholes in designer clothes? He listened. Aside from what appeared to be the sound of wind moving around crumbled buildings and creeping along the burned, ash-covered streets, he heard nothing. The smell of death and now a hint of feces were overpowering, though.

A sense of doom crept into his body. *So this is what the end of the world will look like, the end of everything.* Scalia thought about retreating again, running back to the cemetery, returning to his non-hero persona, back to the coward he knew he was. He would find the cave and the way out of this shit hole. Screw everybody else. A small needling voice somewhere deep in his subconscious stopped this line of thinking in its tracks, a voice that was firm and dominating. It was the voice of Martin D'Cutta, and in a tone just above a whisper it said: "The sword will fuck you up," and that was all it said, but it was enough.

Scalia pulled himself together. He was done being afraid. He would not abandon his friends; he would see this through, one way or another. He touched the Hellstick that still waited in his back pocket and thought, *The pen is mightier than the sword . . . that is, unless you have a Hellstick.*

He regarded the wrecked city with new eyes, better eyes. This place was meant to scare, to terrify, and it was doing a heck of a job on that level, but this place changed and adapted, probably differently for each condemned soul. Scalia realized they messed up, they got things wrong, and he was just dealt a terrific hand. No people, no screaming, and no faceless suits, plus he hadn't been here for twenty-four hours yet, so Scalia was pretty sure he could walk around untouched. What did Farrow say? *As long as you don't get involved in anything . . .* Well, this new person, this new version of Robert Scalia was going to get involved. He was going to retrieve his friends, yes friends, and get them out. Neither he, nor the fighter, belonged here, and they, along with Paula, were leaving.

An aggressive pull from the pit of his stomach told him Farrow was waiting, and he sensed the prizefighter somewhere nearby, somewhere close. Scalia looked out over the city once again, with its dancing flames and isolated pockets of dizzying smoke climbing upward. This was the end of the world, the land of the dead . . . and he was going to get his friends. Everybody else could go screw themselves.

Scalia got back to a crawling position and retreated from the doorway some. Now almost upright, supported only by his knees, he unwound the chain that was wrapped around and hugging his waist. He dragged it to the right side of the humming threshold next to the chisel and mallet. Subsequently, he took the eight-inch chisel and placed its point into the center of the last link in the five-foot length of chain, pounding its thicker side with the mallet. The spike sunk invitingly into the hard ground. With each steady blow, the eight inches became five, then three, until that last chain link was embedded soundly into the ground. When he was finished, he discarded the mallet.

Scalia grasped the rest of the chain's span and pulled on it hard to make sure it was tight, secure. It was. When he was satisfied it wouldn't budge and could more than hold his weight, he pushed the chain out through the doorway. It slowly slithered out and down like a rusty serpent and was left hanging from this existence into the next; a makeshift entry into hell.

The writer poked his head through the doorway and saw the chain floating silently below him. He figured, hanging from its end, and adding his own height into the equation, it would only be a two or three foot drop to the ground, a plunge even he could handle.

"Fuck you, Frank Duran," he said out loud, hopefully putting that ghost to rest forever.

He went through the doorway, first on his stomach, legs kicking into the open space beneath him as he held tightly onto the chain and started down. It swung slightly amidst the wind twisting around him. Descending hand under hand, Scalia lowered himself deeper into hell's final level. He took a single last look at the doorway above him that was cut into the air and the length of chain he was grasping. *No turning back now.* Almost too quickly he came to the last few links, and after just a minor hesitation, the writer opened both his hands letting go of the chain and dropped to the ground.

The two faceless sentries standing just outside the glass wall with their backs to Farrow and Paula paid no mind to all the yelling and racket the prizefighter was causing.

"Open the fucking wall! I'll tear your goddamn arms off! Motherfuckers! Unhook the girl!"

Farrow's fists were bunched together tightly, muscles bursting under his slick skin. He continued to pull at the ring that was keeping his arms rendered useless behind his back. The faceless demons in the black and blue suits ignored his noises and attempts at contact; they neither turned toward him, nor showed any signs of emotion, acknowledgment or interest. They had a job to do and apparently intended on following orders.

Continuing to back-kick the solid wall behind him causing thin vibrations to slide up through his legs, Farrow worked himself into a fury.

"Let the girl go! You're dead; you're so fucking dead! You get on the wrong side of me, you better run for cover!"

His voice rising, dangerous, laced with venom, a bull on steroids anticipating release from its chute.

"I'm going to kill every one of you sick motherfuckers!"

Paula's eyes, still finding a bit of comfort in Farrow's panicked stare, continued to look at him with desperation and urgency. Tears leaked down both her cheeks in slow, measured trails. Her swollen face looked like a huge, bruised plum. The long, slim fingers of her hands were frantically grasping upward, searching for purchase on her tied ankles to steady her now violently shaking legs. Paula needed to keep her feet pulled as close to the back of her upturned head and stretching neck as possible, but her lashed wrists held in place to the small of her back prevented much of the limited movement she was allowed. The wire connecting her ankles to the makeshift noose that wrathfully circled her throat was pulled as inflexible as a circus tightrope.

"Paula, stay with me. Do you understand? Stay with me, don't let them win."

Recognition of defeat covered her expression in a compliant inevitability.

"My God! Paula, honey, hang on! You're a fighter! Just hang on!"

But Farrow could see it in her eyes, the same way he had seen the expressions of dozens of opponents and challengers he had beaten in the ring, spent bodies he had stood over. She was finished. She had given it her best shot and lost. Paula was down for the count.

He could see her fingers uncurl and settle among her painfully tied wrists. Her legs stopped shaking, stopped trying to hold the impossible position any longer, and Farrow heard Paula say a single, hoarse word, more of a hissing croak through a swollen throat actually.

"Sorry."

She pulled her eyes from his and closed them in a peaceful gesture. Farrow saw a single thin streak of blood slowly move down her neck from behind the wire noose on the left side of her throat. The bare soles of Paula's feet bent upward in a surrendering motion.

"Paula! No! No! Hang on! Hang on!"

And then to Farrow's left side, a muffled voice through the glass wall.

"The sword will fuck you up."

He quickly turned his head in that direction, only to see the backs of the sentries, now both headless, crumpling to the ground outside the cell wall in two motionless heaps. A second later, in a washed-out blur, the wall itself exploded. A thousand splinters of glass rained down, cascading onto the concrete floor in a cacophony of sharp edges and glinting white-hot light.

Out of the mist that had been gathering in the hallway just outside the cell, Robert Scalia rushed into the small room, eyes blazing, the Hellstick thriving and pulsating electric blue and yellow in his right hand, its tip burning orange with violence. The powerful smell of sulfur filled the room.

He saw Farrow first, standing off to the right.

"Cut Paula loose! Cut her loose quickly!"

Turning his head and seeing what was about to happen, Scalia stepped toward the brutally hogtied figure on the small table, and with a sizzling downward motion of the Hellstick, touched the weapon's glowing blade to the tight wire between Paula's neck and ankles, severing it instantly. Her legs dropped at once and straightened out as her head pulled forward into a resting position full of relief.

"Good job, writer! Good job!" Farrow said through a large smile. "Now free her wrists and ankles, cut me loose, and let's get the fuck out of here!"

In less than a minute, the two prisoners were free, no longer held by bonds of any kind and the exit doorway was wide open and clear. Inviting.

"I know I told you to get out of here and make it to the exit," Farrow said through a half smile, "but I'm damn glad to see you."

"I . . . I almost didn't come back," said Scalia, his voice quiet and tentative. "I wasn't going to come back, but there was this giant tombstone . . ."

"Yeah, with my name on it, I saw it too. The fucking thing freaked me out and . . ."

"No, no, not at all. What I saw was different. It was sort of a poem mocking us, you and me, almost condemning us here . . . and . . ." his voice trailed off.

"And what?"

"It said something about my wife Kerrie. Her name was written on the damn stone. It said that she killed herself, well . . . according to the date that was chiseled there. We are Catholic; if you kill yourself you come to hell. Farrow, we have to get out of here. I can't be the cause of my wife ending up in this place. She's the only thing that matters to me."

Scalia was getting noticeably excited now, tears brimming below his eyes.

"Okay, okay, listen," Farrow said, raising his hands in a "calm down" gesture. "Nothing is going to happen to your wife, I'm taking us out. Once we're through that cave . . . the Hellmouth, everything will fall into place. I think we are safe until we leave this room. Once we cross into the hallway there," he pointed, "they might be alerted somehow, probably to Paula's time expiration."

Paula, who had not said a word since the wires had been cut from her neck, wrists, and ankles, sat quietly in the corner of the small room with her knees drawn into her chest, the palms of her hands rubbing and circling her ankles working the blood back into her feet. Irritated red welts and dark bruises adorned the parts of her body that had been subjected to the bonds. Her face had regained some of its color and shape, but she kept her head down, staring at her long, bare toes, listening to the two men.

Farrow, remembering the digital time display around his wrist, held his arm up in front of his face.

"Shit! Goddamn it!"

The numbers were changing quickly, counting down at a hurried pace.

"What's wrong?"

"This can't be! How the fuck . . . that can't be right! How long have we been down here?"

"What do you mean?"

"They're fucking with the time."

Farrow held up his arm so Scalia could read the display. 04:35, and then in just seconds it read, 04:34 . . . and then 04:33.

"We have four and half hours to get out of here. Something's wrong with the time . . . if we are even a second longer than that . . . we won't be able to leave, we're stuck here," he paused and looked into Scalia's eyes, then added, "Forever."

The room was silent as Farrow's words sunk in.

"Robert, we can't screw up. It's going to take us almost three hours to get back to the Hellmouth."

"The Hellmouth? What's that? I heard you mention it before."

"It's the cave, the exit out of here. We have to go through it to the end, but they're shaving time from us. Someone's fixing the fight. According to the readout that only leaves about ninety-five minutes of fuck-around time; and the timer is still counting down too quickly, we can't afford any more surprises. When this timer is up . . ." still holding his arm high and tapping the display with a single finger, "we're done."

A profusion of street mist from the hallway swirled into the cell and around the two men as if inspecting them, bringing along with it trails of listless air. A light bulb that had been hanging dormant just outside the room started to buzz on and off, drawing the attention of the cell's three occupants.

"Guys," Farrow said, "I got a bad feeling about this. We have to get going. Robert, where are we? What is the place?"

"Oh yeah, that's right, you wouldn't know." There was a noticeable shudder in his voice. "This is the basement to some wrecked building."

"Wrecked building? What are you talking about?"

"Everything up top has changed. It's like we're now in a city sometime after a nuclear war. It's a real mess up there. Everything is either smoking or burning, a total disaster."

"I guess, if they can take five hours from us . . . somehow speed up the time . . . they could . . . are you sure that's what's up top?"

"Why would I make that up? *Could* I make that up? You'll just have to see for yourself."

The light bulb just beyond the designated cell wall barrier continued to blink, but a bit faster now throwing sinister-looking shadows on the outside walls like the projections at an old time-picture show. Paula appeared next to them looking like she had a hard night and was dealing with a terrible hangover.

"Okay, listen guys," she said, finally speaking, "we're leaving now. Let's go. Let's leave right now. It's time to go." Her voice was raw and anxious, just above a whisper.

"Honey, don't you worry," Farrow said, smiling down at her. "We're leaving and we're going to make it out, I'm taking us out. When we cross the doorway, just stay between me and Robert. I think maybe that will disguise your time limit somehow, or a least confuse them enough to give us the upper hand . . . well, for a little while maybe."

Paula gave a slight smile and a nod of understanding to the prizefighter.

"Robert, how far are we to the rip in the air? You know the doorway we lifted you to?"

"Oh, I know it well," he said, still holding the Hellstick firmly in his right hand, but in the smaller OFF position of the weapon. "Once we get upstairs . . . maybe twenty yards, not very far at all."

"That's it?"

"Yeah, for some reason they didn't move you guys a great distance. Weird, huh? I found you right away, and from the looks of the way things were headed, it was a good thing."

"You bet your ass it was a good thing." Farrow looked over at Paula, "But I don't like it. Except for the fucked up time . . . things are moving along too easy, you found us much too quickly."

Farrow looked at his wrist again, 04:25 . . . 04:24.

"I felt a pull from the pit of my stomach. It led me right to you guys."

"I know, I felt the same thing when I was looking for you earlier. We're connected somehow, but why didn't they put Paula and me farther away, or at least in different locations? Why were we so close to the doorway out of here?"

"Let's go, can we go now?" Paula said, interrupting the two men, hopping from one foot to the other like someone holding in a full bladder.

Both men looked at her.

"Farrow, can you carry me through the doorway? I don't have my shoes any longer and don't want to cut up my feet," she said rather meekly and motioned to the floor blanketed by about a thousand glass shards intermittently glistening in the blinking light.

Smiling down at her, he said, "Of course."

"Once we get upstairs, we can run to the doorway. It'll be an easy jog, shouldn't take us long at all," Robert said. "I found a chisel and a mallet by that big grave marker up top, and I staked down the chain just inside the door, you know the one I had around my waist? It's got a nice sturdy hold, too. It's hanging there just waiting for us. We can climb and pull each other up," he finished, sounding proud of himself.

"Good job, Robert. Good job!" Farrow said, then added, "Chisel and mallet?"

"Yeah, I thought it strange, also, but the tools were there almost as if waiting for me."

"Guys, can we please just go already?" said Paula, sounding anxious.

"Do you want this?" Scalia said to Farrow, holding out the Hellstick, expecting the bigger man to seize the item from his hand.

"No, writer, you hang on to it, you're pretty good with that thing; besides, I got these."

Farrow produced his hands, pre-balled into fists.

"I'll take on anyone," he said. "Ain't scared of a bloody nose."

"Yeah," Scalia said. "I know, didn't figure you'd be afraid of much."

Paula, still looking up at Farrow with big doe eyes, went up on the tips of her toes reaching her arms around his neck like a child greeting her father after he'd spent a long day at work.

"Thank you," she said, waiting for him to lift her off the cold cement ground.

"Don't thank me. Thank Luke Skywalker over there," he said motioning to Scalia with his thumb.

Paula turned her head and silently mouthed the words *thank you*, her eyes filling with tears.

Scalia nodded his head and replied, "No problem." Then he smiled at her.

Farrow bent and scooped Paula up like a rag doll, cradling her in his arms. She brought her legs together and pulled her feet as far up from the menacing glass covered flooring as possible, her arms gently circling his neck. Farrow looked over at Robert who still held the closed Hellstick tightly in his hand.

"Okay, you ready?"

Scalia gave an unsure nod, and the two men stepped out of the cell, glass crackling under their feet, and into the white smoke that inhabited the hallway. The light bulb above them continued to snap on and off with an electric buzz, like maybe an unseen figure of devilish ancestry was manipulating the switch from another location.

Farrow looked down at his wrist. 04:23. He stared at it for some time. The digital readout did not change.

"Hold on a second, guys," he said, still looking at his arm. A minute passed and then 04:22.

"I think we're good," Farrow said, relief in his voice. "The timer seems back to normal, it's not speeding up any longer." He looked up smiling. "It must have been that room, that frickin' cell did something to the time. That must be why we were in there."

Looking at Paula and Scalia now, "Let's get the fuck outta here."

The three looked left and then right. The suits the sentries had been wearing were crumpled in two discarded piles, scattered along the ground. No signs of their bodies were evident. Melted like the witch in the *Wizard of Oz*.

One end of the hallway was pitch dark, nothing could be seen, while the other was somewhat brighter in the now thickening smog.

"I guess we go this way," Farrow said, favoring the slightly lighter venue.

"Yeah, just up the hall and there's a staircase that will get us to the street. It's just a quick run from there that will take us to the chain; then it's up and out. Just . . . be prepared for what you're going to see when we get aboveground. There were no people or anything . . . but it's a sight that's going to stay with you."

Looking at the watch's display, Farrow said, "It will, but only for another four hours and twenty-two minutes, just try not to worry about it too much. They're fucking with us . . . trying to scare us."

"And doing a good job, if I do say so myself," Scalia said.

"Okay, once we get up the stairs," Farrow said, looking at Paula as she slid from his arms, her bare feet coming in contact with a now glass-free floor, "stay between me and Robert, we'll keep you sandwiched, but we're going to go fast . . . got it?"

"Just think, last month I would have gotten paid to do something like that," she said.

Nervous laughter ensued from all parties involved.

"I think as long as you stay between us, our not-yet-expired time limit might protect you, or at least hide your already expired one, from anyone it might matter to. I'm not sure about this. Just a feeling I got."

She nodded. Farrow looked at Scalia whose knuckles were white from the grip he had on the Hellstick. He nodded as well.

"Okay, guys, this is it. Let's rock and roll."

They started down the hallway, heading quickly in the direction of the staircase, the three souls close together, Paula in the middle.

A light bulb at the opposite end from where they now stood blinked on, its electric insect-like drone loud enough to be heard from their position almost thirty feet away. This bulb did not blink, however, did not go from light to dark and dark to light. It stayed burning brightly, bright enough to reveal what had been waiting quietly at the hallway's end in the darkness, waiting and hiding.

ROUND NINE

The wolves, five in all, were the biggest any of them had ever seen, much larger than you might encounter at a zoo or in the pages of *National Geographic.* Two of the beasts were standing on their hind legs in a seemingly second-nature fashion. Their eyes, clouded white, had no pupils. Each of the five animals had thick matted coats and were jet black in color, contributing to their concealment moments earlier. The hallway mist stayed close to the ground encircling the meaty legs of the animals, and all five sets of eyes stared blazingly at Farrow and his small band of escapees.

The two separate parties, ten yards apart, stood motionless, but even at this distance, the fugitives could see mouthfuls of teeth that were both glistening and needle sharp. A low, throaty sound laced with rage slowly filled the hallway. Paula backed into Farrow; Scalia backed into Paula.

The light between them and the wolves was flickering fast now, producing a strobe-like effect. One of the mammoth beasts took a shambling step forward, its eyes in a delirious, rolled-back manifestation, never pulling its stare away.

"Farrow, what do we do?" said Paula and Scalia, cutting each other off, their troubled pleas entwining, looking to the bigger man for leadership.

Farrow kept his voice low and even. Controlled.

"Walk back slowly, altogether. No sudden moves, keep your eyes on them. Paula, stay between Robert and me."

"Shit," she whispered, "sounds like fun, maybe I'll pay *you.*" Nobody laughed.

The wolves started moving as one, forward and slowly, extra-large mouths salivating, eyes pouring white light. The smell of excrement infested the entire area. A third wolf went up on its hind legs. Standing upright, the creature was nearly seven feet tall at full complement; its stride was not at all unlike that of a man.

"Robert, how far back is the staircase?"

"Only about twenty feet behind us to the left, and then about thirteen or maybe fifteen stairs up to the surface."

"And how far to the chain?"

"With a straight run, just about two or three minutes. Not even a quarter of a mile. Paula, your shoes are still at the bottom of the portal. I saw when you lost them earlier. I didn't grab them because I wasn't sure if . . . well, from the looks of those heels, you could probably run faster without them."

"Thanks. And from the looks of those things," she said, pointing a finger at the five approaching wolves, "I think we *will* be running very soon. Besides, I like walking around hell barefoot," she added sarcastically.

"Listen, guys," Farrow said, keeping his voice low, "we're going to keep moving backwards, together." He paused. "Once we hit the stairs, we turn and run."

As he spoke, the three of them moved in a single line in a slow reverse shuffle, Farrow in the back, then Paula, and Scalia up front closest to the wolves, their eyes never leaving the large black animals.

"If any of those things make a sudden move, anything at all, Robert grab Paula's hand and run like your ass is on fire. Get to the chain and I'll be right behind you. Do you have the Hellstick ready?"

Scalia held the weapon high for Farrow to see. It was still in the closed position.

"Oh, trust me, it's ready," he said, not sounding as confident as he did earlier.

The light bulb between the two conflicting parties continued to flicker. The wolf standing in what could be considered the center of the pack let out a roar, a deep, carnivorous sound, then dropped down to all fours, an obvious pouncing position.

Both Paula and Robert looked back to Farrow.

"Here we go, guys, looks like they're getting ready to make a move, getting ready to do something. Robert, switch places with me."

The two men quickly changed positions. Now Farrow was in the front of the line and Scalia was in the rear, closest to the staircase that was growing nearer with each backward step.

Paula turned slightly to the left and reached back with that hand in search of Robert's, her slim fingers instantly tangling with his.

"Don't fire up the Hellstick unless they start coming . . . and don't provoke them in any way," Farrow said.

The two wolves that had remained standing upright, now also dropped to what looked like an attack position, their legs slightly bent. All five animals were now coughing out vicious, gargling bursts full of menace and hate.

"Get ready," Farrow said.

The light bulb flickering above the black wolves dimmed considerably before extinguishing itself completely, throwing the beasts into absolute darkness once again. Their large eyes burned ghostly through the black air like haunted lanterns.

"Keep going," Farrow said. "Keep going nice and slow. Robert, how much farther?"

Without looking behind him, Scalia said, "We should be there anytime now, it can't be much longer. I'm surprised . . ."

The light bulb started to snap on and off again at quick intervals and the wolves came at them. All five, low to the ground, fast and directly.

"Robert, run! Run!"

Scalia and Paula reaffirming the grip on their tightly held hands, turned and started for the stairs that were only a step or two behind them now.

"Get to the chain, I'll meet you at the chain!" Farrow shouted, holding his ground, planting his feet and falling into a fighter's stance leading with a raised left fist. He could hear the sound of confused shuffling behind him.

"Farrow, come with us! There's time! Come now!" Paula yelled to him from a slightly elevated position.

Farrow's eyes scanned left to right anticipating his opponents as they came at him. They appeared to be running in slow motion, light and dark, light and dark, quick snapshots of hair and teeth. The wolves, all five now upright on hind legs stopped charging and stood just a few feet away. The mist on the ground had thinned and was sucked backward along the floor away from Farrow and the beasts, receding like ocean surf.

The animals choked out noises that were both fierce, and Farrow thought, hungry. All eyes were locked on the lone prizefighter who no longer heard sounds of any kind on the stairs behind him. His eyes focused on his clenched fists before him. He could almost sense the hand wraps he was wearing but could not see. His breathing was steady and his muscles tense.

"Come on, fuckers. Let's see what you got."

The sound of his voice seemed to infuriate the beasts as they moved a bit closer.

I have the advantage; they're going to get in each other's way. They'll be tripping over one another. This idea brought a dangerous smile to his face.

The wolves inched forward and then shifted back. A shuddering mountain of black fur, barking ferocious sounds, eyes blazing, saliva oozing in thick wet streams . . . but something was wrong. They weren't attacking. Farrow thought he could hear Paula screaming in the near distance up and outside of this murky corridor. He stood up straight, confused, but at the ready. Why weren't they coming for him?

He took a small step backward and once again stood his ground in a slightly crouched position, fists out in front. The wolves did not move forward, but they did seem to grow angrier. Something was keeping them in place just a few feet in front of him. The light bulb continued to flash, and now Farrow saw the animals in front of him lift their heads upward as if smelling the air, sensing something. He saw the coarse fur beneath their mouths and on their necks knotted thick in tangled heaps, but something strange was happening, if one could dismiss anything up until this point as being strange. The wolves seemed to be whimpering, a high pitched, hurt dog noise. They huddled together and began moving back, away from Farrow.

Outside, somewhere above him, Paula was screaming again and he thought he could hear Scalia shouting his name. The floor shook violently, a loud thunder-crunching boom that rattled his bones, causing small chips to break from the walls and crumble down. Smoke was filling the area, but this time it slid down from behind him, down the staircase, washing around his legs and over the wolves, who were now retreating back into the darkness. Something had scared them. The loud crunching again, Paula and Scalia screaming, something was coming. Something big.

Farrow scanned for the wolves once more, but there was no sign of them. He turned and ran up the staircase, the smell of death filling his nostrils. He took the steps by twos, a third apocalyptic sound, louder now. Whatever it was, it was getting close. A few steps to go, his friends screaming, mist curling around him, he could hear the wolves somewhere below him howling as if in pain. Tommy Farrow burst from the staircase and onto the surface.

Paula and Scalia were yelling from his left side, so that was where he looked first. They were about thirty yards away motioning to him, pleading for him to hurry, and that's when he looked to his right. He wished he didn't look.

As promised, Farrow was standing amidst a broken down, city street. A catastrophe of unknown origin had apparently ended this world. Immobile cars were stopped and deserted as far as he could see. Ash-gray clouds filled the sky and buildings were wrecked and smoldering, huddled in piles or standing ghostly alone. Large black flies swarmed in thick packs.

Farrow registered this, taking it all in instantly, but it was not the incredible landscape that caught his attention, it was the thing coming toward him about two hundred yards away. Another deafening footstep sounded off, rippling tremors through the ground causing windows to implode from their high perches and windshield glass to trickle from the numerous abandoned automobiles that were shifting and quivering in the street under the boom of the footsteps.

Farrow's first impression upon seeing the approaching monstrosity was that of King Kong or maybe Godzilla running amok in New York City or attacking Tokyo or wherever it was those two troublesome fucks enjoyed destroying. But, no, this thing was much worse. Even though it wasn't as big as those fictional creatures, maybe only sixty feet tall, this one looked like a burnt human being, gender unknown. Smoke was filtering off its slim, darkened body and climbing into the thick cloud cover above. It had what looked like the beginnings of giant, leathery wings protruding from its back attached by two horizontal tears starting on its shoulders and ripping downward. The hairless head, slick as an egg, was splotched black and red. Its white, pupil-less eyes resembling that of the wolves, stared in the direction of Paula and Scalia. The creature threw back its head, letting out a roar that put to shame anything he had seen in the movies or could have imagined.

It came a step closer. Its partially extended wings flapped once, kicking up dirt and filth in its wake. The giant abomination, Farrow could see, was actually on fire. Burning. Flames were licking the torso and peppering its legs, neck, and the long gnarled arms, ropy with muscle. The smell of burning, rotten meat was suffocating.

"Holy shit!" he said as he started to run toward his two fleeing accomplices who were still screaming to him, at him.

Paula was halfway up the chain and Robert was holding its bottom taut reaching his arms upward, hanging on the damn thing two feet off the ground. The rectangular escape hatch sliced into the very air itself, waiting and buzzing above, its multi-colored outline calling to them.

There was another cataclysmic crunch. Cars and discarded street rubble jumped inches into the air as the thing took another monstrous step closer, its wings now fully extended, black smoke pouring from its gaping nostrils. Its tortured scream, a monumental roar, filled with steaming heat and ferocity, once again filled the air.

"Paula, climb faster . . . hurry up! It's coming!" said Scalia, his voice elevated to massive proportions. Looking up he could see the filthy bottoms of her bare feet and her ankles crossed around the length of chain as she worked her way up and closer to the doorway. Her time was up and the writer had insisted that she go first. In their haste, her shoes were left on the ground below.

Farrow was almost upon them now; he did not look back at the quickly approaching horror and kept his vision focused on his escaping friends.

"Robert!" he yelled, "Start climbing up the chain, follow Paula, I'm almost there! You have to get out of here, I'm right behind you!"

Scalia looked over his shoulder to see the prizefighter coming on fast, running full out. Behind Farrow, the giant beast was gaining ground. Its wings were now blocking out whatever evidence of sky that was left in this insane asylum. Flames, orange, black and red, engulfed its body. The barbecued head was looking down on them, setting its line of vision on the doorway. The terrible lifeless eyes, two oversized full moons, did not blink.

It stepped closer, its wings blemished, meaty, ripped and raw, flapped a single time, causing the chain to swing in the air, only now with two people hanging on it trying to climb to safety. Farrow was almost there, a few feet to go.

"Don't look down! Climb! Climb faster! Don't look at it! I'll anchor the chain and be right behind you!" he said as he reached the wavering rusty links, his boots leaving partial groove marks in the ground below. Farrow jumped up and grabbed hold of the swinging metal. Reaching, he wrapped the chain once around his right hand and grabbed it tightly above that with his left. He pulled down hard, two hundred and twenty pounds holding it steady.

Dirt and filth moved across the air as the wrecked and broken automobiles were kicked out of the approaching giant's path or crushed altogether. Partially standing buildings were further reduced to powder and useless debris.

"Hurry the fuck up! It's coming!"

He looked up along the chain, through the swirling dirt and mounting dust. Scalia was moving quickly, three-quarters of the way there now and he could just make out the underside of Paula's shins and the tops of her feet sliding in through the portal. The thin electrical outline, which till recently framed the doorway multi-colored, now burned a luminous, steady blue.

Another rumble sounded off in response to a thunderous footstep, the earth-piercing bellow that followed acted as an exclamation point.

Through squinting eyes, Farrow now saw Scalia hanging from the doorway at the waist, half his body erased into shelter while his legs kicked and back peddled in the air on this side of hell while he inched forward. For a second, and among the shifting dirt, he thought he saw Paula's hands, the long fingernails, pulling and grabbing onto the back of the writer's shirt, helping him along, dragging him inside the doorway.

Before Scalia completely disappeared through the exit twelve feet above him, Farrow started moving quickly up the chain. Hand over hand and facing the approaching giant. Its wings dormant for the moment, but each of its three-fingered hands were semi-curled into claws. Farrow continued up, his legs kicking in the air.

"Almost there! Hurry up, Farrow, you're almost in!" yelled Scalia from somewhere above.

This would have been a hell of a lot easier with the staircase, he thought.

The creature, maybe sixty feet away, dropped to its knees and then slammed down onto its hands, or maybe they were claws, into a crawling position. When it landed, Farrow saw the neglected cars and other street vehicles jump almost a full foot into the air before falling in a disharmony of twisted metal, rubber, and surging dust.

All at once, Farrow realized what the thing was doing, making itself as even as possible with the doorway, bringing its head to a twelve-foot height, leveling itself for easier access. It was now crouching low and looked like an angry bull ready to charge.

"Farrow, don't stop! It's coming! Climb faster! Hurry, it's coming! You're almost here! Keep climbing!"

The mixture of voices from above had shaken the prizefighter from a temporary stupor, not even noticing he had stopped progressing up the chain.

"Farrow, cut the crap! Let's go! Climb!"

That snapped the prizefighter out of it; he started up again, just about two or three feet to go now. He could see his friends' hands protruding through the doorway almost as if from nowhere, waiting to receive him, fingers opening and closing, grasping at the air.

"You're almost here, hurry up! Move fast! It's coming!"

Those last two words stopped Farrow briefly again as he brought his eyes to the direction of the massive fiend. It was on all fours, coming fast, charging through the street making a beeline for the hanging chain and the rectangular slice of doorway in the air. It was destroying everything in its path, trampling over and through cars and other obstacles as if they were plastic toys. It let out another deafening roar of prehistoric proportions as its rotating, clawed hands and knees worked over-time in the spinning blur of a horizontal cyclone.

Farrow turned his body around, his back now facing the freight-training creature. He could hear the destruction, the thunderous rumbling of it quickly coming on, Paula and Scalia's reaching hands just a foot above him now.

Holding onto the chain with just a tightened left fist Farrow shot his right arm up with a fighter's speed as both his friends grabbed at his sweat-slicked hand. They had a solid hold on him and started to pull immediately. Farrow let go of the chain, his lifeline, and threw his left arm into the doorway. His legs began kicking in the air almost tangling in the now freely hanging links, anticipating the giant creature at any moment. In a second he was halfway through the door, up to his waist. Paula and Scalia, easing their hold on his arms as he put the palms of both hands on the cool cobblestones before him.

Farrow smiled at his friends only to see their mirrored smiles turn into expressions of shock before being completely engulfed in terror. Paula and Scalia were moving quickly away from the portal, Paula rolling sideways and the writer crab-walking backwards. Under different circumstances the scene might have been funny, but Farrow now felt the steaming breath, a rancid gale of hot air on his back and twisting itself around his legs. He heard a low, bubbling gurgle and knew at once the giant demon was upon him.

He could sense the thing just inches away. Paula and Scalia were still backing from him, cowering. He could see the fear in their eyes, and they his. Farrow then turned his head back far enough so the giant thing behind him filled his peripheral vision.

It was close, an inch or two away. He could see the enormous mouth opening and closing as if getting ready to swallow him whole. *That's most likely,* he thought, *what it had in mind.*

Farrow could now hear thousands of people screaming in terror just as he did when he first arrived. *Was it torture time again?* His little part in the Armageddon scenario was just about over. He waited. Nothing happened. Two seconds. Three seconds.

With his head still turned sideways and his lungs drowning in the smell of sulfur and shit, he said out loud to the giant atrocity, "You gonna pull those pistols or whistle Dixie?"

Farrow braced himself on his elbows, the palms of his hands flat on the ground and his fingers slightly bent grasping the stone for solid purchase. He brought his hanging legs up into his body curling them toward his stomach and kicked out backward, pushing off with his full weight, hitting the creature just above its open mouth and below the black holes that represented its nostrils, his booted feet spring-boarding off the thing's face. Farrow was airborne for just a second as he straightened his legs flying safely in through the doorway and landing in a rolling somersault.

The roar that followed seemed to shake the very foundation of everything in this world and the next. The prizefighter was lying on his side when Paula and Scalia rushed over and pulled him away.

A lifeless eye filled with rage overtook the doorway. It stared, burning at them for almost a full half-minute before blinking once and then disappearing, revealing a sky, peppered once again with falling black ash.

The three souls sat sprawled on the ground, their chests rising and falling. Each quietly trying to catch up with the breathing rhythms common to their bodies. They avoided eye contact with the portal, buzzing just a few feet away.

Nothing appeared to be coming after them; nothing charged in through the doorway and grabbed at or chomped toward them with hungry jaws snapping open and closed. Maybe they weren't scot-free just yet, they still had a ways to travel and time was starting to run on the short side of things, but at the moment, nothing seemed to want them.

There were questions that needed to be answered, as well as asked.

"Do you still think this stuff is going too easy?" Scalia asked, catching his breath.

No one said anything.

Not much time had passed, but it seemed to Farrow who was now standing above his friends staring at the digital readout across his wrist like an eternity. There were just under four hours left to make a trek that, moving quickly, should take them no more than two and a half. He looked to Scalia and then over to Paula who were sitting quietly on the ground a few feet apart from each other. When Farrow finally spoke, his voice visibly startled both.

"Okay, guys, we have a few minutes to gather our thoughts and maybe figure a few things out. If you have any questions, now would be the time."

Paula and Scalia verbally assaulted him immediately.

"Guys, guys!" Farrow started, raising both his hands with his large palms turned outward. "One at a time, speak one at a time. Robert," he said, pointing at the writer, who along with Paula was now getting to his feet. "This whole deal is basically about you, so you start first."

"Okay, okay, I can't believe this. I'm a writer, but now I feel like I'm at a loss for words."

A light breeze floated around them bringing with it a smell resembling burning oak and maybe something else, something like decay. The small holes that had been spitting black smoke seemed to have disappeared.

"What is this place? How did I get here?" Scalia began. "Also, I more than appreciate you being here, but *why* are you here?" he said, looking the bigger man in the eyes. "And what in God's name is that?" he added, pointing above Farrow, at what seemed like a sickle-shaped crescent moon surrounded by a bizarre sprinkle of glowing stars. "I know it's not the damn moon, 'cause this is certainly not earth," Scalia's voice climbing in volume showing a bit more backbone than when the two men had first met just hours earlier.

"No, Robert, it's not the moon. It can't be. I think it's here to create atmosphere, something familiar that's associated with nighttime, to let us know that this scenario, whatever that might be, is meant to be played out during the evening hours."

"This scenario?" Scalia said, a puzzled look washing across his face. "You mean like that Armageddon stuff?"

"Yeah, scenario. I don't think anything we see here is real . . . or at least very real."

"What are you talking about? The giant behemoth or whatever that thing was that just chased us . . . and almost ate you, seemed real. Heck, man, Paula almost cut her own throat with that wire connected to her feet. Was that not tangible enough?"

"That's not what I mean. I think this place evolves from our fears, changes to scare us. You know, the whole area that went on for miles, remember that? The place that had all the chomping mouths in the ground? I know you had your eyes closed through most of it, but it was there and not very pleasant, and there was the broken city we just endured after some kind of Armageddon, like you just mentioned . . . pretty scary stuff, huh? And now it's nighttime, one that features a moon and stars, and in a few minutes we are going to be walking through a graveyard that happens to be set in hell. I mean what's worse than a cemetery at night? Well, I for one sure as shit hope we don't find out.

"So," he continued, "where we are, as I just mentioned, is hell. We are both . . ." He then remembered Paula, and said, "We are, all three of us . . . dead. One way or another, we have died and our souls are in hell. I think this place feeds . . . no, devours itself on our fears and it will conform to whatever it is that might scare us."

When Farrow stopped talking the air around them seemed to grow darker and click a few notches cooler. When he began to speak again, he did so with his arms wrapped around himself. The t-shirt he wore was evidently not enough to keep him warm, and Paula was shuffling from one bare foot to the other.

"Why are we here, Farrow?" Scalia said. "What's going on?"

"Okay, this is what I know. I was fighting for the heavyweight title, a unification bout for a belt in Madison Square Garden against Jeff Johnson . . ."

"Joltin' Jeff," Paula finally spoke again.

"Yes, Joltin' Jeff Johnson. In the tenth round he knocked me down. I mean, I dropped my arm to my sides and he hit me, a solid blow knocking me to the canvas. I can remember him standing over me and flashbulbs popping all around us, and I . . . I don't know, I closed my eyes."

"Yeah, and then what?"

"I woke up on a beach, but it wasn't any beach. It was someplace from my childhood, a place I loved. There was this horse, my uncle's horse . . . I used to ride her along the shoreline with the sun coming up over us. I never felt so alive in my life; together, the two of us were unstoppable . . . and that's where I was, back on that beach. The next thing I know, these two guys, two odd men, are telling me that I died from an intracranial hemorrhage after Johnson hit me."

Farrow looked up at Paula and Scalia who were both silent giving him their full attention. "Anyway, Robert, I was sent here to get you out." Farrow attempted a smile. "The continuing existence of the world actually depends on it."

"I don't understand . . . how can the world depend on you getting me out? I mean, I don't even belong here; I've never done anything wrong . . . well, anything that would justify being sentenced to an eternity in hell."

"You're correct, Robert. You did nothing wrong, nothing to deserve this. You don't belong here anymore than I do . . . or she does." Farrow looked over at Paula who was now looking down at her feet, one on top of the other, avoiding his eyes.

"These two guys I mentioned, they were dressed all in white . . . ya know, robes? Like guardian angels or something. They gave me weapons to fight demons and shit."

"You mean the Hellstick?"

"Yes, that was one of the things they gave me, one of the weapons. I also have, well, I'm wearing hand wraps, they're invisible." He held up his hands and made fists. "I know you can't see them, but believe me they're there. They let me hurt these fuckers when I hit them, kind of evens the playing field."

"Is that it?"

"No, I had something else," Farrow said, his voice lower.

"What do you mean you *had* something else?"

"It was called a Spitfire, a little red pill that when mixed with my saliva and spit out at my enemies, was supposed to cause massive destruction. I was told not to stick around after I used it.

"Why are you using words like *had* and *supposed to?* That sounds like something we could have used against that giant bat-thing that almost had us for dinner," said. Scalia.

"I lost it," Farrow said, as he now joined Paula looking down at the ground.

"What do you mean you lost it?"

"Fuck, I don't know, it must have fallen out of my pocket when I pulled the Hellstick out sometime earlier."

"Oh, that's just great! You only lost what sounds like our most powerful weapon," Scalia said.

"Listen, writer," Farrow said, "I got you this far, didn't I? You were a few hours from getting your balls ripped off, and now for the time being you're basically safe."

"Yeah, after I had to come back and rescue your butt."

Farrow's blood started to simmer, the temperament of a prizefighter. He clenched a single fist.

Realizing what was about to happen if this went on much longer, Paula stepped between the two men.

"Listen, boys, we're in this together. There is no need to argue and fight with each other, because after all is said and done, we're going to end up right back where we are now, and from where I stand that's still pretty screwed. If you want to fight something, fight the problem." She held her arms out separating the two men that had actually come pretty close together. She looked at Farrow long and hard and then over to Scalia. Both men took a step backward.

Scalia spoke first.

"Farrow, I'm sorry. I don't know what came over me. That's not like me. That's not like me at all. I had no right . . ."

"No, I'm sorry," the bigger man said. "That *is* like me, but I have no right starting something with you. It's the influence of this damn place, they want us at each other's throats. You're very important, and we all have to work together to get you out of here. But, Robert, I'll tell you, you seem to be coming out of your shell a bit. That's good, that's real good. We may need this version of Robert Scalia in the near future."

"Yeah," Scalia agreed, "maybe we will, but I hope to heck not. I'd rather take a beating from you than face whatever else they're going to throw at us. So, tell me, Farrow, why am I so important and how did I get here?"

"What's the last thing you remember?"

Scalia thought for a second. "I had just finished a book signing in downtown Manhattan at Basilio Books, a huge bookstore that just opened." He thought some more. "Afterwards, a limo was taking me to meet Kerrie for dinner. My wife is really beautiful, when she gets all dressed up . . . man!"

"Robert, stay focused. You wanna see Kerrie all dressed up again? Then stay on track."

"Okay, I was in the limo, I was meeting Kerrie for dinner. She went to see a show during the book signing, *Phantom* for the fourth time; she really loves that show. Anyway, she's been to so many signings they started to bore her. We were going to eat real late. I think the show ended around 11:00." He stopped talking.

"And what happened next, Robert?" Farrow asked.

"The limo driver and I were driving around . . . just killing some time waiting for the show to end. It must have been a little after 10:00, maybe twenty after . . . a cab, a taxicab hit into us . . . I remember seeing the car door crunching in toward me and hearing all these twisting metal noises . . ."

"Right, they said that, those two guys I was telling you about. You were in a car accident and ended up in the hospital in critical condition. You actually died for a few seconds as they were trying to revive you." Looking at Scalia now, "They would have succeeded."

Farrow stopped talking a moment before continuing, the smaller man staring back into his eyes.

"You were snatched . . . kidnapped is more like it, I guess," Farrow said.

"What do you mean I was kidnapped? How could . . ."

"Robert, what do you remember? What's the very last thing you remember?"

The writer stood perfectly still in quiet reflection for a few seconds, his eyes closed. Before speaking again, he slowly opened them.

"The limo was spinning, I felt like I was being beat up from all sides, and then . . . and then," he said with a smile spreading across his face, "I remember the park. It was the park Kerrie and I used to go to."

"Where you guys first did it," Farrow said, a smile all his own now, and then followed the grin with a wink.

"How could you possibly know that?"

"Those two guys on the beach, John and Keith . . . anyway they told me about you and Kerrie and the park. It was a place from your life that you loved, a place with special meaning to you, is that right?"

"Well, yeah, of course that's correct information, but . . ."

"See? This proves my theory. On the good side of things, we were thrown into happy places from our past, good scenarios. For you it's this sex park, and for me it was the beach."

"It wasn't a sex park . . ."

"Places we loved, places with special meaning to us. This damn place . . ." Farrow straightened his arm and swung it in an arcing motion around them, "is meant to scare us . . . to fuck with our heads. Paula," Farrow said, pointing at her now, "after that asshole shot you, where did you wake up?"

At first neither man thought she was going to respond. After a long silence she finally said, "I don't belong here. It was self-defense, I told you that already. You told me it was self-defense."

She brought her eyes back down to her bare feet, still one on top of the other, rubbing them together for warmth. She was crying now.

"I don't belong here, it's a mistake. I can't stay here!" she shouted, her gaze still pointing downward.

"Paula, honey. Okay, okay, it doesn't matter. We're leaving very soon. We're going to get out of this."

That last sentence seemed to calm her down a bit. She wiped the tears from her cheeks with the back of her arm and didn't seem to be crying anymore. Farrow looked back to Scalia and started to talk again.

"Robert, John and Keith explained to me why you're so important. You see, I died in the boxing ring only about thirty seconds after you did, well, after your soul was taken and before you could be revived. When you woke up in that park, for however brief a period of time it was, you were close to the Hellmouth . . ."

"The Hellmouth? What's a Hellmouth and who is making up these ridiculous names?"

"I don't know who made the names up, but this Hellmouth, it's kind of a passageway between worlds. I told you this already. It's a long cave that connects the limbos we were in . . . to hell. You were close to the entrance to this Hellmouth and something wanted you, something knew how important you were . . . or will be. They must have been waiting for you."

"I don't understand, why am I so damned important? I'm only a writer. I write books about a vigilante, and until a little over an hour ago, I was basically a coward, probably still am. So I couldn't possibly save anyone, let alone the world . . ."

"You saved us," Paula said, looking at the writer now, her eyes bright. Whatever she had been going through seemed to have passed.

"Robert, listen to me," Farrow cut in, "in about seven years, you are supposed to write a book. This book is about a potential presidential candidate. This guy is apparently a real scumbag, lots of skeletons in his closet. You know anybody like that?"

Scalia quiet now, thinking.

"I don't . . . a presidential candidate? Maybe I haven't met him yet."

"Well, anyway, this politician, this guy . . . whoever the fuck he is, will become the President of the United States . . . " Farrow paused a few seconds before continuing, "and he is going to cause a nuclear war. Robert, he is going to end life on earth as we know it if he gets elected."

"And this happens in seven years?"

"This is what they told me, unless that is . . . unless you write this book, that, by the way, is going to become a bestseller. Thousands upon thousands of people will read it and prevent this asshole from getting into office, actually swing the vote."

The crescent moon seemed to climb higher in the sky and the night around them was soundless.

"How can I . . . I mean how does it work, what do I have to do?" Scalia said.

"Once we cross through the cemetery, there's this empty field with a single white tree, the thing looks all twisted, and past that is the Hellmouth . . . this cave I'm talking about. Once we go through and out the other side, we'll both be put back into out bodies. You'll be resurrected in the hospital and I'll open my eyes on the canvas of the boxing ring, our souls will be put back at the exact time they left."

"I'll get to see Kerrie again?"

"You'll more than get to see her again, you can take her back to that park." Farrow smiled.

"And what about this book I'm going to write, the book that saves the world?"

"All I know is your supposed to write it. You're going to meet this politician somewhere, you're somehow going to know his secrets, or at least enough dirt on this guy to write a book and prevent a presidency; but this only happens if we get you out of here."

"What about me, Farrow?" Paula said, "Where will I go? I died before you guys. I can't go back into my body. What will happen to me?"

Farrow remembered John telling him only two souls could come out through the Hellmouth, he wasn't a genius at math, but he did know the difference between two and three.

"I don't know," he said to Paula. "If you don't belong here, and we're that close to the exit, they have to do something with you, with your soul, something more than this." He motioned his arm into the night as a dark cloud sifted into his mind, *Remember, Farrow, only two can come out*. In truth, he didn't know what would happen to Paula, but without Teresa he had nothing to go back to, so maybe only two souls would be leaving this terrible place.

"Robert, I know all this is hard to grasp, real hard to swallow . . ."

"No, you know what's hard to swallow? A giant man-bat thing, flaming and charging at me like I was dinner. And, oh yeah, those wolves walking on their hind legs don't go down too easy either. How about that doorway ripped into the air?" He pointed in the direction at the buzzing rectangle. "That stuff is all a little hard to swallow, believe me. If you say I'm going to save the world, then that's what I'm . . . we're going to do."

"When we get out of here, we won't remember any of this, none of us will."

"How do you know that?"

"That's what they tell me. We can go on about our lives, whatever pathetic lives some of us have left."

"Now what is that supposed to mean?" Paula said. "You're a prizefighter, a famous prizefighter. I mean, I'd ask for your autograph if we weren't stuck in hell. You're really telling me that Tommy 'Heatseeker' Farrow doesn't have a life to go back to?"

Farrow was silent for almost a full minute.

"Remember when I told you about Johnson knocking me down, right before he scrambled my brains and sent me here? Remember how I said I dropped my arms . . ."

Paula and Scalia nodded.

"Well . . . I did that on purpose." He looked at his friends with an embarrassed expression masking his face.

"Why would you drop your arms? Aren't fighters supposed to protect themselves at all times? Keep your arms raised? Isn't that like the number one pugilistic rule? Did you *want* Johnson to kill you?"

Farrow dropped his gaze to the floor and then looked back up.

"I wanted him to hit me, I wanted him to beat me and punish me. I deserved every blow that Johnson was able to land. I wanted to make things easy for him."

"What on earth for?" said Paula.

Looking at the digital readout, "It's a long story and we should get going. We still have to cross through that damn graveyard. Something I'm not looking forward to."

"No," Scalia said, with a heightened sense of authority, "give us a few minutes, Tommy, what's the deal?"

And just like that Farrow began to talk, the confession pouring out of him, its flow not stopping until he was finished. He kept his voice low as the sky around them grew darker.

"I met Teresa, that's my wife," he said, looking back and forth between Paula and Scalia, "just before I started to get some real good fights. Ya know, bouts against 'name' contenders. I beat everybody they threw at me. My popularity, as well as my rankings grew, started to soar actually, and with that came the money. I was unstoppable, but I earned every penny I made. They sometimes call boxing 'The Fight Game,' but boxing is not a game, you don't play it. You endure it, and you overcome it. You train longer and harder than the guy you're going to fight, and you gotta have heart. That's what really wins fights. I've been fighting my whole life, it's what I do and I'm good at it. It's what I love."

His small audience was listening intently, captivated.

"In the beginning, Teresa was great. She'd come to all my fights, there was always a ringside seat in the third row reserved for her. She got to meet and hang out with a lot of famous people in those seats . . . all kinds of celebrities. We were headed for the big time . . . together. We were . . . we are . . . well, I'm still in love with her. We got married not even a year after we met. Teresa was always so enthusiastic when I fought. She'd be a vision of beauty sitting there in the third row, cheering and yelling for her man. After beating whatever opponent that was stupid enough to get in the ring with me, I'd walk over to the ropes on the side of the ring she was sitting on . . ."

He stopped talking again, this time for an extended period. Paula and Scalia weren't even sure he would continue, when he did start again, the air around them seemed to dip even colder than it had been just seconds earlier.

"She would have this giant smile across her face." He seemed lost in thought for a second. "Teresa was . . . *is*, a real stunner, she always dresses to perfection, but what I love the most about her . . . is something she does at the end of every fight."

Farrow stopped talking again. Paula and Scalia realized the story must have been hard for him to tell, so they just waited for him to continue.

"She . . . Teresa, would always have an arm in the air . . . her right arm flying above everyone else's heads, with a single finger pointing toward the ceiling as if to say that I was 'number one.' But she didn't just mean because I had won the fight, she was telling me that in her life," he paused again, a tear streaking down his cheek, "I was number one. I loved her so much when she did that. Her hand held up high . . . the single finger pointing . . . it made me feel like we were the only two people in a sea of thousands." He brushed the tear away with the back of his fist.

"Anyway, about a month and a half before this fight against Johnson, she asked me to stop fighting . . . give up boxing. You know the story, you've seen the movies. She was afraid I was going to get hurt. I'm thirty-six years old now; and that's actually starting to get up there for a fighter. She felt my career had run its course. I mean, I had plenty of money, so it wasn't about that. We could have lived six lifetimes on the cash I made from fighting, but Teresa couldn't understand why I would want to risk my health or maybe something worse . . . and looking at our situation now," he said, twirling his finger in a circle around them, "I guess I did get something worse. I once heard Joe Frazier say that boxing is the only sport where you can get your brain shook, your money took, and your name in the undertaker book . . . well, it looks like I'm in that book."

Farrow let that part of his story sink in before continuing.

"So, I have this fight coming up against Johnson, and I compromised with her. I promised just this one last fight and I would retire. She and I would ride off into the sunset together. You see, the fight against Johnson was a unification bout, I'd get another belt and for some reason, I really wanted it. I know, I know, boys and their toys. Anyway, I watched hours of tape on Johnson and had him all figured out. There was no way I could lose, but Teresa gave me an ultimatum."

He paused a second or two.

"*'This is how it is,'* she said. *'If you fight Johnson, you lose me.'* That's what she said. Can you believe it? She wasn't gong to watch me wreck my body any longer or destroy my mind. *'Look at Ali, for Christ's sake,'* she argued. It's a hard thing, a very hard thing to give up something you love, to walk away from the only thing you know . . . I mean, fighting has been such a big part of my life. So . . . I called her bluff. I just knew if I fought Johnson, Teresa would give in, come to the fight and everything would be fine.

"Anyway, at that late date, cancelling the fight would have cost us millions. It was being billed as 'The Fight of the Century.' But after all was said and done, my mind was elsewhere while I was actually fighting Johnson, and when you fight someone like that . . . your heart as well as your mind has to be in it. Completely focused. I kept looking over the ropes, ringside, into the third row where Teresa's reserved seat was, the same location for all my fights . . . she wasn't there. I couldn't walk away from glory, but I walked away from what I would call a once-in-a-lifetime love. I got disgusted with myself as the fight went on, I acted like a selfish child. You know the song, money can buy almost anything, but it sure as fuck can't buy you love. So, I dropped my arms and stopped defending myself. I wanted Johnson to hit me, to punish me. I let him hit me and hit me until . . . until I guess he killed me, and here I am!"

Farrow threw his arms in the air as if to say ta-da!

"Guess he punished me alright," he said looking around at the bizarre nighttime sky around him. "I guess being sent to hell on a suicide mission for the dead is sufficiently punished, wouldn't you say?"

Neither Paula nor Scalia said a word. And it was Farrow again who finally broke the silence.

"Now you know, I'm selfish, and even if I can get us out of here, I have nothing to go back to. I'll never see Teresa with her finger in the air again shouting, 'Number one, Tommy! Number one!' I won't see Johnny Laguna my trainer, or Jimmy Conn my cut man, in my corner wearing huge smiles waiting to slap me on the back or lift me . . ."

"Holy cow!" Scalia said loud enough to startle both Farrow and Paula. "For the love of Hemingway's ghost!"

"What?" Farrow said with a puzzled look that replaced the solemn one he was wearing.

"What were those two names you just said? Your trainer and the other guy?"

"Who? *Johnny* Laguna and *Jimmy* Conn?"

"Johnny Laguna and Jimmy Conn! How could I have been so stupid?" Excitement was now brimming in Scalia's voice.

"Robert, what are you talking about?"

"I'm sorry, Tommy. I'm sorry for what happened with you and Teresa, but Holy God damn!"

Paula was staring at the writer now, extreme interest in her eyes.

"Well, spit it out, Robert! What have you got?" she said.

Scalia seemed almost proud of himself when he said, "Jon James. Jonathan James!" He said the name again, yelled it out into the night that actually seemed a bit warmer.

"Okay, we give up, honey," Paula said. "Who the hell is Jonathan James?"

Scalia stood there and smiled like the cat that swallowed the canary.

"Robert, we've got to get moving, we don't have the extravagance of time. If you have something to say, let's have it."

"My dad died when I was fifteen years old, he was a city firefighter, died on the job, chemical explosion. Strong, outgoing, fun to be around, and he saved people's lives . . . the exact opposite of me. I couldn't, and I can't play sports . . . well, never really liked 'em much. I'm not big, and sure as hell not a fighter. So I wrote stories. I wrote about people I wish I could be, or be more like. My most famous character, the one that pays the bills, is a vigilante named Martin D'Cutta, based partially on my father. Anyway, I became a professional writer. Pretty good at it actually, but recently I've grown tired of the character that's made me lots of money."

"This Martin D'Cutta guy you mentioned?"

"Yes, you never heard of him?"

"Sorry, Robert, I don't read much."

"I heard of him," Paula chimed in. "Actually read two of the stories, you should try one." Looking at Farrow, "I bet you'd really identify with 'The Cutter.'"

"The Cutter?"

"Martin's nickname. He kills people with a sword."

"Ahhh."

"Well, I wanted to . . . or, rather, want to prove to my fans, and I guess myself, that I could write something more than just vigilante nonsense. I have been, for some time now, considering something in the non-fiction genre."

"So you're going to write about this Jonathan James?"

"I'm not sure who, or what I'm going to write about, but, yes . . . maybe. A little while ago you asked me if I knew any presidential candidates I might write about, you know, this whole saving-the-world thing."

"Yeah."

"Well, I don't know any presidential candidates, but my mom who hasn't dated anyone since my father passed, who had refused to date actually, has recently had a change of heart. I guess eighteen years is enough time and my mom is still a very attractive woman, hell, she's only 53 years old."

Scalia looked around at their surroundings as if maybe he had heard something before continuing, his cautious gaze turned back to his friends and he started up again.

"My mother has been on exactly four dates with a man named Jonathan James. I had the *honor* of meeting the guy once. I think it was before their second date. I stopped at her house to drop off some signed paperbacks. Anyway, the guy was a real jerk, a super know-it-all jackass. I saw right through him almost instantly, but I guess my mom couldn't. I just think she was happy someone was interested in her."

"And is there anything special about this creep?" Paula said. "Does he fit into our little puzzle?"

"Yeah, maybe. He's a New York senator. He told me, well, asked me I guess, to vote for him in 2016. I just thought the bozo was kidding, you know, the way all bull-shitters talk, and who knows with these asshole politicians. I figured my mom would grow tired of him soon enough, I mean he's nothing like my father was. I didn't think someone like James would be her type, I mean he's so full of the stuff he's shoveling even his eyes are brown."

The small group stood farther apart now, it seemed the air was heating up. *Maybe,* Farrow thought, *it was like the game of hot and cold, the closer you were to the truth or the answer, the warmer things got.* But he also remembered this was hell and he didn't want things around here to burn.

"What if your mom keeps dating this guy, this senator? Shit, what if she marries him?" asked Farrow.

"I guess it's not out of the question, it could happen, anything could happen. I mean, look at us, we're in hell. *That* happened."

"If your mom married this guy, you might get to know him pretty well. You could find out, or, perhaps, your mother could tell you stuff, share secrets. If this guy is the prick you say he is . . . or think he may be . . . he could be our man. He could be the person you're supposed to write about. This could be the world-saving book you are meant to write . . . that is . . . if we can get you out of here."

Scalia thought about it for a second.

"It seems to fit. I mean, my mom just met this guy a few weeks ago and now I'm out of the picture. If I had lived, seven years would have been plenty of time for me to get to know him and what he's really about . . . and write the book. It all fits."

"First things first, Robert, you are not out of the picture. You are on an operating table in Manhattan, and even as we speak the doctors are trying to revive you, and in less than three hours . . . they will."

Paula and Scalia moved in close to Farrow who was now looking at his wrist display. 02:56.

"We don't have much more time, guys. We have to get moving."

"Do you think this Jonathan James guy is really going to cause a nuclear war and end the world if he becomes president?" Paula asked Farrow.

"I'd bet my soul on it."

The trio began to walk. The two smaller bodies fell in behind the prizefighter, Paula between the two men as they made their way up the cobblestone path toward the large gray stone that marked the beginning, or the end, of hell's graveyard, depending, of course, on the direction you were traveling.

Round Ten

The moon seemed to curve and lengthen, resembling a reaper's sickle. On both sides of the path, blackened trees reached toward them with twisted limbs. The gnarled branches emitted ghostly trails of smoke into the night air.

"Farrow, how much time do we have left?" Scalia said to the bigger man, calling to him from the last position in the small convoy.

The prizefighter didn't answer directly, and Scalia was not even sure he had heard him until Farrow raised an arm and looked at his wrist.

"Just over two hours, our little chat ate some minutes up, but we'll be okay."

"How much time did we start with? How much time did they give you to get me out?"

Farrow, still moving forward, turned his head to the left so Scalia could hear him more easily.

"Thirteen hours and thirteen minutes."

"That's an unusual time limit. Why 13:13?"

"I think it's supposed to be some kind of joke on Satan's part . . . or Lucifer, whatever you want to call the asshole that runs this place. John from the beach called him Beelzebub. You know, 13:13, if the number thirteen is unlucky, then thirteen twice, is doubly unlucky. I guess the prick with the horns has a sense of humor. I think he kind of set the rules like some sort of messed up game. That's the time limit he gave us. It started as soon as I crossed into the Hellmouth from the beach, but when Paula and I were locked down in that cell below the city . . . I don't know . . . time sped up somehow. It's almost like we are doing better than we should

159

be, and whoever is in charge over here fixed the game in their favor. Cut some of our hours away."

"Hmmm," Scalia said, contemplating this. Then after a few seconds of silence said, "Farrow, I'm sorry about your wife, I'm sorry about Teresa. When you get back, when *we* get back, I'm sure you two can patch things up. I mean it was only a fight for Christ's sake."

"Not sure if I'll be going back," Farrow said quietly, under his breath.

Neither Paula, who was a pace behind him, nor Scalia had heard him though.

The small band pressed on. They moved forward into the night like a snake sliding through wet grass. Just ahead Farrow could make out the large grave marker that had had his name chiseled across it earlier, the same one Scalia had seen, but with a much different message branded into the stone's face. Farrow wondered what surprises it would hold for them this time. Behind him, he could hear Paula and the writer talking softly to each other; he neither listened to what they were saying nor cared. He was dealing with his own demons.

"So, Paula," Scalia said, "really, where did you wake up? I mean, you know after . . . well, after that gangbanger shot you?"

Paula was silent at first.

"It wasn't a gangbanger. Somebody was hiding in another room. I didn't know he was there. Probably buying drugs. I was taken by surprise, Donell's blood was all over. It sprayed up onto me."

"You cut his throat?"

"Yeah, I told you that already. The asshole liked to beat me."

"Why didn't you just run away or move away . . . why . . ."

"What is this, twenty questions?"

"I'm sorry. I'm sorry, I didn't mean to . . ."

"Robert, it's okay, I just want to get out of here. I don't want to relive a nightmare while we're still stuck in one."

"So, where did you wake up when you got here? Was it someplace from your past, somewhere good, like . . . from when you were a kid?"

"You know something, for a writer, you're not a very good listener. Didn't you hear a word I said earlier? I told you my story. There was no place in my childhood that was any good, unless you think that being raped by my father is something agreeable. There's been no happiness in my life . . . ever." She was quietly crying now, all worked up.

"Paula, listen, I'm sorry, I didn't mean . . . don't worry about it."

"No, you listen, my life has been a living hell, and now it's a dying hell, too. I don't deserve this. Who the fuck makes the rules? You guys talk about a nice beach or a beautiful park . . . that shit never touched my life. God turned his back on me. I don't like pain, I don't want to suffer anymore. I can't be here forever."

Paula was getting louder now, Farrow stopped walking and turned toward the commotion.

"What's going on back here, guys?" he said.

"Please, you have to take me out of here!" Paula was getting hysterical now. "I can't be chained up like an animal and cut up into pieces every day forever. You have to get me out of this fucking place!"

Farrow and Scalia were both trying to calm her down now.

"Robert, for Christ's sake, what did you say to her?"

"I asked where it was she woke up after she died and she started to freak on me. That's all, just making conversation."

"Didn't you get the idea earlier that she didn't want to talk about it?"

"What do you want me to say? I'm sorry, my mind is not in the right place at the moment . . . ya know, being in hell and everything."

"You want to know where I woke up?" Paula said, her voice singing through the night. "You want to know," looking at Farrow now, "what pleasant scenario I emerged from death into? Fuck the both of you! I woke up kicking and fighting those assholes wearing the black and blue suits. You remember, you know . . . the guys with no faces? I woke up screaming in terror! Clawing and scratching, and then they locked that giant ball around my ankle. You still want to know where I woke up? I woke up here! Right here in fucking hell."

As suddenly as she started screaming, Paula fell silent. The two men looked at each other.

Something wasn't quite right with Paula, Farrow thought. She was keeping something from them.

"Okay," Farrow, the voice of reason again, "everybody settle down, just stay calm, we're almost to the graveyard. That big, damned stone is just ahead there." He pointed off into the immediate distance. "Once we get past it I want to keep moving and go very quickly. Things have been too quiet around here."

Paula stood nestled close to Farrow, nodding with tears drying on her cheeks. Whatever little makeup she'd been wearing had been smeared to oblivion.

"Paula, I'm sorry," Scalia started, "I just wanted to . . ."

"It's okay, Robert, forget about it. I know you didn't mean anything. I just want to take my mind off my life, my past life. Let's concentrate on the problem at hand and work through it. If there's a graveyard coming up, let's focus on that."

A blanket of silence covered them.

Another two minutes passed before they were upon the large stone marker and standing behind it; anxious to see its face, but staying put for the moment. Each wondered what would be written across its surface this time.

They stood behind the monolith for a few seconds. The burial ground beyond was dark and foreboding. With its many stones poking up from the dirt ground, the land was sprawling and seemingly endless. They could see the path go on for about ten feet before it disappeared completely, sucked below the earth.

They looked back and forth among each other, but Farrow was the first around the large marker, and the first to see what was now chiseled there. Paula and Scalia quickly followed him.

There were no words, just a simple number sequence: 33 31 36. Around each number a circle was carved and across each circle was a diagonal slash that reminded Scalia of the movie poster for the film *Ghostbusters*. The slice mark across the center number '31' was colored in a dripping red that looked almost like a leaking wound.

"They're trying to bully us," Farrow said. "Motherfuckers are trying to bully us, don't you see?"

"Bully us how? How do you get bullying from a bunch of numbers?"

"They're playing with us, Robert, having fun at our expense, taunting. I'm thirty-six years old, how old are you?"

"Thirty-three, but what's that got to . . . oh, our ages."

"And I bet you're thirty-one, is that right, Paula?"

She slowly nodded her head looking at the number with the red slash mark between the other two.

"Just trying to scare us," Farrow said. "Pay it no mind."

"Why does the number thirty-one have a red slice across it?" Paula said, her voice laced with a noticeable quiver. "Why don't the other numbers have it? Just mine?"

"It doesn't mean anything, just ignore it. Like I said, they're trying to bully us, scare us. Get us all ready for the next trick up their sleeves."

"But why just thirty-one?" she said again, suspecting the reason.

"Just stay close, I'm sure it means nothing," Farrow said, not believing the last part of the sentence he had just spoken and remembering Paula's twenty-four hours had recently expired. She was fair game.

They stared at the stone for a few seconds longer. The number sequence seemed to cry out at them, mock them. Without saying another word, they turned around. The graveyard loomed darkly in the blush of the crescent moon. Above, ominous clouds were gathering.

"Shit," Paula said, "there's something wrong with my vision. Everything looks wrong, all the colors around me look washed out . . . almost . . ."

"Almost like an old black and white movie?" Farrow said, finishing her sentence.

"Yeah, I guess so. Yeah, exactly like that."

"Mine, too," Scalia joined in. "My vision is screwed up as well. Everything looks black and white, like a film from the twenties or thirties."

"When I was a child," Farrow started, "my dad used to make me watch those old Frankenstein movies. He was a movie buff, he loved westerns and those old horror films, and I guess I did, too, but I'll tell you, some of them scared the shit out of me. Frankenstein's monster was in my dreams for weeks. When I came through this way earlier, there was a thick fog low to the ground and stuff was skittering beneath it. At least things seem a bit cleaner now. They tried to get in my brain before with this scenario, but I'm not a child anymore. How about you, Robert? Paula? Does any of this scare you?"

Robert hesitated before he spoke.

"I was . . . well . . . I was afraid of *Night of the Living Dead* in my youth."

"Oh, God!" Paula said louder than she meant to. "You tell us that now? While we're standing in front of a graveyard? That's great." She pointed off into the distance. "You can go first."

"Sorry," he said, "I just wanted to be honest with you guys . . . I just . . ."

"Listen," Farrow said, "cut the shit and get behind me. I'll lead. We're going to march right through this place, there's no turning back."

Reluctantly, Paula and Scalia fell in behind him, but not before exchanging nervous glances.

They trod upon wet dirt and slick patches of grass, the smell of earth strong in their nostrils. Rotted tree trunks featuring warped branches appeared to reach for them every few feet. The black and white illusion caused Paula and Scalia to blink their eyes in an attempt to rectify the vision problem while Farrow just accepted it.

"Do animals really see in black and white?" Scalia asked. "'Cause if so . . . this is messed up."

About twenty paces or so into the graveyard, Paula turned her head to look back at the large stone branded with the three numbers, their ages. It was no longer there, erased by the night. Looking from side to side, taking in the grounds, she was amazed by the amount of stones surrounding them.

"Hey, Farrow," she called to him, "if we're dead and we're in hell, why is there a graveyard sitting smack in the middle of it?"

"I told you, I think it's just here to scare us. This place feeds on our fears. You know how I was afraid of those old Frankenstein movies, and our writer friend," he motioned toward Scalia, "is afraid of the living dead? Maybe this is a mock-up of that. They're trying to get into our heads. Don't worry. I have the hand wraps and Robert has the Hellstick. If anything comes at us we'll fight it off."

"Yeah, sure, you guys are all set. What do I have?" Paula said.

"You have us," Farrow again.

The grave markers and the scattered trees seemed to press in closer around them as they moved deeper into the burial grounds. The uneven light across the stones created deep pockets of shadows between the trees. Things were quiet and it was almost as if three friends had decided to go for a walk on a crisp autumn night. They could hear the crunching of dirt and maybe small rocks beneath their feet. The walk was almost cathartic.

"We should be able to see the wall soon," Farrow said.

"Wall? What wall?"

"Oh, I didn't tell you guys. There's a huge wall surrounding the cemetery, strangest thing. It spans the whole length. Seems to go on in both directions, as far as I could see anyway. Guess it's just part of the effect, part of the scenario. If we stay in the direction that we're headed we're going to come to a huge entryway, almost like an underpass, maybe ten feet high and five or six feet wide. That's our way out. It'll lead us to the field with the weird tree and the Hellmouth beyond."

He looked down at his wrist display. "Should be about another fifteen or twenty minutes, and then not much further after that."

"When I was growing up," Scalia said, "my parents and I lived across the street from a cemetery. It was just outside our front door and to the right. That one had a fence, too, but it was only about five feet high. When you are just a kid that seems tall, but it really wasn't. It was made of iron and I was so skinny I probably could have slipped through the bars, but I was always too afraid to go anywhere near the place . . . and look at me now. All kinds of courage," he smiled to himself.

"Goddamn! The ground is getting hot," Paula said, as she shuffled from foot to foot.

"Hot how? I mean, how hot is it getting?" Farrow said, clarifying his sentence.

"The ground, the dirt is starting to burn my feet. I can almost feel the heat coming up . . . you know, like on a beach when the sand has been baking in the sun too long and you have to run to your towel."

"You could just wear flip flops at the beach," Scalia said.

"I know you could just wear flip flops at the beach, but I don't have any footwear at all, Robert, and as you might recall, we are not at the beach. I hate the fucking beach, my dad used to take me there and . . ."

"When did this start?" Farrow asked, cutting her off. "How long have you noticed the ground heating up?"

"Just a little while ago, maybe two or three minutes. It felt comforting at first and I didn't think anything of it, my feet have been so numb, but then it seemed to be getting . . . too hot. Now, it's just really, really uncomfortable . . . I mean, I can deal with it, guess I have to . . . but it's weird."

"I'm sorry, I should have grabbed your shoes at the bottom of the chain, but I was in kind of a hurry."

"It's okay, Farrow, I'd rather go barefoot than walk through all this dirt in those heels. Probably just end up taking 'em off anyway."

Farrow stopped abruptly, putting an arm out as if to block Paula and Scalia from advancing any further.

"What is it?" Scalia said.

"The ground, look at the ground."

They both did.

Thin fingers of smoke were slowly materializing from the dirt with a gray, old-film quality. The mist stayed low, maybe hanging only a foot off the surface and quickly consumed the whole area as far as they could see.

"This is what I saw on my first trip through this place," Farrow said. "Paula, how are your feet? Still hot?"

"Yes, but not burning. The ground temperature is manageable, I'm accustomed to it now, just can't see what I'm stepping on."

"Should only be dirt and rocks like before," Farrow said, remembering how something had disturbed the ground fog during his earlier walk, something he didn't get a look at. He shifted his eyes around the area, the low mist only covering the tops of his boots; the three of them listened in silence for a few seconds.

When Farrow was certain nothing was very much out of the ordinary, he motioned for them to continue by waving his arm in a forward action.

"Let's go," he said, starting to walk.

Paula and Scalia followed.

They were just about midway through the graveyard when they heard the first moan, a long rasping sound that moved through the tree branches like an icy wind.

"What was that?" Scalia said, raising his head to listen.

No sooner had he spoken before a second moan, drifting over somewhere from their left, joined the first. The mist below them glowed intensely like an overexposed film negative.

"*Night of the Living Dead*, huh?" Farrow said, looking at Scalia.

Paula stumbled.

At first she thought the band of iron was back around her ankle locked tightly, mercilessly. Her right leg was pulled behind her in mid-step.

"Hang on a second, something's wrong!" Panic in her voice. "I can't walk. My foot is caught!" she said, frantically looking at Farrow who was turning to face her. Scalia, stopping short, almost trampled her.

"Paula, what's wrong?" the writer said. "Why did you stop?"

Another long moan oozed out of the night, this time in front of them.

"Oh, God, it's my leg . . . my ankle . . . I'm locked again. That giant ball, it's that . . ."

"I don't see a ball . . . there's nothing . . ." said Scalia.

"Hold on," Farrow said, bending behind Paula to where her leg stretched out behind her.

He waved his open hand back and forth among the low mist trying to clear the area to see what the problem was. Maybe a discarded tree branch had snagged her leg or perhaps some extra long weeds, sticky-wet, had hold of her.

Farrow saw the problem almost immediately, and it was none of the above.

A hand was jutting up from the dirt, milky white with peeling skin, and black, cracked fingernails. Maybe a foot and a half of it was exposed from mid-forearm.

"Oh my God! Get that fucking thing off me!"

More moans sounded off, floating in the night and surrounding them. The mist circling the gravestones and covering the ground bubbled with a disquieting intensity.

"What's happening?" Paula said, tugging on her leg, her voice in a furious panic. "What the fuck is happening?"

"Farrow, what do we do?" Scalia said nervously. "Oh, God, what's that? What in the hell . . . ?" The writer was looking in the sky above Farrow and Paula; the two turned their heads upward to see what he was talking about.

A giant white eye looked down onto them. The same eye Scalia and Farrow themselves had mistaken earlier for a full moon; but it now revealed a pupil as black as a bead of oil. It stared blazing, almost as if to say, "I see you."

The moans around them continued, raucous sounds. The night seemed choked with pain and vengeance.

The giant eye blinked twice then disappeared from the sky.

"Robert! Nevermind the moon . . . or the eye . . . whatever the fuck that was, help me over here."

As he bent lower to free Paula's ankle from the unforgiving grip of her assailant, he noticed more of the arm was exposed now. Whoever or whatever belonged to the lanky appendage would soon be aboveground. The crescent moon that was on the opposite side of the sky from where the eye had been looked like a sideways mouth locked into an evil grin.

Scalia dropped down instantly joining a squatting Farrow, amid the mist that seemed to be boiling up from the ground.

"The Hellstick!" Farrow said. "Light up the Hellstick!"

Scalia didn't have to be told twice, he sat upright on his knees stuffing his right hand deep into the back pocket of his jeans to retrieve the weapon. In an instant the Hellstick was produced, squeezed, and extended to its full length, strong with the smell of sulfur, the tip burning orange.

Farrow straddled Paula, covering her with his body so that only the bottom part of her pulled back right leg stuck out from in between his own. The dead fingers grasping her ankle tightened like a vice, the rotten fingernails cutting into her flesh and drawing blood. Paula started to scream bloody murder.

"Now!" Farrow shouted, "Robert, do it now! Cut the fucking thing off!"

The writer, both hands clasped around the thick base of the Hellstick, swung down at the arm aiming just above the wrist in a fierce arcing motion. Flesh hissed and then separated at once. Farrow and Paula went tumbling forward. The half-arm oozing up from the dirt flung back and forth, spraying the ground around them in a sepia expression of blood. The hand locked around Paula's ankle tightened another click before falling off and landing on its back with the fingers twitching in the mist like a large, dying spider.

The moans around them seemed to be multiplying quickly. The three stood up, back to back to back. The Hellstick was still tightly gripped in Scalia's right hand. Dark shapes that weren't there moments ago started to define themselves against the darker background. The mist was alive under their feet and the sky started to flash periodically with the promise of one hell of a light show.

"What is it going to rain?" Paula said.

"Yeah, may that be our only problem," Scalia responded sarcastically.

For just a second, Farrow was reminded of standing in the center of a boxing ring with the cheers dancing around him and flashbulbs shooting light. Only this time he wasn't fighting for a belt. No this time he would be fighting for his life, his life . . . and theirs.

The shapes, still not close enough to make out any features, seemed to be of human proportions. They came on clumsily, slow and plodding.

Farrow, Paula, and Scalia looked back and forth, this way and that, side to side. They were being surrounded.

"Oh my God! Oh my God! Oh my God!" Paula kept repeating the three words; the tone in her voice revealed her sanity was seconds from cracking.

"Farrow, what are those things? What do we do now?" said Scalia, the Hellstick pointing at the ground, his eyes searching for anything that might be coming up through the mist.

"I would guess they're zombies. Thanks for that, writer."

"My God, what have I done?"

"When things look bad," Farrow started, "and it looks like you're not going to make it, then you gotta get mean, plumb mad-dog mean, 'cause if you lose your head and give up, then you neither live nor win," he said, then added as he raised his arms and tightened his hands into fists, "that's just the way it is."

"What is that supposed to mean?" Scalia said.

"I don't know, heard it in an Eastwood movie."

"Yeah, I caught your 'Whistle Dixie' comment earlier. Okay, I don't want to give up. What do we do? There are so many of them. What would Clint do?"

"You ever see *The Outlaw Josey Wales?*"

"Yeah."

"We whoop 'em," said Farrow.

As the human-shaped things negotiated their way closer, their features were better defined, almost like an old Polaroid photograph slowly developing.

In the faded light, the one closest to them looked like it had spilled something on its shirt, there was a dark wet splotch there. Its clothes were torn and it walked with a stop and start lurching motion that looked drunken. Its face was swollen and lumpy and the eyes were clouded over with a milky white film. The ones behind it and around them moved in a similar fashion, arms were outstretched, reaching . . . wanting.

Moans now filled every inch of the night. Shapes seemed to be rising from the mist everywhere, shadowy with sinister intentions.

"Farrow!" Paula screamed. "What do we do?"

"Robert, you have the Hellstick ready?"

"Damn right I have it ready."

Pointing in the direction they had been going, and straight into the path of several of the undead, Farrow said, "Let's go!"

The prizefighter interlocked his fingers with Paula's and headed his small band of souls into the pack of zombies before them. Reality appeared to change, things seemed as if they were going in slow motion. Every detail was clear, time moved frame by frame, like an old motion picture.

"Robert, go for the necks! Take off their heads! That's the way it works in the movies. Kill the brain and you kill the ghoul."

"Yeah, I know, seen that one a hundred times."

They reached the first three creatures almost immediately. Letting go of Paula's hand, Farrow swung at the ghoul closest to him. His fist came hurdling at the thing's head hitting it just above the right eye. There was a cracking sound not unlike wood splintering as his fist punctured a hole into the advancing creature's skull. He pulled his balled hand out, wetly shaking off what was assuredly part of its rotting brain, the pieces raining around his feet. The thing fell to the ground instantly and unmoving, in a heap of ruined flesh.

"Kill the brain," Farrow said.

The writer was already swinging the Hellstick with an electrical hiss and the strong smell of sulfur. In less than two seconds the remaining zombies in their immediate area had fallen to the ground, headless. Blood fountained from the two empty neck stumps, one into the night while the other across the front of Paula's body. She threw her hands over her face, coughing and hunched over, before clearing the gore from her eyes.

"Nice one, Robert, thanks a lot."

The moans emanated around them, if they didn't move they'd be surrounded in a matter of moments. The tortured limbs of the leafless trees decorating the area, beckoned for them to hurry on their way. The pale ground mist complemented the black and white scene in a bizarre homage to the old Universal horror films.

"Bet you never gave head like that before," he said smiling at her.

"Yeah, real funny, writer. It's so nice to see you coming out of your shell," she said, still wiping the clammy mess from her face and the front of her body.

"Sorry," he said shyly. "I didn't mean . . ."

"Guys, we have to go," Farrow said, grabbing Paula just below the elbow.

"Oww! Take it easy, big man. You're going to break my arm."

Farrow silently slid his hand down back to her hand and interlocked fingers once again.

"Sorry, we just don't have a lot of time to . . ."

Two brilliant flashes of lightning sputtered behind the now cloud-infused sky illuminating the graveyard. There must have been two hundred ghouls standing upright with arms outstretched and hands raked into claws. The main concentration, however, was behind them with only small pockets of twos and threes advancing in their path. Fierce hissing sounds whispered and barked all around, the mist below danced upward with each footstep.

"Oh no! Oh God!"

It was Scalia.

Farrow and Paula turned to see two sets of arms appearing from the mist grabbing at the writer and pulling him to the ground. The Hellstick skittered from his hands buried under the fog a few feet away. The ghoul's eyes, filmed over with cataracts, were locked onto Robert's throat, their mouths opening and closing, anticipating flesh, the teeth clicking hungrily as they moved closer to the writer's neck.

"Farrow! My God, Farrow!"

Scalia, now on his back, kicked his legs up and down on the heated ground as the ghouls huddled over him for their midnight snack. Farrow scanned the area quickly before attending to his friend. In another minute things would be out of control and all would be lost. Paula, he saw, was already making her way over to help the writer, and Farrow, with a prizefighter's speed quickly joined the party.

The two ghouls were pressing their heads down upon Scalia. His arms extended fully with his palms against their chests, were bending at the joint. The smell of rotted flesh was substantial in his nostrils. A thin flap of skin hung loosely off the ghoul braced by his left hand just under its right eye, and it wore a rictus grin on its pale face. The teeth on both creatures continued to gnaw up and down hungrily.

And then Paula was standing over him; he could see her just over the top of the thing's head. A second later Farrow was there as well.

Paula put both hands on one of the ghoul's shoulders, her painted fingernails sharp as daggers. She dug her naked heels into the dirt ground and pulled the creature off the writer. They both went tumbling backward into the mist in a swirl of knees and elbows.

"Hang on, buddy, I'm here," Farrow said.

The fighter now stood over Scalia and the remaining ghoul, straddling the two. Robert's legs continued to drum on the ground, but he now had both his hands around the menacing creature's throat, keeping the mouth as far away from his neck as possible. The thing compensated by snapping at his forearms. He saw Farrow draw a large balled hand behind the undead atrocity and shoot it forward.

The prizefighter's fist ended up inches from Scalia's nose sticking out through the center of the ghoul's face, an explosion of blood and gray matter cascaded down, slick and revolting. Farrow pulled his arm from . the back of the ruined head, and Scalia saw him smile at the end of the ragged puncture framed by the obliterated skull. When he did, the thing collapsed on top of the writer.

"Put that in your next book," he said.

Paula started to scream. Farrow turned his head and Scalia sloshed the limp corpse from his body and started to get up.

"Go find the Hellstick, I'll take care of Paula."

Scalia hesitated a second before nodding his head, and went off with his arms bent low fishing through the mist in the neighborhood of the dropped weapon.

It only took Farrow two steps to reach Paula. Like Scalia, the thing was on top of her, but Paula had her legs scissored tightly around the creature, her feet crossed at the ankles. The small of her back was off the floor as she squeezed the squirming ghoul, its arms cratered with sores, reaching for her. Its mouth a gaping hole, blackened teeth chomping, its saucer-like eyes were burning white.

Farrow stepped behind the thing and put two meaty hands on the sides of its head and gave a quick twist. The neck resisted some before relenting almost too easily. A loud crack followed. Farrow continued to turn, he wanted to see his opponent's face. He spun the head a bit more and it was staring at him. The pupil-less eyes no longer had intent behind them, a thick dark tongue protruded from the dead mouth, its hair was full of worms and dirt. Farrow gave the head another single but vicious rotation, and the head came off in his hands, separated from its neck like the removal of a bottle top.

A hot, inky downpour sprayed from within the headless stump in a flowing shower, and, as before, most of it bathed Paula. She uncrossed her ankles from behind the creature as it fell off to the side with Farrow's help. She stood up, emerging from the low mist covered in carnage, looking not unlike a ghoul herself.

"Thanks, Farrow," she said, wiping, once again, blood, bone, and sticky filth from her eyes, face, and hair. "I hope this shit isn't becoming a habit with you."

He held out his hand to her.

"Let's get Robert and get the fuck out of this graveyard," he said.

"You don't have to tell me twice, honey."

Scalia was bent low searching for the Hellstick. Just a few feet behind him, ghouls with reaching arms shambled forward drunkenly, flooding around grave markers. Dead moans continued to drift around them.

"Robert, leave it! We have to get out of here. Too much time is passing. They're trying to eat up our time."

He quickly glanced down at the digital wrist display that was once a tranquil blue and was now washed of any color. What had once read thirteen hours and thirteen minutes, now displayed . . . one hour and six minutes!

How time flies, Farrow thought.

"Forget it! We have to go. Now!"

The writer, seconds away from abandoning his search, felt his fingers grasp something below the mist, something sturdy and familiar, something like a roll of quarters . . . the Hellstick! When he had dropped it earlier, it must have retracted down to its original size. He had been looking for the full-blown weapon when he should have been thinking smaller. He closed his hand around it and stood up straight, shoulders back and smiling. He squeezed the small tubular item and it extended to its full length, the tip burning, the acrid smell of sulfur powerful. Looking at Paula and Farrow, and stealing once again from his literary creation Martin D'Cutta, Scalia said, "The sword will fuck you up!"

His two friends smiled.

"Okay, let's go," Farrow said.

A dark figure rose out of the ground fog only a foot or two to Scalia's left side. It was almost as if it were on an elevated lift under the ground. It flowed upward mechanically and when it reached a height of maybe six feet, the white smog thinning, it turned toward the writer and brought its arms forward wanting him, its wrecked, insect-infested features morbidly clear in the wavering moonlight.

Farrow was on the thing next to Robert immediately. Hunched, fists ready, leading with his left, muscle memory working to perfection, he swung a low, right-handed upper cut into the creature's ribs, doubling it over. Next, a hard left to the side of its head, spraying twitching bugs. The thing turned to look up at Farrow, only to see a straight right-handed fist shooting toward its face. The blow connected perfectly, crumpling the creature to the ground, its skull split open displaying part of a rotted brain. Working together, Scalia arced the Hellstick down on its neck severing the head causing it to roll through the mist toward the oncoming army of the dead. The spray of blood this time, however, was not pointed in Paula's direction. She didn't get a drop on her.

The wall of ghouls behind them was quickly approaching.

Scalia looked up at Farrow, and they both looked at Paula.

"Enough fun for one night?" Farrow said sarcastically. "Stay close together, we don't have to kill everyone of these things, just push them out of the way. They're slow . . . and, Robert, just keep chopping at everything that moves."

He grabbed Paula's hand yet again and looked over to Scalia. "Stay behind us, writer, you got a literary deadline to meet."

Following Farrow's lead, they ran for it.

Every few feet something rose from the mist. They would see the reaching arms first, before the rest of the body appeared. They dashed through the graveyard, avoiding the small packs of ghouls in their path. Several times, Farrow had to put his arm around Paula and pull her along. She was having trouble keeping full weight on the ankle the ghoul had ripped open earlier. It was healing, but slowly.

"Keep going, guys! We're almost through," Farrow said.

To the left and right, the ground puckered up into several small hills. Farrow now remembered the old, broken crypts that sat dormant under a wedge of moonlight. He silently wondered if the structures held any evil surprises.

As they passed a single ghoul seemingly lost from its pack or maybe prematurely unearthed, Farrow hit it hard across the face without losing stride. Its head spun to the left, followed by its body in an almost comical descent to the graveyard floor. Behind them the sound of the Hellstick could be heard slicing back and forth accompanied by the strong smell of sulfur and various triumphant shouts from Scalia.

The wall that was nothing more than a solid thin line across their field of vision grew in width and depth as they stampeded closer toward it, closer to the way out.

The ghouls around them seemed to be progressing hungrily in a delirious rush. Farrow and company ignored as best they could the shapes staggering on either side of them. The ones behind were of no major concern at this juncture.

And then Scalia screamed out, the shrill noise his voice made overpowered the moans and hisses around them. Farrow and Paula stopped running, turned back to look for their friend, but all they could see was the line of ghouls in the distance against a black background making their way forward, the muddy shapes growing larger with each step.

"Shit! Where is he? I don't see him! Where is he, Farrow?" Paula said, her voice rising as she spoke.

"Robert? Robert, where did you go, buddy? Scalia?"

The writer screamed giving off his position, which was only about seven feet away. The thriving ground mist along with two large stone markers kept the location momentarily concealed from his two friends. The sound of the cry had drawn goose bumps that raced along the arms of both Paula and Farrow.

They found Scalia lying on the ground, flopped onto his back and almost stepped into a nightmare.

Both his legs close to the ankles and his left arm just above the wrist had been pinioned, held there by rotted hands emerging from a soupy mist that fluctuated around decaying fingers. They held the writer's limbs tightly, jagged bones showing through peeling flesh. But Scalia's right arm was a very different story.

A ghoul that had slid halfway up from the ground and stopped rising just above the waist was bent over the writer; it held Scalia's right appendage down and was dipping its head toward his forearm. A single eye was hanging from its socket swaying this way and that, and parts of its brain had been exposed through a large split in the dirt-encrusted skull that appeared to glow in the insipid moonlight.

"Oh my God, get them off me! Farrow, get them off me!"

Scalia's body struggled in the dirt, his eyes filled with terror. The ghoul's mouth was now inches from his trembling arm. A scream of absolute agony sounded into the night as the thing bit down into the writer's flesh.

"OH NOO! OH GOD! OH MY GOD!"

Farrow set his feet firmly into the ground, bent slightly, and grabbed the creature from behind around its forehead with two large hands and pulled back away from Scalia. A lump of flesh was between the thing's teeth as the mouth greedily opened and closed . . . it was chewing.

"IT BIT ME! IT BIT ME!!"

Farrow flattened his hands around the ghoul's head with his large palms on either side of its face and he pushed them together. The skull collapsed inward like a decayed Halloween pumpkin. The eyeball that had been hanging from the socket connected by thin, intertwined tendons, stretched and fell moistly onto Scalia's chest. The remaining eye popped free from its socket with a thick, meaty portion of brain slowly moving out through the empty cavity like pus from a ripe pimple. The lifeless body collapsed on top of Scalia.

"JESUS! GET IT OFF ME!"

The writer pulled on his left arm and, with a splintering crack, the ghoul's hand that had been circling his wrist broke free and fell away in a scatter of small bone fragments and discarded fingers.

Scalia sat up quickly, the eyeball falling from his chest, and saw Farrow moving to join Paula at his feet.

"Robert, give us your arms. Come on, buddy, your hands," Farrow said, reaching toward him as Paula did the same.

Scalia extended his fingers up to them as they pulled him to his feet, snapping the unearthed wrists that had been holding his ankles. The festering hands landed palm down in opposite directions of each other and, to no one's surprise, went up on fingertip and skittered away quickly burrowing low under the mist like decomposing sand crabs.

"Oh fuck! Did you see that? Some messed up shit," Paula said.

"I've seen a lot of messed up shit in the last few hours," Farrow said.

They crowded close to Scalia, holding him up by the shoulders.

"Robert, you okay? You gonna make it?" Farrow said.

"Yeah, I'll make it . . ." he paused for a second and then looked down at the inner part of his arm where a good-sized portion was missing. "Oh my God!" he said, and started to collapse.

Farrow caught him, kept him on his feet.

"Come on, Robert, stay with us. That wound is nothing, should start healing anytime now, and you'll be good as new."

The ghouls that had been behind them, gained considerable ground and were approaching quickly. Hissing whispers once again filled the night.

"Paula, grab him, it's time to go," Farrow said, taking a hold on the upper part of Scalia's arm, and without anymore small talk they were pulling the writer along, quickly moving through the gravestones and trees.

The markers in their path were thinning out, the bulk of the stones now behind them. Almost continuously the ground erupted in close intervals birthing living corpses and spraying dirt and grime almost as if some giant being below the surface were pushing the ghouls up through the earth.

The three souls ran until the graveyard leveled to an open field. The cool air blowing seemed to push against them and the smell of something burning was now evident.

The wall was there, pale beneath the moonlight, vast and cold, running from left to right, seventy, maybe seventy-five feet away. The large cavernous exit in their line of sight yawned invitingly, about ten feet high and five feet wide, framed by the ancient stone bricks that made up the structure.

Farrow no longer held onto Scalia by the upper arm, he now kept his whole hand circled around the writer's wrist tightly, pulling him along. Paula, her eyes dancing around in a panic, and now separated from the two men, was running close behind them.

"Almost there. The exit is just ahead," Farrow said, pointing a single finger with his free hand. Neither Paula nor Scalia replied to the statement, unless heavy breathing sounds and gasping could pass for comment.

With the massive wall growing large in their view and some distance between them and the slowly dawdling ghouls, the small band changed gears to a slow jog before stopping completely to take in the surroundings, evaluate the situation, and catch their breaths.

Paula and Scalia were both bent over, hands on their knees, sucking in huge gulps of air. Farrow stood above them scanning his eyes over the area and around the immediate vicinity. The approaching creatures were still a ways off, progressing slowly like apparitions in a haunted graveyard.

"You know, when we get out of here, you two should get to a gym more often," Farrow said smiling, swirling a hand in front of his chest. "Some cardio will help with the breathing. Clear out your lungs and give you better stamina."

"Screw you," Scalia said, still hunched over, trying to catch up.

"Yeah," Paula added, "don't worry about me, honey, I have unending stamina . . . can go all night long."

That was something Farrow didn't want to think about as he took in Paula's current appearance.

"I'm sure you can, girl, I'm sure you can. It would be just like taking Carrie home from the prom," he said, referring to another literary figure that had been drenched in blood, although Farrow didn't read the book, he only saw the movie.

"What do we do about them?" Scalia said, through breaths that seemed a bit more regular now, as he pointed at the ghouls.

"Fuck 'em. Once we leave the cemetery grounds and get into the next area . . . I really don't think they'll bother us anymore."

Scalia was silent for a moment, deep in thought, almost somewhere else before he said, "I lost the Hellstick . . . I can't believe I dropped the damn Hellstick." His voice had an almost embarrassed tone underlying it.

"Robert . . . they were gnawing on your arm and, anyway, I think that weapon had run its course. It sure has gotten us through some real shit, though. See that doorway? Through there and across an empty field and we're home free, and we're gonna do it in less than an hour. How's the arm?" Farrow said.

"Empty field, huh?" Scalia said, ignoring the question about his arm. "You really think it's going to be that easy? They're really going to let us saunter across this empty field like we're out for an evening stroll or something?"

"Listen, I've been through that way already. There's nothing over there except for some weird-ass tree . . . and we won't go anywhere near it, we'll stay far out of its path just in case the scumbag who runs this shithole has got a trick up his sleeve. And we're not going to saunter . . . time's getting short."

"Robert . . . how is your arm?" Paula said, squinting her eyes to take a look at the section of flesh just above the writer's elbow where he had been bitten.

"It's nothing," he said, "already healing. One good thing about hell, huh?"

"Ankle's feeling better too," Paula said, raising her foot and rotating it in a small circle.

With the ghouls at their backs, and the crypts flanking them on the left and right with seemingly nothing to offer save for effect and stale air, the three souls faced the exit that was just a few feet away.

Wooden torches that had not been there earlier were set within iron ringlets on either side of the opening. The flames that danced on top should have been alive with bouncing oranges, reds and yellows; but in this world the color was gone from the living flames, washed out to a pale grayish white. The air was still and a bit cooler. The crackling sound the flame made filled the night. Something was wrong.

"Wait a second," Farrow said, turning back around to face the approaching ghouls. Paula and Scalia followed suit.

The undead had stopped their forward progression. They stood silently in a line. Waiting.

"Tommy, what's happening?" Paula said. "Why are they just standing there?"

"I don't know, but it can't be good."

"Farrow, listen," Scalia said, before raising his tone, "something's coming! Listen!"

Footsteps, sluggish and calculated, were approaching, still distant, but close enough to be clearly audible in the now quiet night.

"Paula . . . Robert, get behind me. It's coming from the other side of the wall."

Farrow moved in front of his friends, arms extended slightly from his sides in a protective gesture. The colorless torch flames licked upwards on either side of the large doorway as another display of lightning flashed across the black sky above the massive wall.

The footsteps had a heavy familiarity and sent chills down Farrow's spine. Everything vanished in his mind and there was just that sound. He kept his eyes pinned on the large exit. The mist at the doorway's bottom circled in a disturbed manner as the steps grew closer. The air was stagnant.

Farrow took a step backward, silently willing his friends to do the same. The footsteps stopped. The colorless torch flames seemed to mock him as the doorway was now mostly filled; it seemed even darker than before, blacker. Something man-shaped, but larger, much larger, filled the exit with its huge back, momentarily concealing its identity from Farrow and his friends.

Paula and Scalia looked back and forth at each other, worried expressions washing over their faces.

"Farrow . . . what's going on?" Scalia asked.

"Whatever happens," Farrow said, "Robert has to get through that doorway. Robert has to make it to the Hellmouth."

"Tommy . . ." it was Paula's turn, "what is . . . who is that?"

An extended vein of lightning split the sky as the thing filling the doorway slowly turned around to face them. When it completed that turn, Farrow's blood turned to ice, and for the first time in his life, he was speechless.

Before them, just about six feet away, stood the Frankenstein Monster, but this was no James Whale-directed, Jack Pierce-created representation of the iconic creature. This was the real thing.

Standing seven and a half, almost eight feet tall, the monster stared down at Farrow with lifeless eyes. The dark clothes it wore were too short and too tight for its enormous frame. Adorning its feet were heavy boots. The monster's fingernails were rotted black and the crudely attached limbs were not exactly the same length. On top of two gaunt, hollow cheeks and those dead eyes, a line of large staples were imbedded into the top part of its skull keeping it connected to the bottom half of the creature's face. Its thin lips were turned down into a grimace.

The monster took a single plodding step through the doorway as another surge of lightning quivered above throwing too much brightness on the scene. Every detail was crystal clear, a re-mastered black and white horror film come to life.

It turned its head from left to right, first regarding then quickly dismissing Paula and Scalia, who were both backing away from the immense figure, before returning and locking its dead gaze on the prizefighter.

"Is that what I think it is?" Paula said to Scalia just above a whisper, but the writer could not speak. He just nodded his head.

It took another step forward as Farrow retracted a pace, without taking his eyes off the thing.

"Robert, when it comes for me . . . I want you to get through that doorway. You and Paula get the fuck out of here," Farrow said, scarcely audible.

"We're not going to just leave you here. We're in this nightmare . . ."

"Robert, don't fuck around now. You're too important . . . just do as I say."

In his peripheral vision, Farrow saw Paula quietly take the writer's hand. *Good,* he thought, *they're going together. That'll give them a better chance.*

"I'm going to lead it away from the door . . . and when I do . . ."

The monster, bookended by the two wooden torches took a single lurching swipe at Farrow. The prizefighter ducked the blow and was back up instantly as the creature regained its balance as well, its eyes never leaving Farrow's. *I'd love to see the fight marquee for this one.*

Paula and Scalia, hands firmly grasped were ten feet to the right and moving as silently as oiled smoke. In a few seconds they had achieved a position behind the hulking creature and were approaching the exit.

Good, Farrow thought, *they're going to make it.*

The monster growled and took a second long-armed swipe at Farrow, this time catching him with a solid blow in the upper right shoulder. Red-hot pain exploded down his arm and it immediately turned numb. He hit the deck hard, landing first on his left side and then his back, feeling lightheaded. He didn't think the hand wraps were going to work against this thing.

The monster took another hard step toward him, its thinning black hair matted down across the top of its uneven head, long arms reaching, its fingers were cramped into claws.

The prizefighter was seized by the throat and dragged up onto his feet and easily lifted off them. This monster was not misunderstood as in all those old films; this version of Frankenstein's creation was murderous.

Through parted, cracked lips, Farrow could see its teeth grinding in a strained madness. Bending its elbows, it lifted him nearly a foot and a half off the ground bringing him up to meet its eyes. There was a double sensation of choking and being weightless.

Farrow swung both his arms simultaneously and connected his tightened fists into the monster's ribs. Left, right, left, right. An explosive snarl maybe of pain, but more likely anger, followed as Farrow was lifted even higher into the air. He could see rough stitching and long, lined scabs running across the top of the monster's head intertwining with its hair before he was thrown to the ground in a blur of swinging limbs. Farrow landed hard in a wrecked heap a few feet in front of the creature.

To his surprise he saw the monster gently touching its ribs, running its long fingers up and down the length of its sides as if possibly checking for damage or maybe bruises.

In a half daze and mentally preparing himself for the next onslaught, Farrow quickly trained his eyes behind the monster feverishly searching for a sign, any sign, of Paula and Scalia. In the colorless background, he did not see them.

They made it, he thought.

His eyes fell on the exit just a few feet behind the monster that looked ready to charge at him. Farrow had hopes of seeing his friends running off in the distance; he didn't see that, but did notice something a bit more interesting. The torch with its blazing, colorless flame that had been set on the doorway's left side, was no longer sitting in the metal ringlet attached to the wall. The small circle was empty and the torch was gone. Before Farrow had time to register his confusion, the monster was on him again.

It reached down, its eyes squinting, fingers digging into his shoulders as it let out a catastrophic bellow. Its breath was the smell of a hundred cadavers. The monster started to lift Farrow again, and this time he thought the outcome would not be pleasant.

"Isn't Frankenstein supposed to be afraid of fire?" a female voice.

Farrow looked behind the thing with a quick, distracted glance.

Paula was standing just two paces beyond the monster with the writer at her side. She held her arms out away from her body; in her hands was the missing torch. Extending her reach just a bit further, she touched the lighted tip to the monster's back and it immediately exploded into flames. The monster dropped Farrow and threw its arms above its head spinning in a whirl of rising smoke and involuntary, retching shrieks.

Paula and Scalia gathered themselves around their friend who seemed to be, just for the moment down for the count, and slowly helped him to his feet.

Together they watched the blazing creature move in front of and finally through the doorway. When it passed under the exit, the flames that had completely engulfed it flickered and grabbed hold of a riot of colors that looked almost to be breathing under the night sky. They saw the monster walk four drunken steps before falling to the ground flat on its face, then bursting upward into a flurry of black ash and sweltering smoke that raised in hundreds of pieces to the waiting sky. A low sound of thunder rumbled and Frankenstein's Monster was gone.

"I thought I told you guys to run," Farrow said, attempting a smile, but finding it hard to achieve that particular expression. He looked at Paula first and then over to the writer.

"Whooped em' again, didn't we, Josey?" Scalia said, his hand on the bigger man's shoulder.

"I thought I was the only one supposed to quote Eastwood movies?"

"Oh, I'm sorry, I know, I know . . . I forgot, a man's got to know his limitations . . ."

Still looking at Scalia, Farrow narrowed his eyes down to slits and finally did smile, "Thanks, you guys . . . I couldn't . . . well . . . just thank you."

Paula, now real close, strained up on tiptoe and hugged the prizefighter tight, burying her head in his chest. They stood like that for a while.

The three souls looked back to where the undead spectators had been lined up along the graveyard's dark horizon, but they were gone, faded back into the night.

"Guess we won this round," Farrow said.

Round Eleven

Things seemed safer on the other side of the wall, but they sensed it against their backs, boring into them with unseen eyes. The sky to the east was marked by a thin orange streak, not unlike the one Farrow had seen when he first exited the Hellmouth what seemed like a hundred years ago. It looked haunted in the fading moonlight. The vast field before them opened up invitingly.

The lone tree in the far distance was not easy to spot, just a tiny blemish on the horizon; but Farrow knew it was there and silently stared in its direction.

"Something wrong?" Scalia asked. "You know, I mean besides the obvious?"

"We're supposed to get help," Farrow said.

"Help? What do you mean help? Help how?"

"Those two guys I told you about . . . ya know . . . when I woke up on the beach . . ."

"Yeah," Paula chimed in. "What did you say their names were . . . wasn't it John and Keith?"

"Yep, John and Keith. They told me if I really, really needed something, I just had to ask and I would get it."

"Well, have you asked for anything? Does it work? Ask us out of this place," said Scalia.

"That's not what I mean . . . I have to . . . well, we have to get out on our own, but if a situation arises, say like a swarm of zombies attacking us . . . or a fucking three-story man-bat thing comes charging . . . or the Frankenstein Monster wants to dance . . . I thought it was stuff like that . . . they'd help me . . . help us with . . ."

A wind began to twist along the ground and a new chill came into the air. It was Paula who spoke.

"Don't you see? We have been getting help, we've been helped all along."

Farrow narrowed his eyes suspiciously.

"Yeah? How do you figure?"

She was quiet for a second before answering.

"Well, I originally told you how to open the glass cells in the holding area back when this all started, you know, when you came to rescue Robert over there." She motioned a thumb in the writer's direction.

"Maybe that was a way of them sending help to you . . . they sent it through me. Helped you get the glass door opened initially."

Farrow was silent.

"And then when you and I were captured . . . when I almost sawed through my own neck with that wire . . . Robert came back for us. And, no offense, honey," she said looking over at Scalia, "wasn't Robert a coward? A self-proclaimed coward, before all this shit started going down? I mean . . . you don't *not* have courage one minute, and then have it the next. Am I right? Courage is something that grows over time, not a few hours."

Silence.

"All along we've been working together, you've saved us countless times . . . and I just lit the fucking Frankenstein Monster on fire. Robert has been like Zorro with that Hell-sword or stick, whatever that thing was, and what about that mallet and chisel he found? Why would that stuff even be there if it wasn't meant to help us? Don't you see? Whenever we need help it seems like one of us steps up to help the other. Whenever we needed it most, whenever we have really, really needed it . . . one of us has been there so far."

"Really, really need it. That's what *they* said to me. Whenever I really, really need something, I would get it," Farrow said.

"She's right," Scalia chimed in. "We have gotten out of some messed up situations, and one of us . . . or two of us, has always been there to save the others. I mean," he said, looking at Farrow. "When you saw your name on that giant gravestone you started running . . . right?"

"Well . . . yeah. I was scared."

"Maybe John and Keith sent that down . . . maybe they were the ones who put that there to make you run . . . to make you hurry. I know when

I saw that stupid poem about the writer and the fighter . . . and my wife's name on that damn thing, it sure lit a fire under my butt . . . it was actually the deciding factor that sent me back for you guys. And if I didn't come back to get you two, I would have never made it through that cemetery on my own."

"Maybe you guys are right," Farrow said. "I never thought of it that way. Things have . . . well . . . sort of been going in our favor, with a few bumps and bruises . . . but we keep coming out on top."

"I just don't get one thing," Paula said. "The final time we saw that large stone, why were our names circled with slashes through them . . . and why was mine in red?"

"I'm not sure," Farrow admitted after a bit. "Maybe it means you have yet to play a bigger part in all this." He waved a hand around them. "Maybe we are going to really, really need you again . . . in some way." He didn't elaborate on the red circle, or what it could mean, nor did anyone else.

The three stood in silence for a moment before Farrow looked down at his wrist.

"Okay, guys, we got just under forty minutes to cross this field," he said pointing a finger. "I'd say it's about two miles . . . give or take. It took me nearly an hour to cover this way earlier, but I was going slow, familiarizing myself with the place, and time was on my side. Now we have to hustle. Once we get past the tree and through the Hellmouth, which is also about a mile long . . . we're home free. Moving fast we should be able to make it in thirty minutes or less. That's about ten minutes a mile." He stopped talking for a second, remembering what John and Keith had said about only two souls coming out.

"Farrow, what's wrong? You seem . . ." Paula began.

"No, it's nothing. This shit is just starting to wear on me. Thirty minutes and we're gone."

Paula looked over at Scalia and smiled.

She deserved better than this, Farrow thought. She was a good person; she *is* a good person, and he couldn't just leave her. She wasn't meant for this place. It wasn't right. She didn't belong here.

"Okay," Farrow said, "close to a mile and a half from here, we're going to come to this tree I've been telling you about. We'll keep to its left. Nothing out of the ordinary happened when I moved past it the first time, and if luck is still with us, let's hope that surprise visit from

Frankenstein's Monster was the last card they had to play . . . the ace up their sleeve."

"Wow," Scalia said.

Farrow and Paula both looked at him quizzically.

"Everything alright, Robert?" Paula said.

"Yeah, everything's alright . . . it's just that we can see in color again. No more black and white movie vision."

"Oh shit, he's right," Paula said. "Ya know, you just start to take stuff for granted. I didn't even realize our colors had returned till things lit up around here. Wow! Our vision's back to normal. Fuckin' a-!" Looking around she added, "The sky actually looks kind of appealing."

"Do you think that's a good sign?" Scalia asked, directing his question to Farrow.

"I don't think anything in this place is a good sign."

After a few seconds of silence the three started walking the final leg of their journey, single file and quickly. A huge field and about a mile of cave awaited them up ahead. If hell did have a final trick, the time to play it would soon be coming.

"How are you doing, girl? How are your feet?" Farrow said back to Paula who was silently scurrying behind him.

"My feet? That's a joke. I haven't felt them in a while. They're numb again but still working."

"As long as they still work . . . well, for a little while longer anyway, you're going to be just fine."

"I'm counting on it," Paula said.

They pushed on. The timer on Farrow's wrist clicked down in a display of digital finality.

"What the fuck . . ." Farrow said, and stopped walking.

"What's wrong?" Scalia asked

The prizefighter had spoken of the tree as a white monstrosity reaching for the sky with distressed limbs, but the one coming up directly in their view was blackened.

"The tree . . . the damned tree is . . . black. It should be white . . . I don't like this."

"What do you think that means?" Paula asked.

"I don't know . . . can't be sure. In all the old cowboy movies I used to watch, the hero wore the white hat and the villain always wore the black one. Maybe that earlier incarnation of the tree represented good in some way . . . and this one is bad. I don't like it . . . stay close to me. We're going to walk fast, keep an eye on the thing as we go by. If anything out of the ordinary happens, everybody run for the Hellmouth. It's not going to take us long . . . I promise you."

The ground was hard and water deprived, desertlike. The tree was coming up quickly. The skies brightened almost as if someone had slowly moved a dimmer switch to the full ON position.

With each step the tree seemed to grow larger. Looking around in the apparent daylight, he noticed nothing else seemed to be growing up from the fossilized ground.

Upon closer inspection, the tree was not burned black as originally thought, but painted in a shade so severe, one could almost fall into it and get lost in a starless perpetuity. Its many tangled branches reached into the sky.

They could clearly see the cluster of rocks in the distance just beyond the tree that acted as the Hellmouth's entrance, its rough edges and strange angles stood out even at this distance.

"Just keep walking," Farrow said. "I'll watch the tree. Stay focused on the Hellmouth. It's our way out of here, our way home. Just a few more minutes."

The sign that had exclaimed "Welcome to Hell" on an old piece of wood no longer decorated the tree's front, an observation Farrow kept to himself.

Suddenly, the ground started to shake. A thin tremor snaked below their feet as if something large were passing below them, and then it was gone. The sensation had disappeared.

"Now what was that?" Scalia said.

"I'm hoping we don't find out," was Farrow's answer.

"My God, look at the ground," Paula said, pointing a finger past Farrow who was turned back to Scalia. Both men looked to follow her lead.

The consistency of the ground was changing before their eyes from a cracked, apocalyptic terrain, to a bluish, wet ice with patches of mud and dirt showing up intermittently in a haphazard fashion. The tree now behind them remained statuesque, standing prominently with the brightening sky behind it.

"Hemingway's ghost!" Scalia practically cried out. "What's happening? What's going on with the ground?"

Farrow stopped walking and looked at the writer and then over to Paula who said nothing, but her wide eyes spoke volumes.

Crunching noises were now starting to sound off around them, not sounds of someone walking on ice, but the sounds of chomping and grinding. Farrow looked from his friends over to the Hellmouth, which was now only about fifty yards away. Instinctively he grabbed Paula's hand and Paula did the same with Scalia. With tightened grips all around, Farrow said, "Run!"

Large gaping holes, like the ones they had seen in the lower levels of this damned place, were opening and closing around them. The huge mouths in the ground were salivating with greedy anticipation, chewing on nothing, but with carnivorous intent. Black smoke belched into the atmosphere as before, polluting the air and overcrowding the sky.

The three souls weaved in and out along the ground avoiding the tooth-infested pits, winding through the patches of ice, trying to stick to the muddied areas of ground. A cold wind was picking up, wrapping around their ankles like polar cords and the laughing sound of a little girl once again filled their heads.

All three stopped running, hands sheltering their ears. The entrance to the Hellmouth was just about twenty feet in front of them now. The smell of sulfur bombarded the air. Then the child's arctic laughter stopped as quickly as it had started.

Lowering the open palms that covered the sides of their heads, the three souls turned around under a clouded tumor of a sky that looked destined for rain, and faced hell.

Burning, red-rimmed ash was falling like barbecued snow again, spiraling down from above. Standing maybe thirty feet away from Farrow, Scalia, and Paula, were a group of men, ten or twelve, in black and blue suits. Their faces were faded to smeared blurs and they were slowly advancing. Integrated into this group were several large boars. Even at this distance one could make out the dirty matted coats on the animals. Large protruding tusks pointed upwards in a sharpened, deadly manner. Something that looked like skinless human beings crawled forward on the ground, red and brown organs exposed and sinewy muscles bunched in a tight, ropy fashion. Their wide eyes were locked on Farrow and his friends with a ferocious playtime objective.

In the middle of this group, smiling like something out of a red-eyed dream, but much larger than he had been in life, was Tommy Farrow's ninth-grade math teacher, Edwin Baer, the final trick up hell's sleeve.

"So, Mr. Farrow, down here it looks like you're not the biggest kid anymore," Baer said through a smile so ghastly it could have curdled milk, his voice booming and his eyes blazing with hate.

The high school teacher stood nearly eight feet tall, a gargantuan caricature of the man Farrow had known almost twenty-one years earlier.

"Mr. Farrow? Did that thing just say Mr. Farrow?" Scalia said. "How does it know you? How *could* it know you?"

"That is, well . . . that *was* my math teacher when I was in school . . . we heard he committed suicide a few years after I knew him, cut his wrists if memory serves. His life really went to shit."

"Yeah, okay, but why does he seem to be so pissed off at you?"

"It's time for the next round, Mr. Farrow," Baer's voice was riotous, "and I'm not going down that easy this time, I can assure you." The math teacher hollered across the distance between the two men, his voice seething and filling the area.

"Farrow, what the hell did you do to this guy?" Paula said.

"Well, it was a stupid bet . . . you know . . ."

"What kind of bet?"

"It was actually because of Mr. Baer . . . Edwin Baer, that I became a professional fighter. He had it coming."

"What did he have coming?" Scalia said.

"That prick was one of the first people I ever knocked down . . . and practically out."

Baer moved closer with large sweeping steps, twenty feet away now, his smile, that of a shark, was predatory.

"And from the looks of him now, he has it coming again," Farrow said.

Baer and the rest of hell were swirling around them, tightening. Sizzling blue ice, red ash, and black, wet fire, giant mouths opening and closing, and a chill wind picking up.

"Listen," he said, shouting at Paula and Robert but looking down at his wrist, "we only have sixteen minutes. You guys have to go . . . Paula, you have to get him out . . ."

Something rumbled above them in the sky, a crunching noise reminiscent of falling rocks. None of them looked to see what it was.

"Robert is more important than both of us. You have to take him now. Only two souls can leave, only two will be allowed to go through the exit hole," Farrow yelled.

"What are you talking about? Only two?" Scalia said, shouting back. "There are three of us!"

"I'M COMING, MR. FARROW!" Baer shouted in an operatic bellow, his long legs working double time, just ten feet away now. In the wind-swept ash, the motley crowd moved along with him.

Farrow looked into Paula's eyes. "You have to go now. There isn't time to argue. Take his hand and pull him along. Fuck it, carry him if you have to . . . you and I don't matter! Scalia is the one . . . Scalia has to make it out of here!"

A crumbling sound from deep within the mile-long Hellmouth echoed out and dispersed around the three lost souls.

"The opening is becoming unstable . . . it's starting to close . . . getting ready to close! We haven't much time, get going!" Through gritted teeth, "Get Robert and get yourself out of here. I'll be along in a minute!"

The boars, the skinless humans, and the faceless creatures in the black and blue suits shambled and crawled closer, led by Edwin Baer. The smell of death and filth was thick and overpowering.

Farrow stared Paula down, willing her to hurry the fuck up. Get moving. Ropy lines of smoke circled and curled above their heads and the smell of sulfur was now suffocating.

"Paula, we have to get him out. Now! Everything depends on it." Farrow was still shouting.

A patch of black mud oozed between her toes. The wet ground seemed to suck at her feet, trying to hold her there, glue her in place.

"I used to run the mile in six minutes during my brief stint in high school," she said through a sad smile.

"Well, you have about thirteen minutes to do it now," Farrow said, looking at the descending numbers across his wrist. "Can you handle that?"

Paula grabbed Scalia's hand, a good solid grip, and started to turn. Robert's pleading eyes looked into Farrow's.

"Tommy, please come with us," he said, already turning away. "What do you mean only two souls?"

"Don't worry about it . . . just get going. I'll be along. I have to slow them down or none of us are going to make it out. Maybe one day you can write a book about me . . . you know, immortalize me forever," Farrow said, and then yelled, "GO NOW!"

Paula motioned Scalia into the exit tunnel, the Hellmouth. He turned back a final time to see Farrow framed by smoke. The writer couldn't be sure, but he thought he saw the prizefighter wink at him.

Paula pulled Scalia. The ground turned from sticky, sucking mud, to a harder, stone surface, an environment that would be much easier to navigate.

"Can you run?" Paula asked.

Turning to face her, he said, "You bet your ass I can run."

Something sounding large and very unfriendly roared the name FARROW just outside the Hellmouth's opening, shaking the stone foundations.

"Are you ready for this? We have to go. Farrow will be fine. He'll probably get to the exit before us. That man always finds a way," shouted Paula.

Looking into Paula's eyes, Scalia said, "I'm ready."

With all of hell behind them, and only a prizefighter to fend it off, Paula and Robert faced the direction that would lead them from this place, to an exit that was filled with life and hope for humanity.

They reaffirmed the grip on their hands tightly and made a run for it.

Edwin Baer stood before Farrow looking down at him, the hands at the end of his long arms were pulled into claw-like fists.

"You can turn your exam paper over now," he said through a wicked smile.

"Took that test already," Farrow said, and sank a single, hard fist into Baer's ribs.

The math teacher backed up a step, looked down at Farrow's arm extended into his lower body, then trained its gaze back on the prizefighter, looking him in the eyes.

"That all you got, Mr. Farrow?" the Baer-thing croaked, sounding like his mouth was full of cockroaches.

Farrow answered with a quick left, right, left into his old teacher's new, bigger, hell-infused body, but this time he didn't step backward, just waited for Farrow to finish the onslaught.

"Done?" Baer spat out. The thing's teeth were pointed and decayed brown.

Farrow retreated a few steps, hunched in a fighter's stance, the crowd behind Baer backed up as well, giving the two space under the ash-infested sky. The obscene gathering behind the teacher seemed to be growing in numbers of abhorrent shapes and putrid odors.

Baer's large eyes never left Farrow's face. Taking a single, crooked step forward, the teacher swiped a long, right arm through the air. It passed just in front of Farrow, clearing a visible path through the spiraling ash.

With Baer's body twisted to the right, Farrow moved in with a quick hard left just under the bigger man's armpit and then followed with a blur of a right hand into his breastplate. Baer made a winded, purging sound while backing up under the two blows, and started to say something, but Farrow had enough of his old teacher and went for the face, this time hitting him in the jaw, a shot perfectly executed that was not unlike the first time he had hit the man all those years ago.

Baer went down to one knee and Farrow quickly attacked with a left hook to the other side of his face, snapping the head sideways like he'd been smacked hard. The false teacher immediately stood back up in front of Farrow who was now crouched low and ready to rumble.

The Baer-thing dropped his long arms to his sides. In a fast snorting exhale, two gusts of smoke burst from his nostrils. He turned his head, first left and then right, as if adjusting his neck, working it around, or perhaps he was just regarding the crowd of demons, before coming at Farrow. He slashed both arms in an angry, sideways-swiping motion; his eyes were heated coals. He came fast.

Paula and Scalia, joined hand in hand, didn't have much time to mind their surroundings. The noises behind them faded the deeper they moved into the passageway that was the Hellmouth. The hard, stone ground descended quite a bit, and then evened out for a few steps before a steady, dark incline rose before them. There was plenty of room in the cave-like environment for the two to run side by side. The only sounds, save the fading demonic crowd to the rear and the echoing impact from what might be Farrow's final prizefight, were their own heavy breathing and the sound of Paula's bare feet hurriedly smacking against the stony terrain.

Farrow could see the ragged, hanging strips of discolored flesh low on Baer's forearms just above his wrists where he had apparently hacked the life out of himself years earlier. *Could that be possible? Would the wounds still be there, raw and all?*

The larger-scaled version of Edwin Baer swiped at Farrow with seemingly no plan except to hit him hard and try to cause as much pain as possible.

"We're not in school anymore, Mr. Farrow. There's no one to run crying home to." He smiled with cracked lips and rotten teeth.

A clawed hand raked toward Farrow's face, but by bobbing low, he dodged the blow easily. This incarnation of Edwin Baer, as well as the one he had known while they were both alive, didn't know a thing about fighting. Sure, the asshole was a genius with numbers and fractions, but in the ring, Tommy Farrow was the teacher, and right now, this was his schoolhouse.

Farrow lowered the left side of his body and stepped into a right-armed swing by Baer. His clenched fist sped toward the math teacher and connected soundly with his lower ribs.

"I can do this all day," Farrow said, and hit him across the left cheek with a hard right the bigger man never even saw coming.

Baer stumbled backward a step as Farrow moved in with a solid uppercut to the chin. The teacher's body crumpled to the ground, landing hard on his back among the ice and dirt.

"You're in my class now," Farrow shouted. "My 'sweet science' class."

Standing over Baer, the way he had done to opponents many times over the course of his career, Farrow couldn't help but feel a twinge of pity for the pathetic man.

The crowd of faceless black and blue suits, demons, and whatever other freaks had gathered beyond the now-dazed Baer, seemed to have grown in numbers that had to be in the hundreds.

It had only been a few minutes since they ran off into the Hellmouth, but Farrow could still feel a connection between himself and the writer, a steady pull in the pit of his stomach. *Still here*. He glanced down at his wrist display. *Come on, guys . . . hurry.*

Farrow could see dozens of small fires burning sporadically among the ghastly crowd of fight patrons. Twenty feet away from him, just about where the line of creatures began, a naked woman was horizontally tied tightly to a metal spit. Ropes secured her at the neck, waist, wrists, stomach, knees, and ankles. Two faceless black and blue suits were slowly roasting her over one of these fires, turning her and cooking her evenly. Her flesh gleamed with what was apparently some sort of oil, but she did not start screaming until her hair caught fire.

A line from an old Eric Burdon song crept into Farrow's head, something about "getting out of this place, if it's the last thing we ever do."

Several wooden structures were erected within the gathering of hell's finest, maybe twelve feet high. Farrow could see the rise and fall of flashing silver from between the wooden partitions, and heard a wet, meaty chopping sound. Guillotines. Screams and horrific shouts followed. The ground holes continued to open and close . . . and chomp, but something else was also happening. The sky no longer flicked from dark to light . . . daytime to nighttime. It was flushed red, the way the moon looked on those particular nights that meant brutal heat would prevail the following day.

Farrow pulled his eyes away from those sights and looked down at Mr. Baer, his fists ready for another go at the man, but his old teacher was gone. Only a melted black outline remained; his body, now nothing more than thick liquid tar. He realized that the teacher had just been here to slow him down. He should've fled with his friends.

The crowd was still unmoving, as if anxiously awaiting something or perhaps someone. The stained guillotine blades had stopped their deadly rotations and the woman who had been tied to the spit for barbecue was now nothing more than a blackened lump of meat with ghostly smoke rising off her body. An unsettling quiet fell over the crowd as the sky deepened to a further shade of crimson.

"What the fuck is going on now?" Farrow asked out loud to himself, the sound of his voice not very comforting. He took a backward step toward the Hellmouth's opening. He could still sense Scalia's soul. The readout across his wrist told him it was a little under six minutes to party time.

What was happening? Hurry up, guys! Get out of here! Farrow silently willed his friends. *Paula, get him the fuck out of here!*

An enormous splintering sound drew Farrow's attention up to the left. The ash had stopped falling and the demonic crowd that had been in front of the black tree started to part, making a path before it.

The air grew considerably cooler. Farrow locked his eyes on the abomination. Did the tree move a few feet closer? He thought he saw the monstrosity shift some, lean a bit to the right and maybe trudge a foot or two forward. *That couldn't be . . . that just couldn't be*, he looked back into the crowd and remembered where he was.

Five minutes and thirteen seconds.

A thin voice within his head, an arctic hiss, ice picked into his brain.

"You've heard of 'the tree of life'? Well, I'm 'the tree of death'."

Keeping his eyes on the thing, but now with both hands at his temples, Farrow saw chunks of ice, stone, and muddied dirt spew out and up into the air, as the tree started quickly moving toward him.

"Robert! We don't have time for this!" Paula said to Scalia in a frantic voice.

The writer had stopped running and was now hunched over with the palms of his hands covering his knees.

"Scalia! Robert! Pull yourself together! We're almost there . . . almost at the end. Stand up, man!"

"I'm . . . I'm sorry . . . I just need another second or three . . ." Scalia closed his eyes and kept running the name Martin D'Cutta through his mind. *Martin D'Cutta. Martin D'Cutta. If Martin D'Cutta could do it . . . so can you. You rescued Farrow and Paula back there; you could run a few more feet.*

"Robert! We have to go right now!"

The writer with his head pointed down, opened his eyes. He saw Paula's bare feet bloodied and caked with filth. She had a single, consoling hand on his back and was tapping him vigorously.

"Robert, enough! Let's go!" And then quieter, "Give me your hand." Scalia was silent. "Robert! Your hand!"

Scalia stood up slowly, still breathing heavy, but managed to say, "When we get out of here, I gotta get myself to a gym . . . work on some cardio like Farrow said." He smiled at her.

"Okay, honey . . . you ready?" Paula said, staring at the writer.

Another second or two passed.

"Yeah, I'm ready. Let's do this. Let's finish this thing."

Paula slipped her hand into his, tangling their fingers together tightly.

"Paula . . ." Scalia started, "what's that buzzing sound?"

She pulled her eyes from Scalia and looked up.

"Buzzing sound?"

"Yeah, don't you hear that? Sounds like . . . bees."

Paula then heard the sound as well.

The tree making its way toward Farrow gained considerable speed as it cut its way through the hard ground and along the path that the demons, the ghouls, and the faceless black and blue suits had cleared for it. A line of wrecked ground, solid portions of desert landscape, were left in its wake.

The tree's elongated limbs lowered themselves to its sides now resembling more than ever actual limbs, arms to be exact, and against this strange horizon, the tree seemed to be shrinking, growing smaller. The closer it got, the more he was certain of this.

The crowd moved backward. Even the boars, with their filthy coats and upturned tusks, retreated with the horde.

When the shrunken tree stopped just a few feet in front of the prizefighter, it had reduced itself to just about three feet tall. The vacant space it had originally occupied seemed abandoned . . . almost lost.

A spiraling whirlwind of rock, ice, and thick clumps of dirt, not unlike the spinning Tasmanian devil in those old cartoons, now danced before Farrow encompassing the entire height and width of the tree, and then everything stopped. The pieces discarded, dropped to the ground in a perceptible clamor that registered the only noise, it seemed, for miles.

The dust kicked up by the commotion evaporated and disappeared into the air. A shape formed before him, blinking in and out of reality before holding onto a substantial form.

A small female child stood in front of Farrow, her shadow stretched out behind her for nearly a mile. She was wearing a white dress with fringes on the sleeves. Her blonde hair was pulled into two tight pigtails that stuck out from the sides of her head. Her skin was an inhuman white, almost bleached in appearance. Staring out from that washed-out face were two small emotionless eyes, as cold and dark as onyx.

Her high-pitched voice was laced with ice, and when she spoke a wind sprang up and seemed to howl around them.

"Do you know what little girls are made of?" she said, just above a whisper.

Farrow stared and did not answer. The voice continued.

"Sugar and spice and everything nice. That's what little girls are made of." Then she smiled. Her mouth was full of black teeth, razor sharp.

"No! No! No!" Paula shouted over the hissing and buzzing coming from every direction but whose source was just in front of them.

"We're done for! We're done for!" was all Scalia could manage, his breathing coming in gulps. The two had come to the end of the line. They had run out of cave and stood just about ten feet away from the Hellmouth's exit.

A wall of winged insects that must have numbered in the hundreds stood between them and the way out. A living, twisting blanket of what appeared to be large bees was completely covering their escape route.

"Oh my God! We are so screwed!" Scalia yelled over to Paula. "How much time do you think we have left?

"I don't know," she said, unable to pull her eyes away from the insects. "Can't be much, though . . . not much at all."

The bees, if in fact, that's what they were, resembled large jelly beans with clear, empty bodies, almost translucent; no internal organs could be seen, just empty pockets of space. The stingers at the rear, however, were twice as long as the creatures' bodies and came to a sharpened point, not unlike that of a needle.

The main concentration of the winged insects thrived and huddled together tightly keeping an impenetrable blockade in place for anyone unlucky enough to pass through into the next plane of existence.

"Oh my God!" Scalia kept shouting. "What do we do? Where's Farrow? Where's . . ." But before he could finish the sentence he realized he could still feel the dull pull in the pit of his stomach that connected his soul to the prizefighter, and could tell he wasn't close. They were on their own.

"I think he's busy about now," Paula said. "We're going to have to figure this one out for ourselves."

"Yeah, you may be right," Scalia said, a hand over his stomach, his eyes in a panic. "But how . . . ? What can we do?"

The writer took a step toward the exit . . . and the bees. Nothing happened. The wall continued to throb and move and buzz. He took a second step. The sound of tiny wings grew in volume as if agitated, a protective pit-bull guarding its master.

Scalia turned to face Paula; she was a sorry sight in his line of vision. The woman standing just a few feet away was almost unrecognizable. When he had first seen her in the glass cell next to his wearing the intimidating ankle bracelet, he secretly thought her relatively attractive. The woman who stood before him now, however, was filthy with mud, dirt, dried blood, and smeared makeup. Her eyes were swollen, almost shut, and her hair was matted with grime. Paula looked like . . . well, she looked like she had been through hell.

"Paula . . ." Scalia started, taken aback by her appearance and then thought, *Wonder what I look like?*, "Do you think we could dive through them? I mean like . . . just run into those things . . . and break on through to the other side? Get out of here?"

"Robert, I . . . I don't like bees," Paula said backing away some. "It's been a childhood fear of mine as long as I can remember . . . my whole life." She sounded almost embarrassed by this admission. "I can't go near them, I just . . . Robert! Look out!"

Scalia turned his head. Two of the flying insects pulled themselves off the wall and were speeding in his direction in an enraged blur. They quickly set themselves down on his extended arm, and sank long stingers into the exposed flesh below the sleeve of his golf shirt. Paula took a small step forward as the writer's face registered searing pain.

The clear, empty bodies of both bees were filling with Scalia's blood, sucking it up from his arm. Somewhere in his mind he pulled forth a memory, a recollection of a doctor's office, a needle and a long plastic tube; this was not unlike that, but it hurt way more.

The bees, that Scalia had now silently dubbed "blood bees", filled their bodies quickly, gorging themselves to the point that the bloated creatures popped open with a bursting swish, spraying blood up his arm and misting across the front of his shirt.

The empty shells of the things, now not much more than vacant blisters of air, twisted down to the stone ground, unmoving. Scalia dropped to a sitting position, turned and quickly crawled back to where Paula was now kneeling with both hands covering her mouth. The wall of the vile creatures before them seemed ravenous.

"Wanna play, Mr. Tommy?" the small girl said.

Farrow could now see that the tongue in her mouth was slit up the middle like that of a serpent. Not only was the sky red, but everything around him seemed to be tinted in that shade as well.

"You know you're not getting out of here," she said, "and right now my friends are playing with your friends." The girl smiled and then began laughing, a sound that was all too familiar. Beyond her, Farrow saw an endless mob of spectators.

"You don't think you can win, do you? Did you like my little game with the time?" she asked.

He found it hard to take the small child seriously, but would never, not even for a moment, underestimate the girl-thing that now stood before him. This was an evil older than eternity, an evil so pure and absolute, that to misjudge the creature would mean the end of all mankind. It would mean that he failed, and Tommy Farrow didn't fail. Not anymore.

"In just a few minutes I'll own you. In a few minutes we're going to play some special games . . . we'll play them forever and ever and ever," she said in a sing-song voice.

There seemed to be a certain amount of excitement sifting through the hideous gathering, which was now burning. Smoke was pouring upwards from their bodies, coming off their skin in potent waves of black and gray.

"But don't worry, Mr. Tommy, you really don't belong here, your soul is a bonus, so I'll tell you what I'm going to do." Her voice grew cooler, infused with freezer burn. "I'm not going to hurt you, but you will have a front-row seat . . . let's say, for how about 1,000 years?"

When Farrow didn't respond she said, "Okay, 1,000 years it is. A front row seat to watch what happens to your friends." She stared at him with those lifeless, black eyes. "How does that sound?"

When he still didn't answer, the child started in again.

"I'm going to hang the whore by her ankles," the serpent's tongue licked itself across her top teeth as if polishing them. "I'll hammer long, rusty nails into the soles of her feet and clamp hundred pound weights from her tits . . . all this after I saw her arms off with a butter knife." She stopped talking again waiting for a reaction from Farrow. The thing's voice deepened, "I'm going to slowly peel the skin off her body a hundred times a day."

Wind was now pushing the smoke, shooting it upwards from the crowd, as the sky began to change again, starting to pop and flash.

"I'll pull the writer's fucking eyes out and force them down his throat. I'll make sure he swallows them, before I stuff his cock into his mouth . . . and then his fingers . . . and toes . . . and you know what? You get to watch. You get to watch the whole thing . . . over and over and over. You won't be able to help them. You're going to beg and plead to help them . . . but I promise, it will be at least 1,000 years. Who knows? Maybe 2,000 before I get around to you."

She stopped talking again. Farrow still showing no reaction. He kept his expression blank, his mind clear, his breathing even.

"Every time your friends get hurt, every time I pull them apart . . . it will seem like the first time . . . for you as well as them, again and again." Then with a sly look, her eyes tightening to thin slits, she said, "Right now I'm in the process of arranging for your wife . . . or is it your ex-wife, to come stay with us for a while . . . a long while." She proceeded to laugh in a small playful way.

Something was wrong, terribly wrong, Paula and Scalia were in trouble. He could sense it, feel it in the pit of his stomach . . . feel Robert's soul calling to his, like before when he first found him in the glass cell. He had to do something. Farrow clenched his fists and looked down at the child.

"You leave my wife out of this," he said. His eyes locked on the two black chips set deep into the small girl's ghostly facade.

"Teresa is going to be hogtied naked and drowned in a pit of boar shit." The child's voice was changing now, ringing with a more jagged quality, like she had been eating glass. "How does that sound, Mr. Tommy?"

Steam started to come off the girl as her black eyes flashed.

"Don't you know, children are supposed to be seen and not heard," Farrow said.

Almost instantly, a sensation like an ice pick actually made from ice, worked its way into the center of his head starting at the top portion of his skull. It felt as if his brain were slowly being pulled apart within. He could feel it ripping into two large sections, and in his mind's eye, he could see it happening as well.

Farrow threw his hands up to his temples and immediately dropped to his knees screaming. He slammed his eyes shut, tightly, silently willing that small act to help relieve some of the pain, which it did not.

"Who do you think you're talking to? You have to pick and choose where and when to be a wise-ass, and this time you chose wrong. Like the way that feels?" she said.

The strong impression, the certainty that his brain was coming apart in two equal pieces along with the searing pain, continued.

"Stop it! Stop it! Stop it!" These were the only words he could manage. He just kept repeating the small sentence over and over.

"Time's almost up, Mr. Prizefighter. We're going to have such fun."

Farrow was now reduced to a leaning position on his forearms pushing both palms against the sides of his ears, attempting to keep his brain from oozing out through his fingers. He was on the verge of going mad, the toes of his work boots pounding up and down as he kicked his lower legs violently into the already cracked ice and stone ground beneath him . . . and then the pain stopped.

"Oh," she said, enjoying this, "we're going to have such a good time together."

Farrow, with his eyes still closed, spoke under his breath.

"John . . . Keith," he said, whispering into the ground, his hands still over his ears, "I need a way out of here. Scalia's in trouble . . . I can't get to him fast enough, there's not enough time. I need a way to reach him . . ."

No magic voice in his head answered.

"Can you hear me? I need to get to Robert. I need to help him. I need your help . . . I really, really . . ."

Farrow moved the large hands away from his ears, his head surprisingly not hurting, his brain apparently intact. The pain had receded as quickly as it had come.

"Get up. I want to play some more. You're like a new toy, Mr. Tommy, you and your friends, and this is Christmas morning." Her voice now had an edgier, more adult-sounding quality and a dangerous tone.

"I said get up, prizefighter!" she screamed.

If Farrow knew how to do anything, it was how to get up, how to pick himself back up. It was something he had done his whole life. It was something he should have done against Johnson, and it was something he was going to do now.

He opened his eyes. His vision somewhat blurry came into quick focus. Sitting on the ground, not more than six inches from his nose, as if waiting, was a little red object, shaped exactly like a pill. A wave of red-hot adrenaline pulsed through his body. It was the Spitfire.

He shifted slightly on the ground to conceal the deadly item from the small child who didn't seem all that small anymore.

The thing must have fallen out of my pocket when I first got here, when I pulled the Hellstick out of my pocket that very first time. It must have been just sitting here, waiting.

Farrow did a good job of hiding a smile. Getting awkwardly up to his feet, halfway putting on a show, he snatched the Spitfire and quickly obscured it in the creases of his right palm.

I wanted to use that damn thing so many times, various snapshots raced through his mind, *the wolves . . . the zombies . . . that giant fucking bat-thing. It would have been wasted; it wouldn't have been available when I really, really needed it most.*

He silently thanked John and Keith, and wondered if he was *meant* to drop the damn thing, and if they had a hand to play in it. He thought probably yes, but he still needed a way out of here. He had to get to Paula and Scalia. He couldn't run, he would never make it in time. He wasn't that quick.

"Didn't anyone ever tell you to respect your elders?" the girl croaked, sounding like she had been gargling with pieces of cement.

It seemed that all of hell was behind her. Every bad thing he could think of, every terrible spectacle and obscene display, gathered just beyond the child, albeit much closer now. Generous flames danced up and down her arms, jumping from limb to limb and twisting over her torso, discoloring her once white dress to that of a darker shade in a multitude of relentless embellishments and cruel heat.

"How about a hug, Mr. Tommy?" she said, smiling with all those pointed teeth crowding out of her mouth that now seemed unhinged, three times larger than it should have been. "How about you and I . . ." and then the child's gaze shifted from Farrow, to a point behind him, just over his right shoulder, and all the deadly playfulness drained out of her bleached expression.

The sky behind her and above the large crowd started changing colors with the fluidity of someone changing television channels, in and out from yellow to red to callous gray, to pitch black and purple, a prelude to Judgment Day.

A white beam of light funneled from the sky, spinning in a cataclysmic cyclone. It reached up miles into the air as far as the eye could see. A crunching reverberation, as if a giant fist punched into the ground, crashed behind the prizefighter, a mind-numbing boom. Small pieces of ice and broken rock fell in a frenzied downpour. Smoke, dirt, and ground dust from the event filled the area before quickly dispersing and settling again.

"Wha . . . what's that?" she said, her black eyes unmoving, her vision still trained to a point behind the prizefighter.

A picture of a beach flashed through his mind, a quick snapshot of the Atlantic Ocean. His soul filled with hope and he quietly thanked John and Keith. Tommy Farrow, his eyes filling with tears, knowing what he would see, turned around.

The Arabian mare whinnied softly in the middle of the chaos; she stamped her front hoof once as if to say, "Come on, let's get going." Her eyes were burning embers. A sensation, almost of ecstasy, washed over Farrow, dowsed by the reality that he had no time to cherish the moment with his long-lost friend.

Heatseeker stood tall and proud, her mane shining to perfection, her black coat gleaming and flowing seamlessly. White steam belched from her nostrils as she brought her front hoof up and down a second time, hard.

Come on old friend, there's no time. Let's go!

Farrow made his way over to the animal. The elation that filled his body, which filled his whole being, was indescribable. The mare bowed her head slightly and stamped her right hoof a third time, however, more gently.

Hello, old friend.

The familiar smell of leather saddle oil filled his nostrils as a dozen good memories flooded into his head. With the horse only steps away, Farrow turned back to look at the child, the Spitfire closed up tight and secure, hidden in his balled, right fist.

"Where do you think you're going?" she hissed.

"I'm leaving," Farrow said. "I have to go help a friend. You know, he's got a book to write . . . I hear it's gonna be a bestseller, stop some asshole from becoming president."

The child screamed, and just as Farrow reached the mare, touching his left hand to her warm coat, his brain started to rip in two again, but the pain immediately dispersed like smoke in the wind. The prizefighter realized at once that as long as he had physical contact with the animal, the child could not hurt him.

He lifted his foot and put the toe of his boot into the waiting silver stirrup that was shining so brightly it might have been polished only seconds earlier. Farrow grabbed the saddle horn and pulled himself completely onto Heatseeker, the memories were coming fast, the best times of his life.

Thank you, Keith. Thank you, John.

The animal neighed loudly, white-hot mist now streaming from her nostrils. She turned her body, hooves making hollow sounds on the ground where patches of ice had melted, so Farrow could face the child.

Absolute rage was flaming behind the girl's black eyes, which were the size of half-dollars. The fingers on her small hands seemed to grow longer and the flames that had consumed her body now simmered down to an inch of propane blue, a stove burner turned to a lower temperature.

"I'm going to eat your fucking heart! I'm going to slice your cock into sushi . . . pound it into chop meat!" the child said viciously.

"That may be so, but you'll have to wait until I get back," Farrow said, smiling down at the girl. He brought his closed right hand up to his mouth and slipped the concealed Spitfire between his lips, careful not to drop it. He sloshed it around, mixing the item with his saliva, remembering how to do it, remembering what John had said to him.

After it mixes for a few seconds, you spit the thing in the direction of your enemies and then get your butt out of there.

The child was now shrieking, a high-pitched sound that was filled with hatred and intended retribution. The array of fiends around her howled, a mob of vigilantes readying themselves for a night of brutal activities and almost certain carnage. The sky continued to flash over the whole scene.

"I've had enough of you," Farrow said. "Go to hell!"

He brought the pill to the center of his lips, hesitated for just a second and then spit the thing at the false child.

It sailed easily through the air; Farrow could see it as if things were happening in slow motion: the red pill-shaped weapon, flawlessly cutting a straight path, landing on the ground, bouncing once and coming to rest just about a foot in front of the burning girl with the tight pigtails.

She looked at it with a puzzled expression that might have been humorous under different circumstances. Her eyes narrowed and a crease appeared across her stark forehead. The child picked the thing up, holding it between her thumb and index finger, bringing it up to her face for closer inspection.

"And what is this, prizefighter? Is this supposed to scare me?" Some of the venom was now sucked out of her voice, an unsure quality to her tone. She held the small item above her head, the gathering of demons, now swarming around and passing her, charging.

"No," Farrow said loudly. "It's not supposed to scare you, but it might take you down for the count."

A blast of sulfur reached Farrow as the child started to scream. "Your soul's gonna burn in a lake of fire! I'm going to boil the skin from your fucking body . . ."

From his elevated position on top of Heatseeker, he looked down; all of hell was washing toward him, murderous. Farrow said, "Get ready to rock."

He gripped the mare's reins, pulled back and dug his heels into her sides a single hard time. The horse reared up onto her hind legs, the front set pedaling in the air before them, thick smoke and screams swirling, the sky flashing.

Dropping the reins, he now grabbed the saddle horn with his left hand as memories of the beach assaulted him. The horse returned to the ground hard, and spun around once, almost as if showing off.

"Are you ready, girl," Farrow said, "to save the world one more time?"

Just before the demonic mob reached them, Heatseeker was speeding into and down the yawning throat of the Hellmouth and swallowed whole.

For the first time in twenty-one years, Tommy Farrow was flying.

The exit portal was now completely lined with flames; a phenomenon that started slow, but quickly gained momentum, bright orange and deep red, licking upwards towards the dark stone ceiling and framing the swarm of blood bees that seemed anxiously awaiting another sanguinary treat. Paula looked over to Scalia, an expression of defeat washing over her.

"I think that's it," she said. "I think they've won . . . I'm so sorry, Robert." Her eyes were filling with tears. "I tried, I really tried . . . this is just too . . . this is just too much. Too fucking much!"

She came over to him, her arms outstretched in need of comfort.

"This isn't fair. We tried! We all tried. It can't end this way!" She fell into Robert, her head buried in his neck, sobbing now. "I'm sorry. I'm so, so sorry."

Scalia pushed her away almost violently and wrapped his arms around his stomach. He fell to one knee.

"Robert? What's wrong? My God, Robert?"

It felt as if a giant fist was wringing his insides, pulling with certain urgency.

"Robert? Answer me! What's happening?

The writer looked up to face her, smudges of dirt streaking his skin. Over the crackling and snapping of the growing flames and the buzzing hiss of the blood bees, through a half-smile Robert said, "Farrow's coming."

The growing explosion of heat was so intense that Heatseeker almost lost her footing in between long powerful strides. Farrow felt the searing temperature against his back for almost ten seconds as the flames from outside the Hellmouth funneled into the long cave and rushed at them from the rear like a relentless blast of water flooding into Manhattan's Midtown Tunnel.

When the Spitfire had first gone off, the screams were incredible. *Everything out there*, Farrow thought, *must have been completely consumed*. He held on tightly to the saddle horn with his left hand, while his right arm reached for the sky, just like old times.

The animal's powerful legs rotated in a blur as her hoofbeats gave off a hollow pounding sound against the hard stone, sparking thin, yellow, and orange flashes. Unstoppable. Nine hundred pounds of flesh and muscle. She seemed to know where she was going . . . seemed to know the way.

Farrow actually made a victory fist with his right hand held up high, as quick flashes of the beach and the spray of saltwater consumed his thoughts. *This is good,* he thought, *even if this is the last time, the last hurrah . . . it's the perfect way to finish things.*

Then his thoughts turned to Teresa and his mind darkened. She would probably be better off without him, she deserved better, much better than him, a better life. He hoped she would find it. *I have nothing to go back to. I've lost her.*

His eyes were tearing now, and not only because of lost memories, but also from the air rushing into his face. Farrow felt as if he were sitting on top of a living missile.

Teresa. I love you. I love you . . . I miss you.

Up ahead he saw the end of the line, the end of his ride. He saw Paula and Scalia and the pull in his stomach calmed down to a dull throb.

The horse skidded to a stop, its hooves leaving thick streak marks along the stone ground. Farrow could see his friends huddled near the Hellmouth's exit, seemingly in a panicked exchange.

Why hadn't they left yet? What the hell were they still doing here?

Farrow looked down at his wrist. Just over two minutes. He grabbed Heatseeker's saddle horn, straightened the toes of his left foot into the well-adjusted stirrup, and threw his right leg over the horse's back and let himself drop to the ground. He turned and started off fast toward his friends, but stopped in his tracks.

He looked back at the animal. Heatseeker turned her head and nodded slightly, the mare's large eyes, locked on his. She neighed quietly, each understanding this would be the last time in the other's company. Farrow got lost for a second in a triumphant harmony, knowing that now he would be able to give the horse a proper farewell. He ran his fingers through her thick mane; the animal seemed to squeeze into him. Farrow threw a big arm around her neck, his first love, his eyes again brimming with tears.

"We did it, girl. One last time, we really did it."

The horse whinnied again and seemed to rub her head into Farrow's neck. The prizefighter closed his eyes and when he reopened them a moment later, she was gone. He was standing alone.

Blinking away any remaining tears, Farrow turned to face his friends, turned to face the final problem, and if it couldn't be solved in two minutes and thirteen seconds, they would all call this place home.

He ran at them.

"The fuck you still doing here! We don't have time for this shit! I told you two . . ."

Then Farrow saw the bees, hell's interpretation of bees, or at least that was his first impression. The exit from the Hellmouth was covered completely, teeming with writhing, winged insects. He had remembered hearing the buzzing sounds upon his entry through that doorway just hours ago. He pushed passed Paula and Scalia toward the hissing abominations.

"No, Farrow, wait!" Scalia shouted out in a panic. "We tried it already. The closer you get to them, they'll attack, and it isn't pretty."

He stopped short and turned back to face his friends with a quick glance down at his wrist.

"I can't believe we've come all this way to be stopped by some fucking bees," Farrow said.

"There's too many of them and they're thick in that passageway. Farrow . . . when they sting you, their bodies swell with your blood until they explode. It's not a pretty sight and it hurts like a mother. Two of them hit me already."

Farrow looked over at Paula who was silent, then back to Scalia. His mind was working fast, contemplating their options.

"Okay, here's what we are going to do. I'm going to . . . going to . . . run into those things, right into the center of the passageway. Can I assume that they'll be all over me?"

"Yeah," Scalia said in a terrified voice. "Yeah, they'll cover you alright. It'll be a feast. Those things will sting you and suck you dry."

Looking down at his wrist, one minute and forty-eight seconds.

"Listen, guys, we don't have any time . . . I want no arguments from either of you." Farrow's hands were opening and closing, the muscles in his arms pushing up against his skin. "I'm going over there. When they cover me, I'm going to spin away from the exit. I'll let as many of those things come at me as I can handle. When I move away . . . it should open a clear spot . . . a path for you to move through." He stopped talking for a second. "Now don't fuck around. When you see your chance, go through that exit."

Looking Paula in the eyes, "We have to get Robert out of here. Do you hear me? Do you understand how important he is?"

She dropped her eyes.

Farrow looked back at the pulsating curtain of insects, carnivorous and deadly.

Just like everything else in this damn place, he thought.

"I told John and Keith I'd give them a real showstopper . . . well . . . here goes."

He took a single step toward the living wall, but it was Paula who stopped him.

"Tommy . . . wait. I'll go. I'll do it."

Looking at his wrist, a minute and thirteen to go.

"Paula, don't mess around, not now . . . I need you to drag him through that thing." He motioned to the bees, the sounds they made seemed to grow louder with insatiable anticipation.

"Farrow . . . Tommy," she started off slow and then broke open like a bursting dam. "You take him out . . . it's you who's meant to survive . . . not me. You said you are supposed to get what you need . . . you got *me*; this is the reason I'm here. This is the reason I was allowed to come with you guys." Tears were filling her eyes. "I know that for sure now."

Forty-six seconds.

"You were influenced to take me for this exact reason. This was my purpose. You said only two souls can go out . . . well, hurry the fuck up! Go!" she yelled.

Scalia's eyes shifted back and forth from Farrow to Paula. *Were they really doing this now? Were they really arguing who was going to stay here and be tortured for eternity?*

"Guys," he said, his voice quivering. "Guys? We have to do something fast." He was close enough to Farrow to see the digital readout across his wrist dip under thirty seconds. Scalia took a step toward the exit, closer to the bees, two steps beyond Farrow and Paula.

"I belong here," Paula said, fully crying, but speaking clearly enough for both men to understand her. "I wasn't shot by someone hiding in a back room after I killed my pimp, like I originally told you . . . I . . . killed myself." Her voice was quiet now. "My soul is damned. I couldn't live with the fact that I killed someone . . . even someone as vile as Donell Mosley . . . so I took my own life. Don't you see? I . . . I belong here." She dropped her head, sobbing.

Farrow remembered John, or was it Keith, telling him that if they were in hell . . . they were there for a reason. So this was Paula's secret. This was why she seemed to be hiding something at times, and Farrow finally realized why the circle around her name on that tombstone was outlined in red.

"Farrow?" Scalia said. "What are we doing? Whatever it is, it has to be fast!! Very fast!" The writer's body was shifting nervously, his skin slick with sweat. "Are we going or are we staying? Somebody better make a decision in about fifteen seconds."

Paula lifted her head, looked at Scalia and smiled, then turned her gaze to Farrow and said, "Thank you."

In a frenzied dash, Paula Yannicelli, also known as Cherry Moore, threw her body into the Hellmouth's exit and was completely covered by hungry blood bees.

"Paula! Noooo!" screamed Scalia.

They swirled around her momentarily as if picking just the right spot, Paula standing in the middle of a living tornado. The droning sound emitting from the bees grew in an anxious volume with deadly intent, and then just like that, she was gone. Head to toe, the small plump creatures were on her, consuming every inch. Paula raised her insect-coated arms above her head and shrieked as she simultaneously spun away from the Hellmouth's exit.

Bright light poured into the cave with a sense of hope and warmth. Paula's cries of pain, now consumed that of which the blood bees were making.

"OH MY GOD! IT HURTS! OH GOD! FARROW, IT HURTS! IT HURTS!"

The readout on the prizefighter's wrist now read twelve seconds, but he and Scalia could not take their eyes away from the horror before them. Paula was swatting her arms and kicking her legs. They could see the clear bodies of the bees filling with her blood, fattening and ripe, before bursting and shooting dark crimson on the ground below and cascading against the walls almost six feet away. Paula closed her arms around herself and started to sink to the stone floor.

"OH GOD! FORGIVE ME! OH GOD! OH MY GOD!"

Scalia stood close to the exit, but paid it no mind; he could not break his stare from the horrific sight just a few feet away.

Eight seconds.

The bees were bursting wetly with Paula's blood, an appalling audible pop echoed loudly in the cave around them, not unlike air-blisters used for packing, only these had been filled with scarlet fluid.

The exit opened, stretching before them, filled with white light.

Six seconds.

Now. Farrow thought. It had to be now.

Before he pulled his eyes away from the screaming thing that had once been his friend, if just for a few hours, Farrow thought he saw Paula look at him. Yes, a spot on her face cleared momentarily. The insects danced away and he could see a rather large portion of Paula's face.

Farrow would have bet his soul that in that brief moment he saw her smile at him, just before her mouth was filled the with hungry blood bees.

Five seconds.

The prizefighter looked over at Scalia who was only a few feet away, but still watching wide-eyed, unable to pull his horrified stare from the obscene feast taking place in a red mist, the brilliant, blinding exit just beyond him.

Blood bees were now speedily finishing up with Paula, who lay on the ground in an unmoving lump of depleted meat, and making their way back to cover the Hellmouth's exit, three or four of the engorged creatures were being joined by others. In a moment their chance of escape would be lost.

Four seconds.

Farrow hoped that sometime in the future, even if only in a dream, he would be allowed to remember Paula Yannicelli and what she had done for them. But right now, he had a canvas to get up from, and a wife he loved to get back to. Fuck it . . . together he and Robert had a world to save.

The crazy shit you think of at times like this.

Three seconds.

He ran at Scalia like a linebacker, the considerable traction on his boots digging into the stone ground. It only took two or three steps to reach the smaller man, but when he did, Farrow wrapped his enormous arms around the writer in a freight train of a bear hug and, diving, propelled both their bodies through the gathering blood bees and into blinding light pouring in from the Hellmouth's fiery exit.

Two seconds.

ROUND TWELVE

The Heavyweight Championship
January 20, 2013
Madison Square Garden

Two . . . Three . . .

Farrow's eyes snapped open, the way the characters in the horror movies of his youth would do to alert the audience that they were far from dead and ready for the next in an unending succession of sequels. Not unlike that.

But there would be no sequel for Farrow. No rematch. No tomorrow. Now. It had to be now.

"I simply do not believe what I am witnessing," Jim Lampley shouted into his headset, leaping from his seat at the announcer's table and nearly knocking it clean off in the process. "Farrow is not only lifting his head off the mat, but is now hauling himself up by way of the ring ropes."

"Stunning," Larry Merchant added. "I have been around the fight game all of my life and have never seen someone so close to defeat, or let's be honest, death, rise again like this outside of a Hollywood movie. Nothing short of a miracle."

Farrow was standing fully erect at nine, beating the count and surviving the round which ended only two seconds later as the referee and doctor, Johnny Laguna and Jimmy Conn, all tried in vain to inform Tommy that his night, his fight, his heavyweight championship reign were all over.

"Not after what I've just been through," Tommy said with much effort. "If any of you call this fight, I'll take turns kicking all of your fucking asses in this ring."

The frightening determination of this outburst, followed by a brief examination by the New York State Athletic Commission's appointed physician, convinced all involved, allowing Farrow to continue.

"I promise you this," asserted the referee, poking a bony finger into Tommy's chest before stalking off to center ring, "the next time you take more than two head-shots in a row, this fight is over. I'm not having your death on my conscience."

Farrow smiled through a hideous, bloody grimace.

"Dying ain't much of a living," he said.

Shoving his mouthpiece back in, Farrow was attempting to regain a clearer focus of his surroundings in the forty or so seconds remaining in the interval preceding the start of Round Eleven.

Everything beyond a ten-foot radius still swam in an ethereal pool of maddening mist and haze. The ringside seats began to emerge from the fog and take on a certain clarity, and through it, Tommy thought fleetingly, two of the faces seemed somehow familiar. White robes? Before he had too much time to contemplate their identities, the bell sounded.

"And so, inconceivably, begins Round Eleven of what should have been certain defeat for Tommy 'Heatseeker' Farrow," Lampley said.

"Farrow's eyes are decidedly alive as he bounces out of the corner, he seems to have gotten out of the funk he was in last round," said Larry Merchant. "Mere seconds ago, there was no spark of life in there whatsoever. Now, they are filled with intense desire."

"More like murder," said Lampley.

Tommy bobbed and weaved with malicious intent deep into Johnson's corner, trapping him before he could react, and let loose a single body shot, the rib-breaking volume of which spectators and sportswriters would all recall long afterward.

"Johnson is down to one knee!" yelled Jim Lampley. "This is without precedent. Unbelievable. I can not believe what we are seeing here tonight!"

Farrow hovered momentarily over the kneeling Johnson in the fashion once employed by Jack Dempsey, before retreating to a neutral corner became mandatory standard practice.

Johnson appeared as though in an act of supplication, visibly clutching his crushed left ribcage as if trying to hold the splintered pieces inside his body, praying for some divine intervention in the matter.

Given the reminder to back off his fallen opponent, Farrow stormed backward without taking his eyes off Johnson.

"In the time that it took Farrow to retreat, Johnson is up and banging his gloves together," Merchant observed.

"In a not too forceful or convincing manner, I'm afraid," said Lampley.

Adding to the confusion and excitement was the fact that when the referee turned back toward a now-standing Johnson, he had forgotten to administer the standing eight count.

"Farrow is actually reminding the referee to give Johnson a standing eight," laughed Lampley uproariously. "This night is just getting more bizarre by the second."

Merchant agreed. "Tommy is fighting and officiating at the same time."

And in a fighting spirit he was. No sooner did the referee wave the two combatants together once again, Farrow nearly sprinted to center ring, ducked a weak and half-hearted Johnson roundhouse right, and unloosed a thunderstorm of violence, which began with an uppercut that very nearly, defying logic and physics, spun Johnson's head around the axis of his collarbone, Linda Blair-style.

As Johnson was in the process of collapsing to the canvas like a tree felled by the killing blow of a lumberjack's axe, Farrow connected with a devastating right-left combination.

"Johnson's mouthpiece just sailed into the front row," Lampley screamed. "I would say that there is no way he is getting up from that, but we have seen stranger things already happen tonight."

The applause and simultaneous roar of the crowd produced a terrifyingly awesome earthquake-type effect, shaking the Garden's very foundations, the championship banners earned by the Knicks and Rangers blowing as if in a stiff breeze.

"This is a night not only for the record books," Larry Merchant said as the referee concluded the superfluous ten-count, "but for the history books as well."

Even as the ring became instantaneously deluged with Farrow's handlers, well-wishers, and would-be interviewers, Tommy sought out the two familiar faces sitting ringside he remembered from just a few moments ago, both in white robes, one with a gray beard and the other sporting an odd bowl haircut, thinking that maybe, just maybe, he had a vague recollection of who they might be and what part they played in making this moment possible.

Attempting to orient himself amidst the bedlam that the arena had devolved into, Farrow fixated on the exact spot to discover instead Teresa pressed against the metal barricade, smiling and extending her index finger heavenward in her trademark "You're Number One" gesture.

Seeing him looking at her, Teresa mouthed in words he, of course, had no chance to actually hear above the ensuing cacophony, "I love you, Tommy."

He now understood that the path on which his life was to unfold had a direction and meaning more profound than he ever could have imagined and that none of it, the undisputed heavyweight title, unified or not, the money and all the material objects it could buy, none of it would mean a damn thing if not for her.

"After he went down at the end of the tenth, I figured I had it won," former champ Joltin' Jeffrey Johnson told a press conference full of eager reporters behind a pair of dark shades which couldn't quite conceal the bruising and swelling beneath. "When he got back up and was cleared to come back out for the eleventh, I don't know, man. All the fight went out of me then and there. This guy," gesturing toward Farrow who just now joined him at the table, "he's more than mortal. He's superhuman or something. I don't even know, man."

"What are you feeling right now, Tommy?" one of the indistinguishable blurs shouted inanely from a few feet away.

Smirking at the asinine query he got after every win and loss, he gave his smart-ass stock response. "I'm feeling like I want to give you the treatment I just got back there, and then ask you how you feel about it. But, seriously, I feel like tonight, from this moment on, anything is possible," he said looking at Teresa. He lovingly caressed her hair with a broken and bleeding hand. "Like life is worth living as long as you have something worth fighting for."

"Well, you are now the undisputed Champion of the World," another phantom reporter chimed in. "Two belts . . . are you going for a third?"

He almost corrected this statement out loud, that titles and fame and fortune were not at all what he was alluding to, but decided against it. *Let them think whatever the hell they want*, Tommy thought as he gave Teresa's elbow a gentle squeeze. She looked into his eyes and they became lost in each other up there with flashbulbs bursting and questions flying. Just like the crazy teenagers they once were and felt like all over again.

As long as she knows, Tommy thought silently to himself, *that's all that really matters.*

EPILOGUE

In a small room facing east on the sixth floor of The Mount Sinai Medical Center, several miles from Madison Square Garden, Kerrie Scalia sat next to her husband Robert's bed. Thirteen days earlier, a now-retired Tommy Farrow had beaten Jeffrey Johnson in the eleventh round and unified the WBO and IBF Heavyweight Championship belts.

Kerrie held onto Robert's hand tightly.

Today is the day. Today.

A taxicab had run a red light, smashing into the limousine carrying Robert. He had suffered a spleen laceration that caused bleeding into his abdomen, followed by a drop in blood pressure. He was taken to the emergency room by EMS. Because of complications during surgery the blood flow to his brain was temporarily cut off and he slipped into a coma. He was legally pronounced dead for three seconds before being revived. A CAT scan was performed in the OR and his spleen was removed.

While in ICU, Scalia's vitals stabilized, there was no further bleeding, he was breathing on his own, but remained in a coma. After seven days connected to IV fluids and a feeding tube, he was sent to a medical floor.

Kerrie Scalia was dressed for a winter that was just starting to kick in. The climate had been manageable through December and most of January, but that was changing fast. February had come in with a bitter fury. She wore heavy, fur-lined boots, jeans, and a thick sweater.

Kerrie had had a spa appointment that very morning. She wanted to look her best for Robert when he awakened. She wore very little makeup, but didn't need much.

Sunlight splashed in from the two large windows, covering Robert in a comforting hue. His chest rose and fell and his breath was soft. He could have been sleeping.

Today is the day.

Kerrie willed today to be the day that Robert would wake up. It had to be. She missed him so much. It just had to be today.

She kept her large blue eyes on her husband's face, and it really came as no surprise when he did awaken. Kerrie immediately started shedding tears and brought both hands up to her cheeks, her long fingers framing her mouth. She kissed a fingertip and touched her husband's lips to make sure that this was all real.

"I love you . . . I love you . . . I love you," she said and wondered why she was wasting time with fingers as she bent over Robert and kissed his dry lips.

He kissed her back as best he could.

"I love you, too," he said. His voice was barely audible.

Robert's eyes began to fill as well.

"How do you feel?" Kerrie asked.

It was a stupid question, and she realized that as soon as she had spoken the words, but could think of nothing better to say at this moment of absolute bliss.

"I feel okay," he said through a whisper.

"Actually," a little louder now and looking into her eyes, "I feel like a million bucks . . ." He paused before adding, ". . . like I could save the world."

ACKNOWLEDGMENTS

During the writing of this novel, the following people provided advice, criticism, encouragement, and enthusiasm for which I'll always be more grateful than they could possibly know:

David Abrahamson, World Middleweight Kick Boxing Champion Tommy 'Bee' Battone, Christopher Benedict, Michael Benfante, Regina Galoppi-Benfante, Laura Savino-Classi, Warren Day, Thomas Fierro, John Lacognata, Dr. Leonard Savino, Robert Scalia and Paula Yannicelli

I would also like to thank my parents for their love and unending support.

About the Author

James Classi is the author of *Nine Lives*, a chilling collection of short fiction. He lives on Long Island with his wife and children. *Heatseeker* is his first full-length novel.